TAP, TAP

David Martin

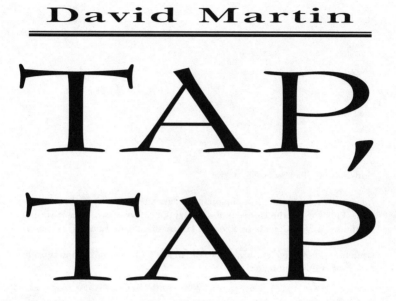

TAP, TAP

A NOVEL

Random House

NEW YORK

All rights reserved under International and Pan-American Copyright Conventions. Published in the United States by Random House, Inc., New York and simultaneously in Canada by Random House of Canada Limited, Toronto.

Grateful acknowledgment is made to the following for permission to reprint previously published material:

EMI MUSIC PUBLISHING: Excerpts from "Wild Thing" by Chip Taylor. Copyright © 1965, renewed 1993 by EMI Blackwood Music Inc. All rights reserved. International copyright secured. Reprinted by permission.
THE GOODMAN GROUP MUSIC PUBLISHERS: Excerpts from "Tell It Like It Is" by George Davis and Lee Diamond. Copyright © 1966 by Conrad Music, a division of Arc Music Corporation and Olrap Music Publishing. All rights reserved. Reprinted by permission.
JOBETE MUSIC CO., INC.: Excerpts from "My Guy" by William Robinson, Jr. Copyright © 1964 by Jobete Music Co., Inc. Excerpts from "Nowhere to Run" by Brian Holland, Lamont Dozier, and Edward Holland. Copyright © 1965 by Stone Agate Music. Reprinted by permission.

Library of Congress Cataloging-in-Publication Data
Martin, David Lozell
    Tap, tap / David Martin.
        p.   cm.
    ISBN 0-679-41055-4
    1. Vampires—Fiction. I. Title.
PS3563.A72329T3   1993   813'.54—dc20   93-38838

Manufactured in the United States of America
24689753
First Edition

Book Design by Tanya M. Pérez

Arabel, every way

Coleridge once jotted in a notebook, "The Prince of Darkness is a Gentleman." What is so beguiling about a specialist predator is the idea of intimacy with the Beast! For if, originally, there was one particular Beast, would we not want to fascinate him as he fascinated us?

. . . has not the whole of history been a search for false monsters? A nostalgia for the Beast we have lost? We must be grateful to the Prince who bowed out gracefully.

—*Bruce Chatwin*
The Songlines

TAP, TAP

ONE

Tap, tap.

He opens his eyes. Philip Burton's brain, the part of the brain that remains on alert while the conscious mind sleeps, has been monitoring that tapping noise for ten minutes now. Having finally nudged Burton awake but unable to articulate its concern, the brain's never-sleeping guardian triggers a chemical release that imparts within Philip Burton a sense of dread.

He turns toward the bedside clock, bringing the red-liquid numbers into focus, 3:40 A.M. What's wrong? Why has he awakened with a dry mouth, his armpits damp, emotions taut?

They say you sometimes experience a terrible foreboding right before you have a heart attack, this thought causing Burton to monitor his chest, the left side of his neck, checking for signs of thready pain, bracing for an internal explosion, a vessel rupturing, blood loose everywhere in his chest cavity—

Tap, tap.

He exhales relief. So *that's* what woke him, a noise downstairs, probably a palm frond blowing against a window or that blasted raccoon on the veranda steps again.

He waits. Nothing happens. No heart attack, no more tapping. See, there's nothing to worry about.

While downstairs the beast in a pin-striped suit with white shirt and red tie, wearing wingtips, lowers his hand from the mahogany banister against which he has been tapping like this—two short raps, then wait a few seconds before repeating—for ten minutes, hoping to draw one of the Burtons down here to him. The beast has disabled the alarm system, has cut the phone lines, and now it's simply a matter of getting their attention. He wouldn't want to attack them while they're sleeping, wouldn't want them to miss out on all the fun.

Tap, tap.

There it is again and now Philip can't get back to sleep worrying about that noise. If it's only a palm frond or raccoon, why does it sound like it's *inside* the house? He sits up and puts his legs over the side of the bed, causing his wife, Diane, to stir, to mumble sleeping questions about what's wrong and where is he going, which Philip doesn't bother answering because Diane is already grumpily pulling the sheet over her bony shoulder and descending back into that deep, dead sleep of hers. As soon as Philip stands, he feels an urgent need to pee.

Sixty-three years old, Philip Burton has doglike features, fat-lidded eyes, and a receding hairline that has dragged his forehead halfway back onto the top of his sun-spotted scalp. He looks remarkably like Gerald Ford only dumber.

As Burton heads toward the bathroom, he begins mumbling a recitation of "The Raven," which he first performed at his grandfather's ninetieth party, attended by great-aunts and dubious uncles and of course the patriarch himself, who was thought by the other members of the Burton family to be literate.

Burton is just reaching the bathroom door when he makes the connection, realizes why "The Raven" has come to mind.

Standing at the toilet trying to squirt urine past the doughnut squeeze of a swollen prostate, he begins again:

"Once upon a midnight dreary, while I pondered, weak and weary,

"Over many a quaint and curious volume of forgotten lore—

"While I nodded, nearly napping, suddenly there came a tapping . . ."

Ah yes, know every word of it.

Unfortunately the birthday presentation to his grandfather turned out to be a disaster, the nervous trouser-pinching young Philip Burton delivering the poem in a pathetic monotone, proud of himself for not missing a word of the eighteen stanzas and then humiliated when his grandfather said, "The literature of our English language is blessed with some of the most beautiful poetry ever written, more lasting proof of civilization than anything built of stone or brick, and yet you choose to occupy a portion of your limited intellectual capacity with that drivel."

The old turd.

When Philip wags his flaccid dick he manages to get a few last drops of urine on his hands, tsking as he steps over to the sink, turns on the tap, and looks into the mirror.

"Ah, distinctly I remember it was in the bleak December;

"And each separate dying ember wrought its ghost upon the floor . . ."

Pleased with himself. How many times has he recited it? *Hundreds.* At the table for dinner guests, at the yachting club's smokers, every year at the island's Halloween party for kids.

He turns the bathroom light out, then immediately back on again. What's this, a business card stuck into the lower edge of the mirror. Burton pulls it out and holds the yellowing card at arm's length: CURTIS BIRD FISHING CHARTERS. HAMBRIENTO ISLAND, FLORIDA. Then the address and phone number.

Burton turns the card over. On the back someone has written in black ink, "20 years."

Initially spooked by the card, Philip shakes his head and harumphs. Not my fault that Bird killed himself. He had no business running a commercial operation on Hambriento, don't care if it had been going on for three generations, it was still a *business*, and Hambriento is a private island, it isn't Sanibel, not yet at least. Besides, the man had no character, because if Bird had had character, he wouldn't have shot himself, he would've had the good sense and moral fiber to pick himself up and start over again.

Sixty-three years ago Philip Burton had the good sense and moral fiber to be born rich. His family's fortune originated in steel, those nineteenth-century Burtons building factories, employing thousands of men, firing enough steel to dent the earth's crust. Then, a hundred years after it began, Philip's father oversaw the closing of those factories, firing men not steel, putting assets not men to work, altering the Burton family business from making steel to making money. And now Philip doesn't know the difference between pig iron and pork chops.

His brothers manage the family fortune on Wall Street, but Philip never had the head for it, never made sense of that barrage of ridiculous terms, leveraged muni funds and earnings-to-something ratio, Philip preferring to specialize in memorizing lunch menus, improving his golf swing.

His brothers moved him out of New York and down to Florida, where Philip's "job" was to look after the family compound on the sleepy but exclusive Hambriento Island. His wife, Diane, redecorated, bought furniture, added windows, put in gold-plated bathroom fixtures, had parquet floors refinished, then had carpets laid over those refinished floors, Philip meanwhile overseeing construction of a new pier and directing palm trees to be moved around the grounds the way Diane rearranged furniture.

Tap, tap.

Hearing it again as he reenters the bedroom, Philip wonders if he should call Security or buzz one of the servants or what. Of course if it's only a palm frond or raccoon causing that tapping noise then everyone will have a good laugh at his expense, the way his brothers did after he recited "The Raven" at their grandfather's birthday party. Curtis Bird laughed at him too—for different reasons of course—but guess who had the last laugh in *that* little matter.

Standing there trying to decide what to do, Philip looks at his wife's face illuminated by moonlight coming in the floor-to-ceiling windows facing the Gulf of Mexico. Her wrinkle-puckered mouth hangs open and she's drooling slightly.

Diane Burton's small and doll-like features made her passably cute as a young woman but now that she's sixty her face appears almost monstrously featureless. Remnant nose. And does she have lips or doesn't she? Decades of playing golf have leathered her skin to the texture of a work glove, the color of mahogany. But she *is* fit, supplementing her three-day-a-week golf outings with daily sessions of power walking, wearing weights on her wrists and ankles as she strides the pathways of Hambriento pumping arms and kicking legs in a manner so wildly exaggerated that she looks quite demented. No fat on Diane Burton. And when she dies she won't have to be embalmed because she's already too sinewy and tough to rot.

Nothing occurs to Philip as he looks at his wife's moonlit face, not affection or disgust, neither regret nor appreciation. He might as well be looking at a pillow he's slept with for nearly forty years.

Tap, tap.

My God, sounds like it's right there at the top of the stairs.

Where the beast pauses to imagine how he will describe all of this to the one he loves, describe how he kept tap, tap, tapping his way up the stairs until finally old man Burton came out into the hall and that's where I took him, where I razored his throat and . . . But he's getting ahead of himself, it hasn't happened yet, there's still the possibility of dogs.

Tap, tap.

Philip Burton is convinced that one of those awful fishermen has broken into his house.

On weekends they come to fish the pilings of the Burton compound's pier, lower-class working men who wear baseball caps and have tattoos all up and down their arms, accompanied by overweight wives and equally fat children, playing radios and drinking beer, occasionally landing their cheap little boats on the beach.

As long as they stay below the high-tide line they aren't trespassing on Burton property. At least not legally. But of course their mere presence is a trespass on Philip and Diane's sensibilities.

So Philip has devised a little game. He takes up a hiding position behind the curtains on the screened-in veranda facing the pier, waiting for those dreadful people to settle in, his two perfectly matched snowy-white Samoyeds, Ronnie and Nancy, waiting with him. When the time is right, Philip opens the outside door and tells the dogs, "Sic 'em."

Spoiled and disobedient in all other matters, Ronnie and Nancy love harassing poor people. The two Samoyeds run out onto the pier and bark at the boats, then come back around to get to the beach where they charge, barking and stiff-legged, to scare those awful people, even the ones who are legally below the high-tide line, right out into the water.

And the things those people say! Cursing at the dogs, threatening to come back and shoot them, screaming up at the house, where of course Philip remains hidden behind curtains—he has no intention of getting punched in the nose again.

Which reminds him. He looks down at the business card that he's inadvertently carried with him from the bathroom. How did it get there, who stuck it in the mirror? They've already been upstairs, those awful fishermen who hold me responsible for what happened to Curtis Bird, who hate me for siccing my dogs on them, who—

Tap, tap.

Right out there in the hallway! Call Security, *now.*

Philip heads for the phone while muttering in a singsong voice that which he can't get out of his head now that he's started remembering it.

"Back into the chamber turning, all my soul within me burning,

"Soon again I heard a tapping somewhat louder than before . . ."

Phone's dead.

He disconnects and tries again, still no dial tone. Philip drops the receiver into its cradle with disgust. Ever since those crybabies broke up the phone company . . .

Pushing a button on a small console that will activate a buzzer in the servants' quarters, Philip notices that the red light next to the button hasn't come on, meaning that the buzzer isn't sounding.

TAP, TAP.

Only one thing to do now, one last line of defense—the dogs.

The Samoyeds' success at chasing the fishermen and their families away from private piers has made Philip and Diane minor heroes to their elderly rich friends because, really, what's the point of being wealthy, living on an exclusive island, and otherwise ideally ordering your life if every time you want to stand on your veranda and look out at the ocean you're forced to see some tribal collection of perfectly awful poor people standing below the high-tide line? I mean, really. This isn't Bangladesh, not yet it isn't, although you have to wonder where Hambriento is heading now that the property owners association has yielded on condominiums.

The whole point of getting rid of Bird's charter operation was to maintain the island's exclusiveness. The Burtons, along with their ally, Kate Tornsel, put tens of thousands of dollars into that battle. And then, five years after Bird killed himself, construction began on the causeway and bridge, condos have been built, and now you can't go anywhere on the island without bumping into tourists—which means of course that getting rid of the charter captain and his family didn't accomplish anything in the long run.

Except a certain personal satisfaction, of course.

TAP, TAP.

Heart pounding, Burton puts on a robe and slides his feet into leather slippers before hurrying to the adjoining door between his bedroom and the dogs'.

The Samoyeds sleep in separate beds. Nancy is spayed, Ronnie castrated. Smelling their master in the doorway, the dogs don't stir, not even when Burton whispers their names, pats his legs, begs them to come, and finally whispers an excited "Sic 'em, sic 'em." The dogs are tired and moody. They had their weekly off-island trip to the groomers today, a two-hundred-dollar ordeal that always ends in them being muzzled and tied down, so their attitude now is "Screw you, Phil. You want someone sicced, go sic 'em yourself."

Nothing works, he laments. Not the security system, not the phone, and now not even the dogs.

What should he do? Open a window and start screaming for help? The groundskeeper lives in a cottage a hundred yards away from the main house, maybe he'll hear me, he'll know how to handle a break-in, he's black.

Philip is just stepping to his bedroom window when he smells something awful, rotting fish.

Then, me thought, the air grew denser, perfumed from an unseen censer / Swung by seraphim whose footfalls tinkled on the tufted floor . . .

And turns to see, standing there in the doorway leading to the hall, a slightly built man wearing a dark suit, white shirt, tie.

Philip is instantly relieved. Must be someone from Security checking on why all the systems are down. "What's going on?" Burton asks in an urgent whisper.

The man motions for him to come out into the hallway.

Philip looks over at his sleeping wife and nods.

In the hall that odor of rotted fish is overwhelming. "What smells?" Burton asks, still whispering.

"Chum," the man replies.

"What?"

The little man smiles.

"You *are* from Security, aren't you?" Philip asks nervously.

"I'm from hell, from your past."

"What are you talking about?"

"Revenge."

The little man smiles broadly as he reaches out one hand and uses his knuckles against the walnut molding.

Tap, tap.

"What . . . who are you?" The fear almost making Burton void what's remaining in his bladder.

"Don't you remember me, Philip?"

Wait, he *is* vaguely familiar, that oddly accented voice, the strange combination of a small-framed body but long spidery arms, that little bow mouth. But *who?*

"I remember *you*," the intruder says softly, almost fondly. "Every year at the Halloween party. Quote some of it to me now, Mr. Burton. Say, 'Get thee back into the tempest and the night's Plutonian shore!' "

"My wife's jewelry is in the bedroom."

"The debt you owe can't be paid with jewelry."

"Debt?"

"The debt you owe Curtis Bird."

The business card. "Good Lord, man, that was twenty-some years ago."

"Twenty years ago exactly. Interest has accumulated."

"Well, I'm sorry for what happened to him of course but surely you can't hold me responsible, a man takes his own life, obviously he's unstable—Wait, I know you!"

But before Philip Burton can say anything else, the man moves toward him with such speed that to Burton's astonished eyes this appears to be a visual trick. Once grabbed, Philip swoons like a carica-ture of a Victorian lady, caught before he falls.

He is held securely by two thin powerful arms, one clawed hand at his chin and twisting his head to the side, exposing the lower-left portion of his crepey neck, forcing Burton to speak through tightly clenched teeth, "Get thee back into the tempest and the night's Plutonian shore!"

Bitter laughter.

Then razored pain, then teeth and *then* Burton struggles wildly. But it does him no good, he is held as easily as a child would be.

Philip croaking, "Take thy beak from out my heart!"

He stiffens from the shock of what's being done to him, struggling again only briefly before slumping, gone limp, held now as a lover would be and feeling as a lover would the soul-deep suck of it.

Not a red drop falling to the white carpet on the hallway floor, there where Philip Burton is laid out supine by that small cranelike figure, wiping his mouth and quoting, "Nevermore, motherfucker."

. . .

"Philip?"

What is going on, an irritated Diane Burton wonders. First he gets out of bed to pee, then he rattles around in the hallway making enough noise to wake the dead, and now *this*.

How odd. What time is it anyway?

A hand runs up under her nightgown, cupping a withered breast, murmuring encouragement, not like Philip at all.

"Philip, *really*."

She doesn't like to be awakened for any reason, certainly not for this nonsense, fingers finding a nipple and working it in ways that strike her as *different*, not the usual pinch and pull of Philip's technique. Now those fingers are massaging the nipple, playing around its brown circumference, quite pleasant actually.

"Philip?" Her voice has softened.

His other hand reaches between her legs, parting them with a distinctly un-Philip-like authority, one finger touching her clitoris, Philip's never been so unerring, with him it's usually just a poke and prod . . .

"Goodness," she whispers as the lower hand expertly rolls her now oily clitoris while the upper hand squeezes and rubs both of her breasts, increasing the tempo, heightening the sensation, raising the stakes.

Smiling, Diane reaches around behind her to touch a flank, oddly bony—has Philip lost that much weight recently?—but when she moves her hand, Diane is reassured to find a familiar rounded little belly, which feels drum-tight, making her wonder if he's going to start passing gas again, a development that would certainly break this wonderful mood he has created.

One more thing to check before she commits herself. Still reaching behind her, she moves her hand down to grope for his member, curious how hard it will be this time because, really, what's the point if it's so squishy she has to hold it with both hands and sort of stuff—

Touching it, she pauses.

Not Philip's.

When Diane screams, the man who'd been caressing her from

behind, too large and hard to be her husband, leaps from the bed. Buck naked, he crosses the bedroom in three loping, animally strides to exit through the open doorway and out into the hall, laughing as he goes.

Diane can't get her breath. Where's Philip? Oh dear God what's going on, are the poor people rioting?

While out in the hallway the beast, still chuckling, takes Philip's body in his arms, he can't wait to tell the one he loves about this, this is going to be *rich.*

Diane is just reaching for the phone to call Security when she hears singing coming from the hallway outside her bedroom door, a woman's voice or a man performing a soft falsetto.

"Nothing you can say can tear me away from my guy . . ."

Transfixed, Diane keeps her eyes locked on the open doorway.

"I'm sticking to my guy like a stamp to a letter . . ."

Having never paid any attention to that awful rock music, she is unaware that the voice is a perfect replication of Mary Wells, singing in a bouncy but unhurried tempo.

"I'm telling you from the start . . ."

And just then her husband comes into view in the doorway.

"PHILIP! PHILIP!"

But he's being held by someone, by that creature who was in bed with her, *he's* the one who's singing, singing and embracing Philip around the waist, holding Philip's left arm out, dancing with him. A ridiculous sight, though Diane's terror doesn't allow her to appreciate the folly of it. The intruder is naked, half Philip's size, as if a naked child is dancing with her husband.

". . . I can't be torn apart from my guy . . ."

Except they're not really dancing, Philip is being carried along, his toes—one foot bare, the other with a slipper half on—are dragging the floor, his head lolling back as if he is drunkenly examining the ceiling, as if his neck has been broken.

His robe has fallen open to expose Philip's slack belly, beneath which his genitals have shrunken as if in fright so that all that can be seen poking out from his sparse gray pubic nest is what appears to be the white-skinned head of a miniature anteater and the rounded tops of two small hen's eggs.

Dancing Philip into the bedroom, carrying him as if he were weightless in spite of their size difference, the intruder keeps his back, his bare ass, turned toward Diane and continues singing in that woman's teasingly sultry voice.

"My opinion is he's the cream of the crop. As a matter of taste . . ."

And here the little man stops singing long enough to bury his mouth into a large purple wound on the lower left portion of Philip's neck.

Diane screams as the intruder twirls Philip around so swiftly that lifeless arms reach outward.

"No handsome face could ever take the place of my gu-uy . . ."

Philip is danced over to the bed and turned so that his blanched face can be shown to Diane, her husband's half-closed eyes and parted lips and upward-turned face making him appear to be experiencing a kind of ecstasy.

Meanwhile Philip's dance partner continues singing in that soft and playful voice.

"He may not be a movie star but when it comes to being happy, we are . . ."

Diane is still screaming when Philip is dropped onto the bed.

Screaming with the unconscious regularity of breathing, screaming in and screaming out as the dreadful creature offers a perfect and loving mimicry of Mary Wells, the voice pouting and groaning, bumping and grinding, repeating over and over the final words Diane Burton will ever hear, *"There's not a man today who could take me away from my guy . . . there's not a man to-day who could take me a-way from my-y gu-y."*

Then he's in bed with her, kicking the lifeless Philip out of the way, climbing onto Diane and silencing her screams by covering her mouth with his own stinking flesh-rot, blood-wet mouth, taking her breath away as she desperately tries to crab sideways to avoid being impaled.

He slides down to her neck, but before Diane can resume screaming she feels quick pain at the base of her throat, next to her windpipe.

The wound there is sucked as the intruder grinds against Diane and produces sounds that she recognizes, that for nearly forty years she's heard Philip making atop her.

She experiences a seizure that stiffens her body plank-rigid, Diane suddenly thrusting her flat ass up off the bed, briefly holding both herself and the man aloft, then collapsing while deep in her leaking throat she manages a final coital groan.

After long minutes the dreadful creature's mouth comes away from Diane's neck with a loud theatrical *smack* that spews a fine red mist of blood, the creature then gulping in air as if, having pulled too long and deeply on a bottle, he has built a huge oxygen debt and is grateful now to repay every precious cubic centimeter of it.

"Oh Dondo!" he shouts, laughing, beside himself. "Dondo, Dondo, Dondo, it's dee-Dondo-licious! I'm in love!"

Then he speaks in another voice, another woman's voice, black and street-sassy, taunting, *"When I say I'm in love you best believe I'm in love, L-U-V!"*

TWO

The beast at the door brushes off the front of his overcoat and adjusts the tilt of his homburg. His stupid heart is jumping more wildly now than it did last night in the Burton mansion. Oh be still. How long did it take him to get dressed for this reunion, how many different shirts and ties did he try on, how many pairs of cuff links? *Cuff links.* I should've bought him cuff links. No, he doesn't wear French cuffs, he's more of the rolled-up-sleeves type. But I could've brought him a silver pocketknife. Or a manly bouquet of tiger lilies. Don't be stupid. But the beast *is* stupid, he knows he is, stupid for who's going to be filling this doorway in a moment, tall and broad-shouldered, tousled light brown hair, that all-American, all-boy face. Oh be still!

Smiling, beside himself with giddy anticipation, the beast reaches for the door.

THREE

Tap, tap.

I got up and headed for the door wondering who might be visiting us unannounced that Sunday evening. I expected a neighbor, a salesman, solicitor for a good cause, someone who had the wrong house—anyone but Peter Tummelier.

Yet there he stood, my childhood friend. And seeing him I felt immediately and profoundly . . . inconvenienced. On Peter's previous visits—ten, twelve, fourteen years ago—I was single and in my twenties and still enamored of the late-night life: bars and booze, impulsive red-eyed trips to Las Vegas, nose candy and women whose names ended in *i*. A visit from Peter back then meant a well-financed, week-long party.

"Peter!"

He smiled but spoke my name casually. "Roscoe Bird."

I felt like saying, *This is not a good time for me because* . . . Because I'm settled: settled in and settled down. Because I have to go to work in the morning and I haven't gone to work with a hangover in years. Because I'm all grown up now and I don't want to play with you anymore.

"Are you going to ask me in?"

Chagrined, I stood aside.

But Peter didn't enter, he just smiled and raised his thick brows as if he was in on a joke that I and the rest of the world was yet to get.

A short and slightly built man my age, thirty-six, Peter wore a luxurious boy's-size wool coat every bit as black as his eyes, which dominated a face that otherwise had all its prominent lines running vertically—the furrows between his dark eyes, the long, thin nose, the prominent widow's peak barely seen under the ridiculous homburg hat he wore. His mouth, so small and delicate as to be girlish, was puckered.

"May I?" he asked, rocking forward on his toes.

"Yes, of course, come in, come in." I stepped even farther aside.

He walked into our central hallway and shook his shoulders as if to dislodge snow. It was March 13th, about forty degrees here in Washington, D.C.—but no snow.

"What brings you to town?" I asked.

"Here to speak with the best friend I have in the world," he said, taking off his coat. "Oh dear, I've embarrassed you."

I laughed and thought, Here we go already with his games. "You don't see a lot of homburgs these days," I said, taking his hat.

"Not in the States, no."

"Are you still living in Europe?"

"Eastern Europe, the Caribbean, wherever I hang my homburg is home. What have you been up to since last we met?"

"I got married."

He lost his jolly expression. "You're joking."

"No."

"Children?"

"No."

"I came into my inheritance this year. The *plan* was, when I came into my money, we were going to buy a boat together and go on a cruise around the world."

"That was the plan all right—back when we were teenagers."

"When I visited you ten years ago it was still the plan. We weren't teenagers then. You said—"

"She's upstairs studying," I interrupted. "Would you like to meet her?"

Peter looked at me hatefully but then recovered a smile, though much dimmer than the one he wore when I opened the door. "Of course."

I was halfway up the stairs when he called to me. "Oh Roscoe, you said she was studying. Doing her numbers? Have you taken a *child* bride?"

"Graduate school."

"Ah."

Walking toward the spare bedroom where Marianne had her study I wondered what her first impression of Peter would be, that he was an Old World patrician from an old family with old money and superior attitudes? That he was privileged, droll, disdainful? Yes of course, all of that. And funny and weird and a little spooky too.

As soon as I knocked and opened her door, she asked, "Who was that?"

"Who *is* that, he's still here. Peter Tummelier."

"Peter . . ."

"*Toom*-ah-leer," I carefully pronounced it for her. "From Hambriento. I've told you about the Tummelier brothers, Peter and Richard."

"Oh yeah, the Nehru jackets, right?"

"Yes. Except tonight Peter looks like a Swiss banker. I'm sorry but it seems you're going to have to come down and meet him."

"Of course." She closed her books and shut off the light on her desk. "I hate it when people don't call before they visit. How do I look?"

"Beautiful."

"Right. He's dressed like a Swiss banker and I'm in sweatpants and one of your old shirts."

She patted my cheek and we went down the steps together, the small and elegant Peter Tummelier looking up expectantly at us.

"Oh Roscoe!" he exclaimed before we'd reached the bottom step. "She's a gamine! How absolutely brilliant of you to marry her!"

Marianne laughed.

"Marianne," I said, "this is Peter Tummelier, a friend from Hambriento Island where we grew up together. Peter, this is my wife, Marianne."

"How do you do." She put a hand out to shake.

He looked at that hand as if it were a small gift, finally taking it gently in both of his large hands. "Charmed, my dear, absolutely charmed to the very tips of my toes. You are the most strikingly beautiful woman I've ever had the pleasure—"

"I doubt it," she interrupted. "But it's kind of you to say."

I tried to see my wife through the eyes of someone meeting her for the first time: a slender young woman with short dark hair, large brown eyes, a small nose, a nicely proportioned mouth, her face wonderfully animated regardless of what emotion she was displaying, anger or happiness or just quietly listening to conversation. With her short hair, small breasts, and slender hips, she also looked remarkably boyish and I wondered if Peter was going to comment on this.

When Marianne tried to withdraw her hand, Peter held on. "You *are* beautiful," he insisted. "And that's the truth. And beauty *is* truth."

"Truth beauty," I mumbled idiotically.

Peter turned toward me. "And?"

"And . . . and so on and so on."

"Typical product of an American education," he said gleefully.

Marianne gave him one of her unnervingly steady stares, saying, "Beauty is truth, truth beauty, that is all ye know on earth, and all ye need to know."

"Oh my dear *dear* lady." He raised her hand and kissed it, Peter speaking in a lascivious whisper, "Ah, to make delicious moan upon the midnight hours."

Marianne tried to withdraw her hand again but Peter still wouldn't release it. For a man who was only five and a half feet tall, he had unusually large hands and oddly long arms, as if, when he had been put together, those particular parts had been taken out of the wrong bin.

He turned to me and said, "She's enchanting and I'm sure you don't deserve her."

But Marianne wasn't having any of his oily charm, telling Peter bluntly, "Let go of my hand."

Surprised, he did so immediately. Then Peter faked one of those accents he used when he was unsure of himself or trying to impress someone, this time it was upper-crust English. "Roscoe, dear boy, said he hadn't taken a child bride but you're as dewy fresh as—"

"Thirty-three," she announced.

"Oh never tell your age, dear, leave the allure in place."

"The allure of a woman's age arises from an era when a woman was valued as a breeder." Marianne wasn't smiling. "You know, heifers, fillies, virgins."

"Uh-oh," I muttered.

Peter was perplexed, knowing he had committed a faux pas but not quite sure of its nature.

"Let's all go into the other room and have a drink," I suggested.

"Yes," Peter replied, "but I'll need to sit somewhere comfortable where I can extract my foot from my mouth."

This disarmed Marianne enough that she took his arm and said, "We'll get along just fine, Mr. Tummelier."

"Ah, you pronounced it correctly, what a delight you are. I'd consider it an honor if you called me Peter."

"Of course."

After we were in the living room and just as I was about to take drink orders, Peter turned to Marianne. "Roscoe said you were in graduate school."

"Yes, working toward my Ph.D."

"In what field?"

"Psychology. In fact I'm just finishing a paper on sexual deviations."

"Then we *shall* get along famously. *I'm* a sexual deviant!"

Genuinely amused by this, Marianne laughed loudly and I wasn't sure if she caught the look Peter gave me.

"And what is your line of endeavor?" she asked, still chuckling.

"I don't *do* anything, my sweet, I'm *rich!*" he said, elongating that final word into two syllables. "Worth millions and millions." *Mill*-yuns and *mill*-yuns.

She laughed again.

Obviously enjoying the effect he was having on her, Peter bounced a little in his chair as he spoke. "I have to say I was quite surprised to find out Roscoe had married, but the fact that he's married such a delightful—"

"Why were you surprised?"

He looked at me and then back at Marianne. "I've seen Roscoe only a few times in the twenty years since he left Hambriento—he left back when we were both boys of sixteen—but based on what I *did* know about him, I never took him for the marrying type."

"And what exactly is the marrying type?"

"I suppose I mean the settling-down type. The nine-to-five type. The nice-house, mowing-the-lawn-on-Saturday type."

"You mean an adult."

"Well—"

"Well, your old drinking buddy has grown up since last you saw him."

"Since he married you?"

"Precisely."

As I listened to this exchange I wondered why Marianne was being so hostile toward Peter.

He apologized. "I seem to have gotten off on the wrong foot with you. All I meant was, well, to me Roscoe was always the Wanderer. In fact that's what we were going to call our boat, *The Wanderer.*"

"Your boat?"

"Roscoe and I had planned to buy a boat and go on a world cruise."

When Marianne looked at me for confirmation, I said, "Just one of those things kids talk about."

"The Wanderer," Peter said contemptuously. Then he smiled and asked Marianne if she knew the song. "Dion?"

"I hate rock and roll, especially golden oldies."

He seemed incredulous, asking me, "How long have you two been married?"

"Six years."

"Poor Roscoe, you've gone six years without listening to any of our old songs?"

"I use headphones."

In the ensuing strained silence I looked at both of them and thought how evenly matched they were. Not just in their tough-mindedness, their ability to wound with words, they were physical equals too: Marianne taller but Peter with longer, thicker arms. I had an image of the two of them stripped down, greased up, and thrown in a room together to fight it out.

When I laughed at this, they both looked questioningly in my direction. "So!" I said a little too loudly. "Who's drinking what?"

Peter stood. "I'm afraid I'm about to make a crashing bore out of myself."

"I can hardly wait," Marianne cracked.

"Because you see," he went on, speaking to her, "I need to take Roscoe someplace where I can talk with him about an old and very private matter."

The atmosphere in the room, hardly friendly to start with, instantly chilled.

"I realize that's unforgivably rude of me, having just met you, having been offered the hospitality of your charming home, but being alone with Roscoe is required by the very nature of what I must discuss with him."

They looked at me again. "We can discuss it here," I said weakly.

"That's quite impossible."

Well, I thought, here's the other side of Peter Tummelier, because in addition to his quaint, quirky charm he could also be as demanding and imperious as a czar.

"Peter," I told him, "you can't show up like this, unannounced and . . ." I almost said *uninvited*. ". . . and demand that I—"

"I need to finish that paper anyway," Marianne said, standing.

"Oh look, I'm here two minutes and I've put the entire Bird household in turmoil. Please, Marianne." He pronounced it *Mariahne*. "I need to talk with Roscoe about some private, family matters and I need to do it in some neutral setting, some quiet bar. Then he can come home and tell you everything, my dear. 'Share a pillow, share a secret,' I always say. Do let him go off with me. I'll have him back by midnight. Like Cinderella."

"Roscoe can come and go as he pleases, he doesn't need my permission." She was steamed. "Besides, I have writing to do. It works out perfectly."

"Good." As far as he was concerned, that settled everything.

"Peter," Marianne said, offering to shake his hand, "fascinating meeting you."

"The pleasure, my dear, was entirely mine." He took her hand and tried to kiss it again but she wasn't having any of that this time, withdrawing her hand and forcing Peter to settle for a bow.

I followed Marianne out of the room, grabbing for her arm in the front hallway. "Listen, I don't know what this is about, I certainly don't want to go out and have a drink with him."

"I don't mind about that, I just don't like his high-handed treatment." Then she sagged her shoulders and smiled. "But I do have to finish that paper tonight so go out with your friend, have your private discussion, and then don't invite him back for another visit."

"I didn't invite him for *this* visit."

"I know. Do you realize he has a crush on you?" But before I could answer she leaned up and kissed me. "Go on, go. Be back by midnight, Cinderella."

Just then Peter joined us in the hallway. "I have been an absolute prick, haven't I?" he asked, his voice flat and sad, his black eyes darting anxiously between Marianne and me, waiting for one of us to let him off the hook.

Which Marianne did by smiling and then shaking her head as if she was disappointed with herself for not staying angry at him. She told Peter, "Realizing what you are is your saving grace."

Which instantly brightened him. "It is, isn't it!"

FOUR

Peter drove a black Mercedes with a red interior so plush and gaudy that he must've had it custom-installed as a joke. I knew he wanted to talk to me about our long-standing plan that he would buy a boat when he came into his inheritance, I would captain it, and we'd cruise around the world. But, in the Mercedes with him, whenever I tried to discuss it, to explain that the plan was no longer operational, Peter would hunch up his shoulders and put a finger to his lips.

He found a former working-class tavern that had gone yuppie. Four Bauer-and-Bean-dressed couples sat at tables, sipping lite wine and imported beer, speaking softly, no one smoking, no one loud or drunk, the kind of place where hard-liquor bottles gathered dust. We took seats at the end of a long bar with a rounded edge that had been polished by bellies not belonging to any of the current clientele. Everyone stared at Peter in his homburg.

The young bartender, a rosy-cheeked cross between Chippendale and chipmunk, came bounding in our direction with a smile as his spotlight. "Gentlemen, how are you this evening?"

I said we were fine, hoping he wouldn't tell us his name.

"I'm Todd! What can I get you?"

Peter said he would have a Slow Slide Down a Tall Palm.

"Whoa! Can't say that I've ever made one of those."

Peter carefully instructed Todd how to concoct it, using sloe gin, coconut crème de menthe, rum, and some other stuff I didn't catch.

I said it sounded awful and ordered a beer.

"*A beer,*" Peter said disgustedly. "Don't be ridiculous, have a Slow Slide Down a Tall Palm with me. I started drinking them in Haiti. Quite tasty, quite lethal."

"Two of them?" the bartender asked cheerfully.

"*No,* I'll have a beer."

"A beer it is."

After Todd left I told Peter that I thought it was rude of him to demand to be alone with me right after having met Marianne. "And if it wasn't for the fact that she needed to work on that paper tonight I would've never agreed to go out with you."

"Yes, yes, of course. I was unforgivably rude," he said, dismissing the complaint. "But as soon as you discover what it is I'm about to tell you, you'll be *thankful* your sweet wife wasn't around to hear it."

"This is about the boat, right? The boat, the cruise, the—"

"No."

"No?"

"Not exactly."

"So tell me."

"I will, don't worry, booby. But first a tune or two, a few drinks, then down to business."

"Peter—"

But he had already slid off his stool to scurry over to the jukebox. He got back to the bar just as our drinks arrived.

"Hope that Slow Slide is right," the bartender said, obviously intending to wait there until Peter tasted it.

But Peter waved him away.

"I'm sure it'll be fine," I told the young man as he turned to leave.

Peter lifted his glass and said, "To departed friends."

I nodded and raised my stein of beer, watching as Peter took a big drink that left him with a mustache of white foam.

"So—" But I was interrupted by Sam and Dave on the jukebox.

Having taken off his wool overcoat but still wearing the homburg, Peter once again slid off his stool, this time to shout along with the song, instructing the bar's other patrons to get up out of their seats and give him some of that *"oollld soul clapping."*

The yuppies smiled expensively at Peter, who was an admittedly ridiculous sight, this little man dancing around in a dark suit, white shirt, red silk tie, wearing a homburg, singing soul. None of them appreciated Peter's talent for eerily accurate mimicry, but I remembered from when we were teenagers, from when I first introduced Peter to rock and roll, remembered how he learned to sing those old rock songs exactly as he heard them, exactly as they were sung by the original artists.

He came dancing over to me, pushing up the back of his homburg so the front of the brim came low over his black eyes. *"You didn't have to love me the way you did but you did, and you did—I thank you!"*

Peter always made me laugh.

When the song was over, he got a round of applause, which he acknowledged with deep bows.

"That was jolly good fun!" he exclaimed, jumping back up on the stool, draining the rest of his drink, then calling to the bartender and indicating with his finger that we would have another round.

I told him he hadn't changed a bit.

"And I never will, *never.*"

"Wild Thing!" shouted the jukebox.

"Wild Thing!" Peter shouted into my face.

"You make my heart sing, You make everything . . . groovay. Wild Thing!"

"Hey, Peter—"

"Wild Thing, I think I love you . . ."

Then Peter growled along with the Trogg, *"But I want to know for sure."*

When the bartender brought the drinks, I thanked him even though I had finished barely half of my first beer.

"S' come on hold me tight . . ."

I picked up that first beer and killed it.

"I love you."

Peter leaned way back on his stool and did a few riffs of wild air guitar. He acted as if he was drunk already, high on *something*.

"When I finish this second beer," I told him, "I'm leaving, even if I have to call a cab."

He gave me a disappointed look, removed his hat, and said, "This is not the wild-and-crazy, rock-and-rolling Roscoe Bird I grew up with on Hambriento. What happened, has the sweet Marianne *gelded* you?"

"Half an hour with you and it's like the past twenty years never happened."

"Precisely. That's what it means to be friends."

"No, I meant you're still a vicious bastard, that's what I meant."

"Still vicious after all these years," he sang.

I laughed and told Peter that I had indeed mellowed and that, yes, Marianne was the reason. "For which I am grateful."

"The grateful gelding!" he shouted. "How extraordinary!"

I shook my head, there was no talking to him when he got like this, all hyper and weird. I would just finish the beer and leave.

After the jukebox quieted, Peter ordered another round. I said no, but he demanded that the bartender bring the drinks.

"You can line them up here on the bar as much as you want, but when I finish this one I'm out of here."

"Of course, oh grateful gelding."

I started to say something but stifled it with another drink of beer.

When the bartender brought the third round, Peter threw a hundred-dollar bill on the bar. "Bring this gentleman a margarita, rocks, salt. Add a little orange juice, a little club soda, that's the way he likes them. Then keep the drinks coming. As soon as you see we're almost finished, bring another round." He put a second hundred on the bar. "That one's for you, now run along, there's a good boy."

"I'm not starting on margaritas, Peter, I'm leaving after—"

"Yesterday was the twentieth anniversary of your father's death."

I froze.

"Surely you realized that."

I shook my head. Then became angry and hurt and confused all at the same time. "I don't keep the date circled on my calendar, it's not something I celebrate. Damn you anyway."

"I celebrated it last night."

"Jesus." I turned on my stool to face away from him.

I grew up on Hambriento Island, a small barrier island off the southwest coast of Florida, an island accessible only by water. My father was a charter-boat captain, and what I recall from the first sixteen years of my life is nothing but good: fishing, boats, working with my father, a perfect life. I suppose, however, that a portion of this happiness has been imposed retroactively; that is, at age sixteen a line was drawn in my life and everything before that line I remember as good, everything after it as disappointing.

For the first sixteen years I knew precisely how the remainder of my life would proceed. Dad and I had discussed it endlessly. He must have been talking to me about my future when I was an infant, before I was cognizant, because I don't remember a time when I *didn't* know what I was going to do: take over the charter business when my father was ready to retire. Except that in addition to the fishing charters that Dad did exclusively, I also planned to take people on vacation trips, coastal cruising, gunkholing, through the Bahamas and even farther.

I had it all worked out. It would break your heart, this ten-year-old boy earnestly filling page after page of notebooks with fuel prices, insurance payments, maintenance costs, supplies, projected income, estimated profits. *I knew what I was going to do the rest of my life.*

And Dad never laughed at my financial doodlings, he was with me on this all the way, saying that when the time came he would sell his fishing boat to help me buy a trawler and finance my vacation-charter operation, and then he'd work for me as my mate. Not only was this what I wanted, Dad said it was what he'd wanted all his life too—being able to pass along everything to his son just as his grandfather had done with his father and his father with him.

It was all set. The older I got, the more realistic my plans became. Dad told me that the key to running a successful charter operation was knowing how to get along with people, making sure they stay safe but keeping out of their way and letting them have fun, maintaining your dignity and authority as captain but not being an asshole about it. That and a low debt overhead, he said, will make you a success where eight out of ten other small charter operations fail. "That and having your old man as your mate of course."

I can still hear him saying it, can still hear both of us, we must have spent a thousand hours discussing our plans. Anytime I wasn't in school, I was working as the mate on his fishing charters, meeting clients, making contacts, learning. It was perfect, *it was set.*

Then a month after my sixteenth birthday he pointed the muzzle of his .357 Magnum pistol at his forehead and blew out the back of his head, falling off a dock and into the ocean where brown pelicans flocked to peck at floating bits of his brain.

It was after my father's suicide when Peter came up with his plan to buy a boat so we could go on a permanent cruise. He'd finance everything as soon as he came into his inheritance. My contribution would be running the boat. I wanted it to happen, I wanted it desperately, but as the years went by and Peter was restricted to living on income from various trust funds, I thought less and less about ever captaining a boat, living the life that was supposed to be *my* inheritance.

"Don't you still want to kill them?" Peter asked from behind me.

I knew to whom he was referring of course: the Burtons. It was my father's feud with Philip and Diane Burton that led to his suicide. After he killed himself, my mother and two older sisters and I were turned out of paradise and exiled to live in Saint Louis with my mother's bachelor brother in a cramped apartment a thousand miles from salt water.

"You certainly wanted to kill them twenty years ago," Peter said to my back.

I certainly did. On the evening following my father's burial I broke into the Burtons' mansion carrying the same pistol my father had used to blow his brains out. Peter's brother, Richard, had bribed someone at the sheriff's department to get the pistol for me. Neither of the Burtons was home that evening but I was seen by a servant, the sheriff's department was called, and I was taken into custody.

Fortunately, the deputy in charge of the investigation, John Laflin, had been a good friend of my father's and he arranged it so that no charges were brought against me, primarily because I was leaving for Saint Louis with my mother and sisters the very next day. Johnny warned me not to come back to Hambriento; if I did, he would arrest me.

When the new drinks arrived I turned to the bar and took a healthy slug of the margarita.

"That's my boy," Peter whispered.

"Why in God's name are you bringing all of this up now, is that what you came here to tell me, to remind me that it's the twentieth anniversary of my father's suicide?"

"Don't you still hate the Burtons, don't you still want them dead?"

"That was twenty years ago."

"Your father's still dead, you're still not captain of a boat the way your father and grandfather and great-grandfather were, the fact that it's been twenty years has changed none of that."

I shook my head, instantly depressed, not knowing what to say, drinking more of the margarita.

"Do you still hate them?" Peter asked relentlessly. "Just tell me that."

"Yeah, I guess I do."

"Splendid!" he exclaimed, jumping a little on his stool. "Whom else do you hate enough to kill, Kate Tornsel?"

Also a resident of Hambriento, she had joined with the Burtons in their campaign to ban my father's charter operation from the island. The island busybody, Kate Tornsel was also the one who called the sheriff's department when she spotted a girl and me having sex on the beach, when I was fifteen, a year before my father's suicide.

"Roscoe?"

"I hated her and I hated the Burtons but I'm not sure I hate anyone enough to kill them, not anymore."

"I'm appalled."

"Hey, Peter, things change, life goes on."

"Not for your father it doesn't."

"Goddamn you!" I shouted, half standing and, in the process, knocking over my drink.

Todd came running. After he cleaned up the mess, Peter ordered more drinks and slipped him a fifty.

"Still throwing money around, I see."

"Here it comes," he said, smiling tightly.

"All of you people with inherited wealth act the same. I grew up around it. You take being born wealthy as a personal accomplishment."

"Not an accomplishment, no," Peter said quietly. "But neither is it an indictment."

When my fresh margarita arrived I told Peter that when it was finished I was leaving. "I'm not kidding either."

"Of course you're not."

"Don't patronize me."

"I shan't."

I took another drink and suddenly wanted a cigarette; I had stopped smoking shortly after marrying Marianne six years ago. "How's Richard?"

Peter put his hand out, palm down, and twisted it back and forth.

"Still in Europe?"

He shrugged.

"Don't you visit him?"

"Occasionally."

Four years older than Peter and I, Richard had been sent off to a mental institution in Europe shortly after my mother and sisters and I left Hambriento. I was never sure what exactly had happened to Richard to warrant institutionalization. He was a strange kid but no stranger than Peter. In the past whenever I asked what Richard's condition was, why did he have to be sent away, Peter would say only that his older brother had "gone cuckoo."

I finished what I had promised would be my last drink and then informed a subdued Peter that he could either tell me what he wanted to tell me or not, but I was leaving.

"Yes, of course, the time's come, no more dancing around the maypole, time to tell secrets. But first—"

"Oh for crying out loud—"

"No, no, just one thing, tell me whom you hate, whom you *hate-hate*, besides of course the Burtons and Miss Tornsel."

When I tapped a finger on the bar, Todd thought I was trying to get his attention and I had to shake my head at him, wave him off. "Daniel Maring," I whispered to Peter.

"Who's Daniel Maring?"

"I used to work for him. A real bastard, overbearing, ex-military. Irish on his mother's side and terribly proud of it."

"Why do you hate him enough to want him dead?"

"I didn't say I wanted him dead."

"Of course not."

"But I do hate the bastard."

"*Why?*"

"He had just been brought in as vice president of our PR firm, a position I'd had my eye on, and our office was having a retreat, spouses invited. Maring resented that I had friends on the board of directors and after dinner one evening he got on my case about kissing ass. Kept baiting me, asking me why I'd never served in the armed forces. He's a retired colonel. *Quartermaster Corps.* At the office he insisted on being called colonel, except I'd refer to him as Danny. Or to really get his goat, Danny Boy. So there was a lot of hostility between us before we even arrived at the retreat. Anyway after we left the dining room and went into the bar, I started singing "Danny Boy," and when Maring grabbed my arm, I busted him in the mouth."

Peter was delighted. "Good for you! The old Bird temper shows itself. Not *entirely* gelded, are you, lad?"

"A dumb thing to do. Because instead of settling for firing me, which he also did, *Colonel* Maring gets a lawyer and sues my ass. So I hire a lawyer. It goes back and forth. The upshot being I was out of work, had to pay a hefty settlement and an even heftier legal bill, and ended up filing for bankruptcy. Marianne and I lost everything we had saved, all the money she had brought to the marriage. We remortgaged our house, and I had to take a job in a small education association at about two-thirds of the salary I had been making with the PR firm."

"Just like your father. The Burtons and Tornsel ruined him, this Maring character ruins you."

Although Peter had managed to get another round of drinks delivered while I was talking, I didn't touch mine. "What is it you want to tell me?"

"I have an announcement to make."

"Does this have something to do with your sexual orientation?" I asked.

Peter wasn't amused. "You always had that part wrong, you know. What I felt for you, our friendship, the plan for the boat, the cruise, none of that ever had anything to do with *sticking it in.*"

Before I could say anything he took a large drink, carefully set the glass down, then turned to me and asked conspiratorially, "What would you do if a flying saucer landed in front of you, an extraterrestrial got out, the two of you had a conversation via mental telepathy, then the flying saucer departed leaving no evidence that it had ever been there, whom would you tell, what would you *do* about it?"

"Jesus, Peter, I don't know."

"Come on, indulge me."

I absentmindedly took a drink as I thought. "Okay I guess I wouldn't tell anyone. Cops wouldn't believe me, newspapers wouldn't believe me, and if I insisted that it really, really happened, I'd be labeled a nut."

"One of the most profound, unprecedented events that could befall any mortal on earth and you'd just keep it to yourself, not even tell your wife?"

"I suppose I would tell Marianne but I wouldn't insist that she believe me, I wouldn't become a fanatic about it."

"How about those organizations that investigate UFOs?"

"The problem with them is that they're full of nuts and you get tarred with the same brush."

"*Exactly,*" he whispered. "So many *frauds* are involved that it's exceedingly difficult to make *serious* inquiries into the supernatural."

"I wouldn't call UFOs supernatural."

"I've been making serious inquiries for years."

"Into what, UFOs?"

"No."

"What, then?"

"Roscoe, listen to me carefully. Are you sober enough to understand what I'm telling you?"

I laughed. "You pour drinks down my throat and now you're worried if I'm sober enough—"

"Because what I'm about to tell you, *my announcement,* is unlike anything you've ever heard in your life."

"I'm listening."

"More extraordinary than an encounter with an extraterrestrial—"

"Oh for chrissakes, Peter, stick a fork in it, it's done, *huh?* Now, serve it up, *tell me,* or I'm calling a cab."

"Yes, of course." Beads of sweat had formed on his small upper lip. "I was just going to say that what *I* would do if something profound and quite unbelievable had happened to me, *I* would go to my best friend, a lifelong friend who's the only person on earth I would die, lie, and kill for. And I would explain everything to him because he wouldn't dismiss me out of hand, he would try his best to believe me, he wouldn't laugh."

Seeing that he was serious, totally serious, *painfully* serious, I asked, "You think you saw a UFO?"

"*No,*" he grumbled impatiently. "Haven't you been listening to me?"

"What, then?"

There was a pleading in his face that made the hairs on the back of my neck stiffen.

"Peter?"

"Promise you won't laugh. I can't make you promise to believe me—either you will or you won't—but please don't laugh."

"I won't."

"Promise."

"I promise I won't laugh."

His mouth tightened into the strangest, most tortured little smile.

"Peter?"

He leaned in my direction. "I've become . . ."

I waited.

Glancing over at Todd to make sure he was out of hearing range, Peter leaned my way again but said nothing.

"Go on."

He took a breath, held it, then exhaled coconut breath as he said, "I've become a vampire."

My eyes flashed open and I immediately sucked in my lower lip, biting it. But that worked only for a few seconds, then I couldn't hold it any longer, busting out with a horse laugh that made Todd turn around and smile at me.

Peter looked shocked for a moment, then managed his own bitter smile.

I tried to apologize but all that came out was more laughter.

"You said you wouldn't laugh."

Peter's voice was so small and pathetic, his announcement had been so ridiculous . . . I couldn't stop laughing.

"At last count," he said, "there were three hundred and eight vampires in the world, a disproportionate number of them living in the Los Angeles area."

Which made me laugh all the harder. I hollered at the bartender, "Two Bloody Marys here! And when I say Bloody Marys, I hope you catch my drift, *Bloody* Marys."

He actually started making them.

"There are a lot of fine Italian restaurants in the District," I said to Peter, "but let me offer you a bit of advice: Give the garlic bread a pass, huh?"

"Not even clever," he muttered. "At least I expected you to be clever."

"Regardless of what restaurant you go to," I went on, "please, please don't order the *stake.*"

He just shook his head.

While I continued laughing. It was a stupid, drunken laughter that caused me to bend over and heave with the effort of laughing, laughing even more when the bartender arrived with the Bloody Marys, laughing until I had to stand up, knocking over the barstool behind me, then laughing until I fell against the bar and started sliding floorward. Yuppies all around us wrinkled their little noses in disgust at my behavior.

Peter grabbed an arm and pulled me up. "I knew I could count on you."

But I couldn't answer him, I was laughing too hard.

FIVE

On the drive from the bar to my house, some hours later, neither Peter nor I said much. I was drunk, he was angry. Things had gotten ugly. After finishing the margarita and Bloody Mary, I began on Schnapps Shooters. Made some more bad vampire jokes. Told Peter that the only way I'd believe he was really a vampire was if he could say *I vant to zuck your blud* convincingly. He refused to try and I kept drinking, kept badgering him.

I got into an argument with Todd about a Van Halen song playing on the jukebox that had me trying to pull the plug and shouting but laughing, too, about my best friend being a vampire, further claiming that unbeknownst to the world of popular music, Eddie Van Halen was in fact Van Helsing the notorious vampire killer and that's why "Jump" was upsetting my friend, so if Van Halen is ever played on that jukebox again, I'm kicking it in.

Neither Peter nor the bartender thought any of this was humorous, and at one point Peter made disparaging remarks about my ungentle-manly inability to hold my liquor.

I remember giving a speech—I might or might not have been standing on a chair to give it—about not having seen the ocean for twenty years and when I finally did have my reunion with that old scrotum-tightener I was by God going to get down on my knees and lick her briny edges like the salty golden whore she is.

Then *another* argument with the put-upon bartender, who refused to turn the volume any higher even after I told him that "Unchained Melody" was my favorite song in the world, and I ended up accusing the bartender and all the white-bread yuppies there in the bar of being responsible for the popularity of the movie *Ghost*, which in turn was responsible for overpopularizing "Unchained Melody," threaten-ing to turn it into another "Feelings," which would be a crime against mankind because "Unchained Melody," as I kept insisting, was my favorite song in the whole wide world, a song that made me want to write bad poetry and propose marriage to wall-eyed women, and furthermore there was only one version of that song that should ever be authorized for play, and the Righteous Brothers, who weren't either brothers or especially righteous, should've been taken out and shot in the backs of their heads after they cut their original "Un-chained Melody," because once you achieve perfection all you can do from that point forward is fuck it up, I should know, my life was perfect until the age of sixteen but ever since then it's been one fuckup after another.

I remember Peter talking about my father, and by then the bar-tender must have pulled the plug on the jukebox because Peter spoke softly, there wasn't any music. But we were still drinking, Peter invent-ing strange mixtures of sweet and sour, spicy and whiskey, one drink so repellant that I remember pushing back from the bar to spit it out on the floor, Peter quickly clamping a hand over my mouth and insisting that I "swallow it, swallow it, damn you!"

I did. It was either that or choke. Then we almost got into a fight, the bartender stepping between us and insisting we leave, until Peter spread around more bills.

Peter and I must've made up at some point because late in the proceedings I recall him raising a glass and offering a toast, "Here's to your father. He would have died or killed for either one of us but *neither* one of us had the balls to kill or die for him. Until last night."

I didn't know what he meant by that but I was in no condition to make sense of anything.

I remember telling Peter—who of course knew all of this—about how my life was supposed to turn out, how I was supposed to become partners with my father in his charter-fishing operation, then when he was ready to retire he would help me buy a trawler and work with me running vacation charters.

Peter reminded me that he was prepared to make it happen, to buy the boat, he'd come into his inheritance and—

I told him it was too late.

After the other customers left the bar, Peter bribed Todd to plug the jukebox back in. We listened and sang along (I, drunkenly and out of key, Peter in perfect mimicry) with songs I hadn't heard in years. "Five O'Clock World," "I Saw Linda Yesterday," "Indian Lake," and Every Mother's Son suggesting we "Come On Down to My Boat." Lesley Gore gloating now that it had become "Judy's Turn to Cry."

Then in spite of Peter's unending supply of money we got kicked out of the bar sometime around two A.M.

I fell asleep before we got to my house, Peter awakening me when he stopped the Mercedes at our curb.

"What time is it?" I asked groggily.

"Well past midnight, Cinderella."

"Great seeing you again, Peter. Sorry I laughed but—"

"Yes of course. Go run to Marianne. She may spank your bare bottom for being a naughty boy, but after that I'm sure she'll cuddle you to her boyish bosoms and sing you love songs."

"God, you're weird." I opened the door and stumbled out, leaning back down to tell him, "Great hat."

He refused even to look at me.

"Hey, I meant to ask you, have you started smoking?"

He finally turned toward me. "No, why?"

"I was worried about your *coffin.*"

He said he was "utterly" disgusted with me, which made me laugh. I told him good-bye and closed the door, assuming that was the end of our visit, our reunion. Maybe he'd come back in another ten years when I could introduce him to the children Marianne and I would have by then.

I was a few steps away from the Mercedes when Peter rolled down the front passenger window and called to me, "One other thing I meant to tell you tonight."

I made an unsteady turn to face the car again. "Yeah?"

"I killed the Burtons." Then he took off, tires screaming.

SIX

It is almost four in the morning by the time Peter drives into the compound. He has a special pass. Matters couldn't have gone worse with Roscoe tonight and Peter is worried. He parks the Mercedes to the side of the brick cottage and sits awhile trying to figure out how he's going to explain what happened, how he's going to excuse the fact that he never even got around to making the request. Which of course was the entire purpose of this evening, to *ask* Roscoe to be their daytime guardian, to convince him to do it voluntarily.

Peter gets out of the Mercedes and walks to the cottage's front door, which he unlocks. He doesn't bother turning on any lights, the big security light outside illuminates the interior of the cottage well enough for Peter to see. Besides, he'd rather deal with this confrontation in the dark.

Although a far cry from the charming English cottage after which it is patterned, this little brick dwelling is nice enough considering what it houses. There's a large sitting room, one bathroom, and a separate bedroom with a large walk-in closet. Everything's antiseptically modern. No kitchen of course; meals are brought in. Bars over all the windows.

Peter finds Dondo sitting on the couch and says, "Ah, there you are, did you miss me?" He picks up Dondo and holds him on his lap.

It's an unusual doll, two feet tall, crafted in Germany a hundred years ago, the socketed head made of a hard-fired and vitreous china called bisque. The limbs are porcelain, the body is wood. Tonight Dondo is dressed in a red-checked playsuit with big red buttons and a broad white pilgrim's collar.

Turning the doll around to look at its face, Peter can understand why people meeting Dondo for the first time occasionally say he's hideous, although that opinion is usually tempered by a polite addendum, something along the lines of "he's so ugly he's cute."

The bisque head is life-size but appears to be larger than life, especially with those protruding ears. And while the detail work on the face is exquisitely rendered, the overall effect is one of menace: brown brows painted like questioning slashes over the inside corners of gray eyes carved into the china, each eye containing a white center dot that makes the doll's stare overly intense; too much red on the bulging cheeks, as if those bisque cheeks are underlain with broken veins; a flattened nose; a mouth partially opened showing tongue tip behind two upper teeth, one of which has broken off, jagged; and lips blood red, outlined with a fine black line.

It would require either an insensitive nature or a warped sense of humor for a parent to give such a doll to his child.

The porcelain arms and legs articulate onto the wooden body. Dondo's tiny toes are curled as if he's being tickled, and his fingers are apart and bent, grasping.

"I *know* you missed me," Peter says to the doll's face. "I was down in Florida, do you remember Florida?" He bounces Dondo on his knee, holding the arms out, making the doll dance, imagining him laughing. Then Peter stands, puts Dondo back on the couch, and is halfway across the sitting room, when he is halted by an angry, screeching voice.

"About time you got back, Stubby! Where'd you get the hat, Assholes 'R' Us?"

"I—"

"Is he going to do it?" the voice demands.

"I . . ."

"I . . . I . . . I," the high-pitched voice mocks him. "I *what?*"

"I didn't get around to asking," Peter finally admits.

The voice screams. "Then what was the purpose of meeting him? So you could feel his muscles! Do you have to stand on a box to kiss him, you sawed-off little idjit!"

He always makes fun of Peter's height.

"It's not like that at all," Peter says softly. "You know it isn't."

"If he doesn't agree to do it, then we have to *make* him do it, don't we, Stubby?"

Peter closes his eyes. He has come to hate that voice, high and screeching, like a maniacal child on amphetamines.

"Well? Well? Well?"

"Yes," Peter says. "If Roscoe won't do it voluntarily, we'll force him."

"How come you didn't ask him, huh?"

"I didn't get the chance. He laughed at me."

Which sets the voice off onto a laughing jag of its own, a nasal heh-heh-heh-heh that is more madness than mirth.

To stop the laughter, Peter carefully asks, "How does Dondo like his new home?"

"It's a dump! It's a dump!"

"At a thousand dollars a day it hardly qualifies as a dump."

"Not your money! And I don't care if it costs a million a day, if you don't get me the *fuck* out of here, I'm busting out, you stupid dwarf! You promised me a boat, a boat you said, a boat, a boat!"

"It'll happen. Roscoe will—"

"Did you tell him what you did to the Burtons?"

"Yes, but I don't think he believed—"

"Turn up the heat! Kill Tornsel! Turn up the heat!"

"That might not be necessary—"

"Turn up the heat! Kill Tornsel! Turn up the heat!"

"I will." Too tired to take off his coat or hat, Peter sits heavily in an overstuffed chair. "Maybe next week. I'm exhausted."

"Who's fault is that? You partook! You partook! That was your doing, not mine, *yours*. I warned you what would happen!"

"Roscoe's married."

"Ooooooo," comes the voice's long mocking whine. "And now your heart's broken. Kill the bitch, kill her!"

This horrifies Peter. "Roscoe would hardly come with us if we killed his wife."

"I'm hungry!"

"Tomorrow night I'll—"

"Now, tonight, *I'm hungry!*"

Peter stands and walks to a window. "It'll be light in a few hours, I don't have time—"

"Go grab that security guard, he's nice and fat, and I . . . am . . . starving!"

"I can't do that, not right here where you live."

"You got your fill in Florida. What about me? I'M STARVING!"

"Tomorrow night, I promise. I'll bring you someone nice tomorrow night."

"Bring me children!"

"No, I told you, no children."

"Bring me children! Fat little children, stack 'em in the freezer, you know how I love fat little white children!"

"No children," Peter says firmly. Then from behind him he hears the *clink-clank* of porcelain limbs moving against each other, Peter squeezing his eyes shut in anticipation of those limbs striking him in an assault that will be accompanied by that all-too-familiar screeching, both crazed and gleeful.

SEVEN

Had Peter come to me six years earlier, before I met Marianne, had he said *then* that he'd finally received his inheritance and was ready to finance that world cruise we'd been talking about ever since my father died, I would've accompanied him without bothering to give six weeks' notice, without bothering to sublet whatever apartment I happened to be sleeping in at the time—not even bothering to pack because what did I own that would be of any use on salt water, nothing but memory.

The memory of what I'd learned sixteen years on Hambriento, a barrier island six miles long and anywhere from half a mile to a few hundred feet wide, five hundred and fifty acres of man-enhanced paradise. In its original state the island was wildly beautiful but uninhabitable: head-high fields of sea oats on the beaches facing the Gulf of Mexico, mangrove ghettos dominating the bayside, the island's interior a buggy thicket of palmetto and pine, no fresh water, and a resident population of mosquitoes so ferocious that no native tribe had ever established a settlement there. But the island lies near some of the best tarpon fishing grounds in the world and, around the turn of the century, wealthy sportsmen from the Northeast began traveling to southwest Florida for roughing-it fishing expeditions, discovering that the tarpon fishing was especially rich in the pass at the southern tip of Hambriento Island. My great-grandfather was one of the many locals who hired out as fishing guides, but he alone among them realized what this migration of wealthy sportsmen could mean to the area and had the foresight to buy a plot of bayside property on the "uninhabitable" island.

Rich people transformed Hambriento, domesticating its wildness, bulldozing acres of sea oats to build mansions with names like Sea Oats Manor, ripping out the mangroves to accommodate deep-water slips, replanting and irrigating the island's interior, financing dawn air raids that bombed the mosquitoes into little more than a summer-time nuisance. Hambriento remained totally in private hands: no government roads or services, no members of the public allowed. Protected by this privacy, the rich indulged themselves. Libraries and art galleries were opened, antique cast-iron lamps brightened the bike and walking paths that crisscrossed the island, stucco walls and lush flowering bushes were illuminated.

And I grew up in a place of pastel beachfront mansions surrounded by movie-perfect palm trees. No litter, no crime, no strangers. White sailboats on green water stretching to a ruler-straight horizon. I considered the world a perfect place, and for me, for the sixteen years before I was cast out, it was.

I had for those sixteen years worked close to my father and to men like him, large men with rough hands and squinting eyes, men without vanity about their personal appearance but who were fiercely vain about their transactions with the sea, men who spoke to one another as carefully as diplomats, knowing as they did the consequences of the wrong word wrongly spoken. Until age sixteen, I was on salt water. I rigged lines for sportsmen who had codes of behavior. *I saw things.*

And now? At thirty-six I associated with soft-handed men who used moisturizers on their unlined faces, men whose conversations were studded with obscenities and threats—I'm going to ruin the sonofabitch, I'll rip his fucking head off—that had been learned from movies and referred to transactions written on typing paper. I worked in offices where windows were sealed and the very air I breathed had to be pumped in through pipes. No one had codes of behavior and I saw nothing but the clock—and knew exactly why the windows were sealed.

Leaving the house that Monday morning I paused on the sidewalk and thought about Peter's final bombshell from last night, that he had killed the Burtons. I didn't believe him. It was just another of those elaborate, twisted plots he loved to manufacture. But on the bus ride into work I kept worrying about it and wondered what would happen to me if it turned out to be true, that Peter really had murdered the Burtons—would I be in trouble for not having told anyone I knew about it? Is that what's meant about being an accessory after the fact?

I arrived a little before ten at the education association where I worked and didn't shake that Monday hangover until mid-afternoon, when I closed my office door and sat there looking out the window, watching the beginning of what promised to be a snowstorm. It occurred to me that I could call the Burtons' house on Hambriento and if one of them answered, then I'd obviously know that Peter had been bullshitting me.

It seemed like such a simple solution that I immediately called information, got the number, and punched it in without planning exactly what I intended to say.

"Burtons' residence." It was a man's voice with a slight Hispanic accent.

I said I'd like to speak to Diane Burton.

"Who's calling, please?"

I glanced around my office. "John Credenza."

"May I ask what this is in reference to?"

"Draperies."

"Pardon me?"

"Mrs. Burton asked me to call her with a quote on those draperies she's having installed."

"Draperies? For what room, please?"

"If she's not there right now can you tell me when she'll be available to speak to me?" Just indicate to me that she's alive, I thought—that's what I want to know, that she and her idiot husband are still breathing. "Hello?"

The man I'd been speaking to was apparently holding his hand over the phone, talking to someone else. I was about to hang up, when he came back on, asking me nervously for the name and address of my firm.

"Mrs. Burton has all that information. Listen, if she's not there, I'll talk to Mr. Burton."

Another muffled pause, then a different voice came on, another man but this one all-business, official-sounding. "Give me your address, the name of your company."

"I'll call back."

"Hey, buddy, don't hang up on me, I just need—"

I hung up. What the hell was going on down there? Had the phone been answered by a servant who then handed me off to a cop? Did he want me to stay on the line so he could trace the call? I suddenly had the worst possible feeling about this, as if a rotting dock had just given way under my weight and I didn't know how far I was going to fall, how badly I would be hurt.

EIGHT

Tap, tap.

Marianne opens the door and hesitates only a moment before inviting Peter in.

He responds with a little bow, telling her what a delight it is to see her again.

She laughs.

As Peter takes off his coat and hat, Marianne looks out past him. "A real, live snowstorm," she says before closing the door.

"So it seems. Is our boy here?"

"No, probably held up by traffic." Then she quickly adds, "But I expect him any moment."

"Good." Peter pronounces it *goot*.

"Come join me in the kitchen, I was just having a cup of tea."

"Delightful."

Once in the kitchen Marianne directs Peter to sit at the table and while she's bringing down an extra cup from the cabinet she says, "So you and Roscoe tied one on last night."

"That boy never could hold his liquor."

"Milk or lemon?"

"Lemon, please."

When she brings the cups to the table, Marianne catches Peter rubbing his spoon with a napkin. "Dirty?" she asks.

For a moment he thinks she's referring to him, then he looks down at the spoon and apologizes. "I've always been overly fastidious." He clears his throat. "Did Roscoe tell you what we discussed last night?"

"No. I was asleep when he came home, he was asleep when I left for class this morning."

Peter sips carefully at the tea, then says, "You look remarkably like the young Audrey Hepburn, I'm sure you've been told—"

"You can't have him, you know that, don't you? He's mine."

Peter mumbles something Marianne doesn't quite catch, something sounding like *never cut a cold empire*.

"Pardon me?" she asks.

"Of course," he replies, giving her a crafty look.

She responds with her own smirk. Nothing about this strange little man intimidates her. "You're buying a boat and you want Roscoe to captain it for you—that's what this is all about, isn't it?"

"You do cut to the heart of the matter, don't you, dear?"

"Some men are put off by my directness. I don't have a lot of patience for verbal patty-cake."

"Patty-cake!" He laughs. Then tells her, "Yes, this is about the boat, the cruise—and more."

"It's been twenty years since Roscoe was on a boat."

"He might have to take some courses, complete some training, but that's fine, I have all the time in the world."

"And what did he say last night when you proposed this to him?"

Peter taps his large fingers on the tabletop. "He laughed at just about everything I told him last night."

"You can hardly expect him to change his life, leave me, simply because you—"

"Oh, but he doesn't have to leave you, that's what I've come here to tell him, to tell both of you. I'm expanding the offer to *include* you."

"How very generous. More tea?"

"Yes, please."

Watching Marianne use a large knife to slice another wedge of lemon, Peter asks, "That's Roscoe's father's fillet knife, isn't it?"

"Yes."

"It was twenty years ago this month that he committed suicide."

"Oh." She gets a creepy feeling. "I hadn't realized that."

"Neither had Roscoe."

"I understand now." She returns to the table with fresh tea. "You talked about this last night, *that's* why Roscoe got drunk."

"We talked of many things."

"I'm not giving up my life here to go on a cruise and Roscoe's not going to leave me to captain your boat, so if I were you—"

"Ah, but you're *not* me, are you? If you *were* me you would've thought these matters through, you would've designed a plot that's—"

"A plot?"

"A plot that's like a funnel, wide at the top but as time goes on it will become narrower, more inescapable, and soon neither you nor the dear boy himself will have any choice, you'll have to come with me on a world cruise."

"I don't know what you're talking about."

"You'll find out soon enough. Meanwhile if I were *you* I'd be looking at boating outfits, little bikinis and light cotton wear—oh, you'll love the life. Do you need money to go shopping?"

"You're out of touch with reality."

Peter gets up and stands at the counter where Marianne had prepared their tea. Looking out onto the backyard, he says, "It's dark, I have to go. Tell Roscoe I'll be in touch with him—if not with reality." He finds all this immensely amusing.

"I don't much like you," she says evenly.

"We'll have a lifetime to become friends."

"Are you in love with Roscoe?"

Peter smiles.

"In studying sexual deviations," Marianne tells him, "psychologists sometimes use the term *faute de mieux*—are you familiar with it?"

"But of course—'for lack of something better.' "

"Exactly. Men in prison have sex with each other *faute de mieux*, lonely shepherds fuck their sheep *faute de mieux*. And in his younger years, in the aftermath of his father's suicide, Roscoe went along with your plans for a world cruise *faute de mieux*."

Peter starts to say something but Marianne won't let him. "Now, however, Roscoe has something better—our life together—and plot or no plot, you're shit out of luck."

He leaves the kitchen without speaking to her, Marianne following him. At the front door, as Peter is putting on his coat and hat, she tells him, "Give me the knife."

He feigns surprise.

"I saw you put it in your pocket."

Embarrassed, he reaches in to remove the fillet knife from the inside pocket of his suitcoat. "How clumsy of me," Peter says, offering it to her handle first. "I wanted a remembrance of Roscoe's father."

"Stealing from a friend is contemptible."

This wounds him deeply and for a moment she thinks he's going to cry, which robs Marianne of her anger. She's ruthless with arrogant people but can be a sucker for someone in pain. Gently touching his arm, Marianne says, "Wait for Roscoe, he'll be here soon."

Too choked up with shame to speak, afraid to trust his voice, Peter only shakes his head and turns away from her to reach for the door.

"Have dinner with us," she offers.

Peter pauses, then turns back to face her. Except now he doesn't look ashamed or teary-eyed; he has a fierce expression on his face, which frankly scares Marianne.

He says, "I'm going to catch dinner out on the road."

"Peter, I—"

But he already has the door open. "Ask your husband about tap, tap."

"About what?"

Peter raps the door lightly with his knuckles. *"Tap, tap."*

Before she can speak he hurries out, a small dark figure receding in the swirling snow.

NINE

Tap, tap.

Lois Beyer is in a terrible quandary. Forty years old, never married, living alone since her mother died five years ago, she is an exceedingly careful woman. From the Volvo she's now sitting in to the deadbolts on her doors at home, from the Consumers Union publications at her bedside to the therapy sessions she attends twice weekly, Lois has constructed a life that assumes victimization. *Victim* is how she defines herself, a victim of a mother who preferred Lois's older sister, of a father who doted on Lois's younger brother, of a society that prizes women who are thin and giggly, not stout and obstinate. A victim of a short string of would-be suitors who have complained about everything from Lois's nagging voice (a legacy from too many years teaching kindergarten) to her weight (she's convinced it's a glandular problem, victimized by her own genes) to her absent libido—

Tap, tap.

And now this. Returning home from a teachers' meeting that had been canceled because of the snowstorm (Why didn't someone call me? Lois whined to herself. I bet everyone else was called), she has been flagged down by a well-dressed man blocking this little-used road she's on. A black Mercedes, presumably his, is half in the ditch. And he's tapping on her window, making a rolling motion with his hand.

Lois is not about to lower her window. She knows about carjackings, knows to keep her windows and doors locked, don't stop for *anyone*, keep an avenue of escape open. But every time she tries to go forward he scurries to the front of her Volvo and stops her. She isn't sure she can get around his Mercedes in any case. Yet when she looks in her rearview mirror in anticipation of escaping in reverse, all she sees is a curtain of snow.

Tap! Tap!

He looks harmless enough, dressed in a black overcoat, wearing a homburg, smiling, nodding, *white*. Probably a diplomat—several of them live out here in these countrified Virginia suburbs. What must he think of America, Lois wonders, if a person won't even lower a window to speak to him.

Tap, tap. "Madam! Can you hear me, madam?"

She detects an accent in his muffled voice. Swiss? German? Surely a short diplomat from Switzerland isn't going to hijack my car.

Tap, tap. "Madam?"

Reluctantly she lowers the window an inch.

He performs three quick Oriental-like bows. "Madam, I was not sure you could hear me through the window glass. Please. I am extremely aware of crime problems in your country. I do not wish to enter your automobile. I ask only that you stop at some service facility and request please that a service personnel be sent back here to retrieve my auto which is, as you can plainly see, kaput."

It's a safe, reasonable request and Lois is relieved enough to speak to him. "Are you German?"

"Transylvanian," he says, smirking now instead of smiling.

That makes no sense, she thinks, but it doesn't matter. She has been brave, she's allowed him to make his request, which she will fulfill, and now she can be on her way.

"Madam, you will send someone back for us?"

"Yes, of course." She raises the window. Us?

Tap, tap.

Lois lowers the window again, a little farther than she intended to.

"Kind lady, please do not forget, I ask not for myself but for my child. No other autos have come this way and my Mercedes has grown cold inside."

She glances at the rear window of the Mercedes and sees the back of a child's head, the child presumably elevated in a car seat. Lois hadn't noticed this before. Poor thing must be freezing.

"I'll hurry," she tells the man.

"Thank you. You are German?"

How'd he know? "On my father's side." She catches herself right before mentioning her last name.

"Good." He pronounces it *goot.* "Then I know you will not fail in your assignment, good German that you are."

What did he mean by that?

Lois raises the window and looks again at the child in the backseat. From his size she would guess him to be two or three years old, sitting very still. Hypothermia? My God, she wonders, what kind of kindergarten teacher am I to drive away and leave a freezing child in a disabled car in the middle of a snowstorm?

Tap, tap.

"There is a problem?" he shouts through the window.

She lowers it all the way down. "I'll take you and your child to the gas station. You can wait where it's warm while they come and tow your car."

His expression is all wonderment and gratitude. "Madam, you are a saint!"

He hurries to the far side of his car, opens the back door, leans in, and comes around carrying the heavily bundled child. He tries the front passenger door of the Volvo but it is still locked. Holding the child against his shoulder, the man bends down to look at Lois through the window. She's having second thoughts.

But then tells herself, *Stop this.* Stop being so ridiculously cautious. Nothing's going to happen except possibly you are saving the life of a child.

She unlocks the door and he gets in, immediately apologizing for bringing so much snow in with him. "Any damage to your interior I gladly pay."

"It's okay. Is your child all right?"

"Yes, yes, of course." The man has turned the child so that Lois can see only the back of his or her knitted hat.

"It's a boy?" she asks.

"Dondo."

"He's awfully quiet. You mustn't let him sleep, especially if he's been in a cold car for very long."

Holding the child in an odd fashion, grasped by the shoulders, the man brings him close to his face. Then he lowers the bundled child and looks over at Lois.

"Dondo says he is quite warm, thank you very much, but suffers from a large hunger."

She didn't hear the child speak.

"Do you have children, madam?"

"Fifteen."

"Truly!"

It was a little joke of hers. "I'm a kindergarten teacher, fifteen children in my class this year."

"Ah."

"Maybe you should transfer the car seat," she suggests. "It's against the law not to have a child in a car seat."

"Yes, of course." But he doesn't move.

"It would be a good idea. Especially in all this snow."

"You're absolutely correct."

But instead of getting out he looks over the child's shoulder and asks Lois if she's married, if she dates a lot of different men.

Her heart rate jumps twenty percent.

(Looking at her, at the fear in her face, at that sinking realization she's now experiencing—something's *wrong* here—the beast pauses to consider that which has just entered his chest, an emotion, an expression of . . . guilt. How odd. Guilt should be as foreign to him as . . . He can't even think of an appropriate analogy. From where did this arise, this guilt? Seeing Roscoe again! Yes. He's always had strange and mysterious effects on the beast, bringing out the best in me.)

"Sorry," he says, though he doesn't appear to be sorry, not exactly. More like sadness. He's looking at Lois in a way she finds entirely disconcerting. "That's a very personal question, and I was totally out of line to ask it."

What's happened to his accent? Now he sounds American. "Aren't you going to get the car seat?" she asks nervously, thinking that as soon as he steps out she might just speed away after all, send a tow truck or police car back, something's not kosher here.

"Of course." the beast sighs, encapsulates that stray impulse toward guilt, and grins. "Dondo and I were just wondering if to your knowledge you are harboring any blood-borne diseases."

She can feel the pulse urgent in her neck.

"Here," the man says, "you hold Dondo." He lifts the child in preparation for handing him over to Lois but then stops, brings the child back, holds him to his ear. "What's that?" the man asks, apparently listening, though Lois still hasn't heard the child say anything. "Dondo has a question for you."

"Please . . ."

"Dondo wants to know," the man says cheerfully, "if you practice anal intercourse with bisexual, intravenous drug users."

Before Lois can say or do anything, the man turns the child and thrusts him at her, the horrible doll's face extracting from Lois Beyer a gasp that arises deep in her diaphragm.

TEN

When I finally got home that Monday evening, rattled by the snow-crazed traffic of Washington, D.C., and anxious to talk with Marianne about my call to the Burtons, I found her waiting at the door with news of her own: Peter's visit. When she finished telling me—we were in the kitchen by then, fixing dinner together—I said, "You ain't heard the half of it."

Marianne raised her eyebrows and waited.

When I didn't say anything, she asked, "What is it?"

"Last night, after Peter let me off here at the house and right before he sped away, he said he'd killed the Burtons."

"*What?*"

"The Burtons, the people whose legal harassment of my father led to his suicide. Peter says he's murdered them."

Marianne blanched. "Do you believe him?"

"No." I explained Peter's fondness for impressing people with shocking announcements. "I don't even know if what he's saying about buying a boat and taking that world cruise is true. He's been promising that since we were sixteen."

"He sounded convincing when he was talking to me about it this afternoon."

"Peter *always* sounds convincing. The only part that worries me is that when I called the Burtons—"

"You called them? In Florida?"

"It was a spur-of-the-moment thing. I figured that if one of them answered the phone or if a servant said they were out taking a walk—"

"Then you'd know Peter had obviously been lying about killing them."

"I wanted to confirm it, I didn't want to have to worry about it."

"And?"

I told her about the call, how suspicious the two men I talked to sounded.

"And now you don't know what to think."

I was at the counter chopping carrots. "Yeah. I got the worst possible feeling that this is going to be trouble. I threatened to kill the Burtons myself, I was caught in their house with a pistol."

"But that was twenty years ago, you were a teenager. And you haven't been back to Florida in those twenty years, you live a thousand miles away from the Burtons."

"I'm not saying anyone is going to accuse me of actually doing the murders, assuming they really have been murdered, but I might be charged with having knowledge of the crime and—"

"Maybe that's what Peter meant about the plot." Marianne was standing next to me waiting to add the carrots to our salad. "He said he had devised a plot that would force both of us to go on this cruise with him."

"See, that's exactly the kind of shit that worries me."

"Call the police."

"I intend to, I'm just trying to figure out how to phrase what I'm going to say, you know, so I won't sound like a nut. I mean, I can hardly call a homicide detective and say, 'A friend of mine I haven't seen for ten years blew into town last night, said he was a vampire and had killed two people in Florida, would you mind checking it out—' "

Marianne nudged my arm. "Vampire?"

I gave her a stupid look. "Didn't I tell you?" I laughed. "Peter's big announcement, *he's become a vampire.*" Then I waited for her to laugh too.

She didn't. "Do you think he's serious?"

"Serious about what?"

"That he's become a vampire."

"I must be missing something here. Peter said he'd become a *vampire,* how can he be serious—"

"You go ahead and set the table, the tuna's in the fridge."

"Where're you going?"

She was already at the doorway, calling back to me, "Upstairs—I've read some articles on this. There's a professor I met at the university who's done landmark studies on vampirism."

"You mean folklore?" I shouted.

"No, clinical!" she hollered back from the hallway.

Marianne returned ten minutes later with an armful of papers.

"You notice," I told her, "I'm serving red wine for this discussion."

She didn't laugh at that either. "It's a fascinating topic. I wonder, if Peter really has become a vampire, I wonder if he'd agree to be interviewed by this professor. I could—"

"Whoa." I took her hand so she'd look up from the papers that were now scattered on the table. "You said if Peter really has become a vampire—you mean if he really *believes* he's become a vampire."

"Listen to this. 'If the subject believes he is a vampire, if he is convinced that he needs the blood of a human victim to survive, if he acts upon those beliefs, then for all practical purposes the subject in question *is* a vampire.' "

"Oh. I see—"

" 'At least it makes little difference to the subject's victim,' " Marianne read, " 'because being killed by a "real" vampire or being killed by someone who *only* believes he is a vampire is a meaningless distinction to the victim whose arteries are slashed, whose blood is drunk, who dies.' "

"Yeah, but the nut who believes he's a vampire isn't *really* a vampire—he doesn't have a vampire's powers, he's not immortal, can't change himself into a bat, doesn't—"

"Wait," Marianne instructed, holding out one hand toward me while she excitedly paged through the papers with her other hand. "The good professor addresses that specific point. Somewhere . . . Da, da, da, *here.* 'And while the subject isn't equipped with the traditional vampire's traditional powers, neither is the subject limited by the traditional vampire's traditional vulnerabilities. That is, the subject isn't destroyed by sunlight or repelled by garlic or burned by holy water (though he may fear all of these outcomes). The trade-off strikes a remarkable balance: a lack of supernatural powers offset by an absence of unnatural weaknesses. Meanwhile victims are still being killed for their living blood. Given all this, we must conclude that for all practical purposes vampires do indeed exist.' " Marianne looked over at me, her face shining.

"Peter should've made his announcement to you instead of me—you wouldn't have laughed at him."

"No, I wouldn't have. In fact I would've tried my damnedest to get him to go to the university with me."

I raised my wineglass. "Some people have old friends who come out of the closet, I have one who has come out of the coffin—here's to Peter the Vampire."

But Marianne had already returned her attention to the stack of papers. "Here!" she said triumphantly. "I knew I'd read this. Something like three dozen authenticated cases of vampirism have been studied, with ten or more people now institutionalized as vampires in various asylums around the world. In most of these cases the vampire contacted a priest or a close friend, the vampire seeking help so that he could be prevented from doing what he believes it is his nature to do."

"So Peter came here hoping I'd—"

"Hoping you'd help him, prevent him from ever acting on his impulses as a vampire. Or, if he really has murdered the Burtons, hoping you'd help stop him from killing again."

"And the boat and the cruise and all that is just a cover?"

"Yes! Don't you see, he wants help. And I can get him that help. I can put him in touch with this professor."

"And maybe co-author a paper about it."

"Maybe." She took a sip of wine but was still too excited to eat. "I understand now why Peter made that clumsy attempt to steal your father's knife. He wanted to be caught, he wants to be helped."

"Maybe." I looked at the knife, an oversized fillet knife made for my father by one of his fishing clients, who manufactured cutlery in Chicago. My father's name, *Curtis Bird,* had been engraved on the thin nine-inch fillet blade and hand-stamped into the hardwood handle. Dad said it was too big and too nice to use on fish and gave it to my mother, who gave it to me.

"Or *maybe,*" I said, looking back at Marianne, "Peter's plot is to threaten to implicate me in the Burton murders unless I agree to go with him on this cruise, to captain his boat, and maybe he *doesn't* want to get caught, maybe what he wants is to get his way. You don't know Peter Tummelier like I do."

"Tell me about him."

"I've already—"

"Tell me again. *Please.* Roscoe. So much of what I do, working on my doctorate, so much of it is assembling secondary sources that other candidates have already assembled in their own ways dozens and dozens of times before. The opportunity to study and write about a *primary* source—"

"Especially one that might be a real, live murderer."

She sat back from the table.

"You and Peter," I said, "are a lot alike in your intensity."

Marianne just stared.

I took a few bites before saying, "I thought you were writing about sexual deviations."

"If Peter really is a vampire—"

"If he really *thinks* he's a vampire."

She waved off the distinction and continued, "I could switch advisers to this professor who's been doing clinical studies of vampires—"

"Of people who *think* they are vampires."

"Roscoe, I'm asking for your help."

"If Peter's arrested for killing the Burtons and then if *I'm* arrested as an accessory after the fact, maybe we'll be put in the same cell and I could interview him for you."

"You're not going to be arrested, you haven't done anything. Come on."

"Come on where?"

"Tell me everything you remember about Peter and his family, then you can call the police and go on record with exactly what Peter said about killing the Burtons. That puts you in the clear."

I stood. "You're not going to eat anything?"

She shook her head.

"Let's take our wine into the living room, Professor. Then I'll relate the strange and mysterious story of the Hambriento Tummeliers."

We were in the hallway, I was carrying the wine bottle and Marianne was behind me with our glasses, when she said, "Tap, tap."

I stopped so abruptly that she bumped into me, spilling red wine onto the back of my shirt.

Turning, I saw Marianne raise her slender shoulders. "Sorry."

"What do you—"

"All I know is that Peter asked me to ask you about it. 'Ask Roscoe about tap, tap.' "

Nodding, I said, "I'll tell you that story too."

ELEVEN

Who will miss me, who will cry at news of my death? It is altogether fitting for her to contemplate such matters. Lois Beyer knows she's going to die. All her life she's been anticipating something awful like this, guarding against it and yet oddly waiting for it too: the ultimate victim.

During her twice-weekly group-therapy sessions, Lois often tries to explain the pain of having been a middle child, fat and moody, with an older sister who was beautiful and a brilliant athlete to boot, a younger brother who was cute and a genius in school, but Lois's hard-won pain fills only a thimble compared to the barrels of pain produced by the other women in the group, women who have been molested, beaten, raped by grandfathers, married to alcoholics. And so, even in sharing her humiliation Lois is humiliated: telling weepingly of a male principal who once leered at her, undressed her with his eyes, how vulnerable and degraded she felt, while the very next woman to speak offers an angry but dry-eyed account of having to perform oral sex on an office manager to keep her job, which she needed to support three children, her husband having abandoned his family without paying a dime.

No wonder the other women in the group roll their eyes whenever it's Lois's turn to share. Can you be a victim of not being sufficiently victimized? Is that a category Lois could pioneer?

She'll never have the chance to find out. Gagged, tied, blindfolded, *kidnapped,* and brought here, wherever here is, laid out on the floor, about to be . . . what? Raped. Tortured. Murdered.

Victims of crimes often say, "I never thought it would happen to me," but not so Lois Beyer. Because although she's terrified, praying to God, wishing for a rescue, there is yet a portion of her that is experiencing a perverse vindication. Imagine, then, if by some miracle she *is* rescued, imagine sharing this torment in group. Standing to speak because the other women would have heard about her ordeal and would be fascinated, would want to look at her while she shared, would hang on every word. The group's therapist would have brought in several of her colleagues. Special permission would've been granted for a sympathetic journalist to attend the session. Lois would be trembling with emotion, brave tears, *earned* tears, wetting her plump cheeks. She would tap her sternum meaningfully and say, "I'm hurting inside," and not one woman there could deny it, not one eye would roll. Victim. Say it loud, say it proud: "I am a victim."

Eventually giving such a performance assumes, of course, that Lois survives this night, an assumption that keeps slipping from her desperate grasp.

Voices in the next room. Either the malevolent little diplomat has an accomplice or he's talking to that hideous doll again the way he did on the drive here, after having pulled Lois from her Volvo, trussing her in ropes, gagging and blindfolding her, stuffing her on the backseat floor of his Mercedes, which of course was in perfect operating order.

What's he saying? Lois can't quite make it out. An angry voice.

．　．　．

"I'll know if that tub of lard is infected with anything!" the angry voice screeches. "I can *taste* it!"

"She's a kindergarten teacher," Peter quietly replies as he holds Dondo on his knee to remove the doll's snowsuit.

"You'd better get your scrawny little ass back down to Florida, turn up the heat!"

Peter nods.

" 'Cause your little Birdy boy ain't going to hire on with the likes of us until we *force* him to."

"I realize that now."

"I realize that now," the voice mocks.

Peter places Dondo on a chair and leans close. "Will you be all right?"

"Oh, I think I can handle *it*."

"I'll leave, then."

"Squeamish? Too late to be squeamish, dear boy."

"I'm going."

"Not without giving Dondo a hug!"

Then comes the maniacal laughter as tiny porcelain limbs strike Peter's face, inflicting not pain but humiliation.

Tap, tap.

A blindfolded Lois Beyer turns toward the sound, someone tapping a wooden surface, right here in the room with her. "Upsy daisy," a voice says as arms, powerful arms, push under Lois's back to lift her.

"Gawd!" the voice screeches in a Cockney accent. "Fifteen stone if it's a blinkin' bloody ounce."

She's placed upon what she assumes is a table.

"Scared?" the voice asks, pronouncing it *skeered.*

Lois nods her head and tries to ask why are you doing this, but the gag makes a mishmash of her words.

She feels hands working on her blouse, undoing buttons, ripping material to pull it free from the ropes that bind her. A single finger slips between her breasts, under the bra.

"O Ga hease on't ut ee!" she tries to say. Oh, God, please don't hurt me.

"Und now zee question iss, vhat colair vill zee nipples be?"

The finger between her breasts pulls back with such power that the bra is ripped loose, straps breaking at her shoulders, the clasps behind her back torn away.

"BROWN! BROWN! BROWN!"

She feels a face close to hers, smells his bad breath as he does a Boris Karloff imitation. "You know, my dear lady, the lit-er-a-ture speaks of nipples like cherries, like plums, raspberries, blackberries, mulberries, strawberries, an entire cornucopia of fruity possibilities, a bright palette of reds and pinks and purples. But all I ever get is BROWN, BROWN, BROWN!"

Lois's skin crawls when he touches her, his hands under her breasts, pushing them up as his voice takes on a rough hillbilly accent. "The Good Book sez twin roes feedin' among the lilies but looks lak what we got here is a coupla old milk cows been left too long in the silage, har, har."

She's crying, able to see a little under the blindfold but the room is dark and she isn't sure she wants to witness this in any case. Silence, time ticking. Where's he gone, what's he doing?

A sharp pain strikes at the base of her neck, like a bee sting. When his finger touches there she feels him smearing wetness.

"Nummy nummy for the tummy tummy." He smacks his lips. "Absolutely pure. 'Blood, red blood, super-magical, forbidden liquor.' D. H. Lawrence wrote that about a mosquito of all things. Here's an interesting fact for you: Little-boy mosquitoes have penises, little-girl mosquitoes have vaginas. Imagine the possibilities!"

He slaps her across the face.

"Have to get the old blood pressure up," he says with a flat midwestern twang. "I want them bleeders spurtin' like garden hoses, sure do." And slaps her again.

Then mimics a woman's voice. "High blood pressure makes those bleeders pop off in my mouth all hot and salty, good God, we know about *that* don't we, hon?"

He makes sniffing noises and lifts her skirt. "You've soiled yourself! That means you like me! It means we're going steady! I'm in love!"

Then for the longest time, nothing. Lois's blood pressure has, in fact, risen dangerously high, her pulse racing, her heart about to burst with dread, with anticipation. It is said that animals do not suffer pain with the same intensity humans do because animals do not *anticipate,* and it is this anticipation of pain that heightens its impact, sharpens its point, pushes it into the exquisite ranges. And Lois Beyer is filled to overflowing with pain's anticipation: *What's he going to do to me?*

He climbs upon the table, covering her body with his own, his face at her neck. She feels his mouth, a mouth with hair around it, *like a muzzle.* Lois smells him, the odor of mold and something else. Dirt. But not dirt from a garden. This creature atop her smells of the cellar, of decay, of dirt that's been too long wet and without sunlight. Filth. And as that repulsive mouthy hair scratches at her neck, a sassy woman's voice tells Lois: *"When I say I'm in love you best believe I'm in love, L-U-V!"*

TWELVE

When we were growing up on Hambriento Island, I and my two sisters ran with children whose parents cleaned, cooked, and drove for the rich. We were called island rats, a name of which we were inordinately proud, considering ourselves tough and troublesome, though in comparison to what happens today we were model citizens. We would occasionally climb a wall and swim in some mansion's pool while the owners were away, but we never committed vandalism, didn't steal from wealthy property owners, and weren't resentful of their wealth or of the class system that kept us separate from their kids. They were like the sea, the rich, and what would be the point of coveting the sea's bounty or resenting its power over us?

Rich kids ran in their own packs and had their own agendas and I remember them from afar, an ocean I would never enter upon, overhearing their laughter, seeing their bright teeth smile as they walked to and from tennis courts, red and green sweaters tied around their long necks, watching them speed by in convertibles, never waving.

But Peter and his older brother, Richard, weren't among them. The Tummeliers kept to themselves, though I would occasionally see Peter spying on us island rats or walking the beach alone, staring out to sea like the French Lieutenant's Woman. It was on the beach in fact where I first spoke to him. We were both eight years old.

The sun had just set and Peter was poking around in the sand with a four-foot bamboo pole. He was perhaps even stranger as a boy than what he turned out to be as a man: this odd boy alone in the twilight, his dark hair and black eyes and that premature widow's peak making him look like a member of the Addams family. Peter wore a white and ridiculously outdated Nehru jacket buttoned all the way up at the neck, charcoal-gray trousers, and pointy Italian shoes. *On the beach.*

He called to me in that fakey accent he used even back then. "Little boy," he said, embarrassing me because after all we were the same age, "do you know the legend of Gasparilla?"

I said I did. Everyone had heard of the pirate Gasparilla, who was supposedly an admiral in the Spanish Navy before turning to piracy in the late 1700s. He sailed to the coastal islands of southwest Florida where he and his pirate crews preyed on shipping and, according to the legend, buried their pirate loot. Sometime in the early 1820s Gasparilla apparently was trapped by the U.S. Navy and, to avoid capture, wrapped an anchor chain around his body and leapt overboard to his death.

Peter asked me if I knew why Gasparilla had become a pirate.

I thought I did, something about a ruined love affair, but at age eight I wasn't sure how that part of the story went, I was more interested in buried treasure.

"Syphilitic madness," Peter intoned, raising his thick eyebrows meaningfully.

But the meaning was lost on me.

"That plus his hatred for the Catholic church, for Papists."

I was Catholic but I didn't know about Papists and thought they were probably one of those Protestant groups I could never keep straight.

"He buried priests alive here on Hambriento," Peter told me.

I hadn't heard that part of the legend.

"Other priests came looking for them, so the buried priests had to keep tapping on the undersides of their coffin lids—that's the only way they could be found—keep tapping until someone heard, keep tapping before they died of thirst and madness, just keep tap, tap, tapping."

And with each of those final three words, Peter poked me in the chest with that bamboo stick.

"That's what I'm doing out here now," he said, "looking for one of those graves, going to open it to see if the priest was found or if he died tapping on his coffin lid, tap, tap, tapping."

Again with the poke, poke, poking in my chest.

I was a fisherman's kid, I had been bullshitted all my life, and while I didn't mind this strange boy trying to scare me with stories of buried-alive priests, getting poked by that bamboo stick was starting to piss me off.

He said that the priests who'd been buried alive kept their eyes open all the time they were in their coffins. "Waiting to be found, waiting to see sunlight once again, and sometimes the ones who *were* found couldn't close their eyes even after they'd been rescued. For the rest of their lives they had to bathe their eyes in water to prevent them from drying out, those eyes having been permanently stuck open by the terror the priests felt while they were buried alive and tapping against their coffins, tap, tap—"

I grabbed the end of his bamboo pole in mid-poke and told him, "You keep on doing that and I'll shove this up your ass and ride you home like a pogo stick."

Impressed, Peter asked my name and when I told him he smirked, then said, "Roscoe Bird, the fisherman's boy. I'm Peter, Peter Augustus Tummelier." He pronounced it carefully for me, *Toom*-ah-leer, then stuck out his hand. "I'm almost nine."

We shook.

It was dark, and feeling creepy, I told him I had to go home.

"Wait. I'll show you something. Roscoe." He laughed when he said my name.

"Yeah, what?"

"Well, I'm looking for another of those priest graves, but I've already found *one,* the corpse is still there."

"Bullshit."

"Really? How about if I show you?"

So I said sure. Peter led me to this beach where there was a hole in the sand, a grave-sized hole two or three feet deep, and in the bottom of the hole there were some planks.

"The priest's body lies under that coffin lid," Peter told me.

"Bullshit," I said again.

"He may still be alive, still tap, tap, tapping."

Just as I was about to laugh at him I heard this tapping noise, exactly like knuckles against the undersides of those boards. I was petrified. Then the boards moved! Before I could turn around and run away, someone *under* the boards quickly sat up and shouted, "Save me, save me!"

I was so absolutely terrified that a squirt of urine came out, like a little yelp of pee. I started backing up. The "corpse" came out of the hole and headed for me, holding both hands in front of him and stomping his feet like Frankenstein in a bad movie, still speaking in that groaning voice, "Save me, save me!"

I ran. And I heard them laughing behind me. It was Richard in the hole. Peter's twelve-year-old brother. They had put together this elaborate prank to scare the piss out of the fisherman's son. And of course it worked beautifully.

Marianne and I had finished the bottle of wine as I talked. She said she was surprised I became friends with the Tummelier brothers after they tricked me like that.

"I was fascinated by them, creatures from another world, Peter small and dark, Richard tall and blond, both of them wearing ridiculous clothes, white Nehru jackets, straw boaters, gray trousers, those pointy leather shoes. I've told you all this."

"Tell me again."

"I kept wondering if they *knew* how ridiculous they looked and I found out later they didn't. Their parents kept them isolated from outside influences, no television, no magazines. And Peter and Richard were too weird to make friends with the other rich kids who wanted only to play—play golf, play tennis, play on their sailing boats, play charades, play at scavenger hunts, while Peter and Richard preferred telling ghost stories and holding séances and collecting accounts of grisly crimes.

"Whenever I was with them I always had this *sense* that something was going to happen. The summer after I first met Peter, he and Richard told me that there was a haunted house on the island, a guesthouse in which a man killed his wife. The man supposedly had strapped his wife to a table and used a hammer and chisel to crack open her sternum so he could pull out her still-beating heart.

" 'She and his best friend had cuckolded this man,' Richard told me—and then had to explain what *cuckold* meant. 'The man said she had broken his heart so he was going to *remove* hers. He called her heartless, and then to her screams and with blood soaking the table, he *made* her heartless.' "

"Richard was a sick puppy," Marianne said.

"Yes, even stranger than Peter. In fact after my mother and sisters and I left Hambriento, Richard was sent away to some kind of mental institution in Europe."

She was immediately interested. "What happened?"

"I never knew, I was in Saint Louis when he was sent away, and Peter never talked about it. Anyway, back when I was nine or ten, Peter and Richard said they had found the haunted guesthouse and had stolen the table on which the murder took place. And now they were using it for séances. I was invited to attend one, Peter and Richard acting very reverential about the murder table, which was a simple pine table with a top that had been scrubbed white but still showed a red stain across it. I figured that it was bogus, that the Tummelier boys had bought the table at a flea market, then poured red paint over the top. But I lost my cynicism during the séances we held at that table. Things happened, things I can't explain."

"Like what?"

I felt a sudden shiver, the kind my grandmother used to say was caused by a goose walking over your grave.

"Roscoe?"

"Peter and Richard would call on the spirit, the spirit they had named tap, tap, the spirit that had first been summoned to Hambriento by those buried-alive priests. And sometimes the table tapped back at them, sometimes it moved. I didn't want to believe it was true. I kept *saying* that they were playing another joke on me, that Peter or Richard was tapping against the table or moving it with their legs, but the spooky thing was, regardless what I was saying, I *believed* it was true, I believed they had summoned the supernatural. I was . . . thrilled. Terrified but thrilled. Later on when they claimed they had encouraged the spirit to enter their bodies, the possibility that this also was true . . . it just blew me away. The hours I spent during those séances, at that table—they were the most frightening hours of my life.

"I stopped going to the séances after a talk that my priest, Father Mueretto, gave to one of our CCD classes. He told us not to play around with the supernatural because each time you use a Ouija board or hold a séance, it's like shining a flashlight into hell. Once or twice, maybe no harm done. But the more often you try to contact spirits that aren't of God—because there are only two choices in the spiritual world, Good or Evil—and the more passionately you believe it's *possible* to contact spirits that aren't of God, the longer you shine your flashlight down there, then the more likely it is that something evil will notice you and home in on that light you're shining. He said that séances are like prayers to Satan and if God answers prayers, why wouldn't Satan?

"So the next time Richard and Peter invited me to one of their séances, which they were holding almost nightly at what they called the murder table, I told them what Father Mueretto had said, that holding a séance is like shining a light into hell and eventually something bad is going to home in on that light. You know what Richard said? He leaned real close to me and said, '*Exactly.*'"

Marianne raised her eyebrows and stuck out her lower lip in an expression that meant she didn't see anything wrong with Richard's comment. "I have more sympathy for the Tummelier brothers than I do for your Father Amaretto—"

"Mueretto," I corrected her, realizing a beat too late that she had misspoken his name on purpose.

"Your priest was trying to stifle inquiry. His warning about not shining lights into hell were like those ancient map warnings about unexplored oceans, 'Beyond Here Monsters Be.' It's ignorance, it's what built religion: fear and superstition and ignorance. In fact the way I see it, the Tummelier brothers in their own weird way were in pursuit of knowledge, their séances were—"

"The way I see it," I interrupted, "is that Father Mueretto was trying to protect me."

"I guess we don't want to start in on the Catholic church, do we?"

"No, we don't."

Marianne was an authentic intellectual, obsessed with trying to figure out why people do what they do, why they think what they think, and her analyses were ruthlessly rational. On those rare occasions when she attended mass with me, afterward I had to be interviewed: What was going through my mind when I took Communion, did I really think I was eating the Flesh of Christ? How much did I attribute to symbolism, how much to the supernatural? Did I believe in magic? I never came up with adequate answers. How can you explain faith? I couldn't.

But Marianne's curiosity was part of what made her so attractive to me, her enthusiasm for new ideas, the way she'd become bright-faced with excitement when defending her point of view or dismantling someone else's. She was without artifice.

Which sometimes led to problems and misunderstandings on certain matters. Religion for one. Sex for another. Marianne enjoyed lovemaking in the same way she enjoyed a hard game of tennis or a soaking bath. Either way, athletically furious or soft and slow, the idea was to get right in there and *do it*. She didn't have much patience with pretending or creating illusions, and whenever I tried to inject some fantasy into the proceedings, the effects were usually disastrous. Like my suggestion on our anniversary last year that she wear some outrageously sexy outfit to bed. She agreed and on the appointed evening I was called upstairs expecting leather or lace or garter belts. Instead I found her lying there in a clown's outfit she had rented from a costume company: red nose, multicolored fright wig, huge floppy shoes. I have to admit it was funny, especially when she kept squeezing her little ooga horn while we were making love—but it wasn't what I had in mind. I would've preferred to see her wearing nothing but white cotton underpants and one of those little white bras of hers, the kind a young girl might wear, small and hopeful, a tiny blue flower between the cups.

Thinking about this obviously had an effect on me because when I was getting into bed with Marianne that Monday night she pointed a finger and screeched, "Roscoe Bird, you have an erection!"

I felt oddly embarrassed by it.

"What brought that on?" she asked.

"Thinking about when you dressed up like a clown last year."

Marianne laughed. "Men are so weird about sex. Women are supposedly the coy ones, the ones who have to be romanced and seduced, but actually it's men who are the delicate little creatures when it comes to sex, who have to be cajoled, who have to fantasize and—"

"Okay, okay, I think you've made your point."

She raised the blankets. "Oh. Sorry. Maybe you can get it back. Why don't you lie there and fantasize. Let's see . . . Naughty nun? Slutty whore? Virginal schoolgirl? Prim librarian?"

Marianne kept laughing as she ran through what she considered the usual suspects but her reference to virginal schoolgirl reminded me—I suppose because of all these recent recollections about Hambriento—of the first girl I made love to, Debra Rosenthal, so sweet and shy that she'd get red in the face if you said the mildest cuss word in her presence. We were both fifteen, lying out on the beach, watching the moon, our fingers interlaced. We started kissing and when I reached out with the tip of my tongue, expecting to bump against closed teeth, expecting her to pull away and put a stop to it, I discovered instead that she had opened her mouth to touch tongues with me. An electrifying development. As matters proceeded I dared not speak, operating under the adolescent male belief that if you didn't mention or acknowledge what you were doing, she wouldn't stop you, she wouldn't *notice*. So I didn't speak to Debra of the poetry of her tan line, didn't try to put to words the thrill of pulling down her swimsuit top, watching breasts emerge, watching as their color changed from brown to a shockingly intimate belly white, removing the top completely to reveal in moonlight the bruised purple of her surprisingly large nipples. Neither of us spoke as we felt our way through this most curious debut, filled with a thousand unasked questions about sizes and smells, pains and pleasures, procedural questions too—is this the way you do it and how hard should I push, should I squeeze, and now what—all unasked, unanswered.

Holding each other afterward but still not speaking, we were horrified to see a man in uniform walking up the beach toward us. I found out later that the island busybody, Kate Tornsel, had been watching us from her beachfront mansion—which was so far away she must've used binoculars—and had been sufficiently affronted that she called the sheriff's department. The deputy approached slowly enough that we had time to get dressed and pretend we had been doing nothing other than sitting there watching the moon. He was gentle with us, suggesting we might want to go home, saying nothing about our having been observed, a complaint having been lodged. He told me about all of that a year later, because this was the same deputy who took me in for threatening to kill the Burtons—

"Johnny Laflin!"

Marianne, who was still auditioning possible sexual fantasies, suddenly stopped and looked at me with the strangest expression. "You're fantasizing about Johnny Laflin? Pray tell who exactly—"

"He was a friend of my father's—"

"And you have sexual fantasies about him?"

"No, no." I laughed. "He was a deputy with the sheriff's department in Florida, he was the one who picked me up when I was found in the Burtons' house with a gun, after my father killed himself.

Johnny covered for me. I was leaving for Saint Louis the next day anyway and Johnny did whatever he did, talked with the servant who caught me in the house and deep-sixed the paperwork at the sheriff's department so that no charges were brought. What occurred to me just now was, if Johnny's still a deputy I can call *him* and explain what Peter said about being a vampire, murdering the Burtons. If I tried to tell that to some cop here in Washington, he'd think I was crazy but Johnny knows the Tummeliers, he'll understand perfectly."

Marianne didn't say anything for a moment, then she put a hand on my shoulder. "I'm dying to know exactly how your thought processes came up with Mr. Laflin's name while I was outlining possible sexual fantasies."

"It was . . ."

"Your face is red."

"Johnny also . . . a year before my father died, Johnny caught me out on the beach with a girl."

"*Ah-ha.*"

"There's this real bitch who lived on Hambriento—we called her the Bicycle Lady—and she's the one who called the sheriff's department to complain about this girl and me—Oh, Jesus."

"What?"

"Kate Tornsel."

"Your girlfriend?"

"No, *no,* Kate Tornsel was the one who reported us that night, the busybody, but the thing is, she was also in with the Burtons suing my father for running a charter business on Hambriento. She was almost as much to blame as they were—"

"Roscoe, honey, you're not making sense."

"When we were drinking last night, Peter mentioned Tornsel's name! He asked me who I hated enough to kill, did I hate the Burtons enough to kill them, did I hate Kate Tornsel enough to kill her."

"You think he might have gone after her too?"

"I don't know! I don't even know if he's done anything to the Burtons but let's say he has, let's say he *intends* to kill Kate too. It's one thing to have knowledge of a crime *after* it's happened but if I have a suspicion that someone is *going* to be killed . . ."

"You'd better call your Mr. Laflin right now."

"What time is it?"

"Ten."

"I think I still have his home number."

On the way downstairs it occurred to me that I hadn't told Marianne the whole story about tap, tap, that I hadn't adequately conveyed to her how frightened I was, for years actually—frightened that the tap, tap spirit really existed and that Peter and Richard could conjure it, that they might sic it on me. Even after the priest convinced me never to attend another séance, I would lie in bed at night and imagine that tap, tap had found where I lived and was trying to contact me. I listened for tapping in my room. I listened and listened—and had no idea what I'd do if ever I heard it.

And yet, instead of shunning the Tummeliers, this fear they induced in me made them all the more alluring. Part of that fascination was the thrill of being frightened, the reason we buy tickets to horror movies and read books about monsters, but I was also drawn to the Tummeliers because they were otherworldly, and I was curious about and attracted to their power, their fearlessness in calling upon spirits, the possibility that what they were doing transcended the rational: that they had truly tapped into what was supernatural.

I got through to Johnny Laflin at his house that Monday night and after I talked with him I came back upstairs in such a daze that I couldn't focus on Marianne's face. My expression told her it was bad news, and she asked three times if I felt okay. "Roscoe? Has that Tornsel woman been killed?"

"No." I stood staring off into a middle distance. I knew Marianne wanted an explanation, but I couldn't find my voice.

She came out of bed and put both arms around me. "The Burtons?" she asked. "They've been killed?"

I cleared my throat. "They're missing, been missing for a couple of days, missing and *presumed* killed."

"Oh, Roscoe."

"The sheriff's department has a suspect."
"Peter," she said. It wasn't a question.
"No."
"Who, then?"
I finally brought her face into focus. "Me."

THIRTEEN

Kate Tornsel, sixty-seven, walks with a brisk, no-nonsense stride across her bright-white crushed-shell driveway. On this particular Tuesday morning, March 15, she is wearing light blue cotton slacks and a long-sleeved red-checkered cotton shirt. Around her neck is a white silk scarf, on her feet are red high-top basketball shoes, and atop her head is a New York Yankees ball cap, under which gray hair is coiled in a tight bun secured with a tortoiseshell comb. Although Kate's face is deeply creased at the outside corners of her granite gray eyes and is wrinkle-puckered around her tight little mouth, her skin is as powdery white as a child's. A forty-year resident of Hambriento Island, she never goes out into the sun without a hat.

Kate's hands and head shake a little. She doesn't mind. The shaking completes her lifelong fascination with and emulation of another Kate—Hepburn, the flinty, no-nonsense actress.

Flinty and no-nonsense is certainly how Kate Tornsel would describe herself, a tough old bird who never married because no man she ever met could live up to the standards set by the one man she did adore, *her* Spencer Tracy. Daddy. He was a New Englander, flinty and no-nonsense himself, sanctimonious down to his rigid soul, hypercritical of the behavior (especially sloth and self-indulgence) of others, a tightly wound man who inherited from his father the income from patents to a complicated process employed in the distillation of scents used in cheap colognes and toilet waters.

An only child, Kate was bequeathed more than one hundred million dollars from her father's estate, a fortune that has grown over the years and now earns her an annual income in excess of twenty million before-tax dollars. Kate, however, considers herself nothing if not frugal. She has never touched the principal. Neither has she distributed any of the money to her cousins' children, who are in line for the Tornsel fortune once she dies. Whenever one of these expectant heirs comes to her asking for an advance on expectations, Kate counsels that easy money early in life leads to wasted potential. This doesn't apply to her, of course, but to individuals less strong-willed than she. Meanwhile the cousins' children, who are in their forties and who will all become millionaires several times over upon Kate's death, keep their lives on hold while despairing with thoughts of the tough old bird still being vigorous in her eighties, still riding her goddamn bicycle—off of which the cousins' children keep rooting for her to fall.

Kate has given the Hambriento Property Owners Association more than a million dollars for the construction of bike paths throughout the island, but her dream—her vision, her goal in life—is to ban all motorized vehicles from Hambriento and force everyone to do as she does, ride a bike.

That's where Kate is heading now, Tuesday morning, walking across the bright-white crushed-shell driveway toward the shed where her precious bicycle is kept. It's a balloon-tired, heavily framed, single-speed throwback to the forties, which is when Daddy gave it to her. Big wire basket on the front and a rubber-bulbed ooga horn on the handlebars. She considers modern bicycles with all their gears and levers utterly ridiculous and would like to ban them from the island too, but first let's get rid of the cars.

Kate can't drive. Daddy tried to give her driving lessons all through her teens but she found the effort of coordinating the steering wheel with the foot pedals while watching where the car was going completely flummoxing. Kate had always had everything done for her; even her shoes were laced for her every morning as a child. Those driving lessons were the only times that Daddy lost his patience with his little girl. He'd get red-faced and shout in a harsh voice as she once again rolled the big Packard off the driveway and over the azalea bushes. And then Kate would cry and he would have to bounce her on his lap until they both started breathing heavily. He ended up giving her an old chauffeur and a brand-new bicycle.

And now in the spirit of New England Puritanism she wants others to do as she does, Kate being absolutely convinced that by force of will and power of money she will see a car-free Hambriento before she dies.

At ten-thirty A.M. the Hambriento Property Owners Association is holding its annual meeting and Kate has memorized her speech. This year she's going to pitch bicycles on an ecological basis. "Unfortunately," her opening line goes, "pollution, like charity, begins at home. Save the planet but start with the island of Hambriento." She's been writing and practicing the speech for months.

Most of the wealthy residents of Hambriento own bicycles and are charmed that Kate has financed the construction of so many miles of bike paths, leading as they do past small shops carrying overpriced knits and through cozy gardens kept in bloom by an army of soil-kneed gardeners, but the residents certainly don't intend to give up their cars. Kate Tornsel might choose to arrive at an elegant dinner party on her bike but then, Kate is eccentric.

She is known around the island as the Bicycle Lady, or as Crusading Kate, because in addition to her Bicycle Campaign, Kate was also the leader and chief financier of the crusades to ban smoking in all public places, from beaches to streets, over the entire island; to ban all advertising signs from the few restaurants and shops that were allowed on Hambriento after the bridge was built; to establish and then vigorously enforce an architectural code; to make street parking illegal. She also fought unsuccessfully to stop the bridge, which brought even more cars onto the island, Kate spending three million dollars of her cousins' children's inheritance in that lost battle. Kate also speaks out vociferously against sexual licentiousness but can't quite figure how to organize a campaign against it.

When she opens the door to the shed and wheels her bike out, Kate immediately sees that the back tire is flat.

"Paco!"

Her hands and head begin shaking more noticeably than usual.

"Paco!"

Kate checks her no-nonsense Timex watch, a few minutes of ten. It will take her fifteen minutes to ride from her beachfront mansion to the Episcopal church hall where the ten-thirty A.M. property owners meeting is to be held. Except she obviously can't ride there on a flat tire and the ever-frugal Kate doesn't own a backup bike.

"Yes, Miss Kate?" He has run out from the house and is still wiping his brown hands on a towel.

"Paco" is the same age as his employer and has worked for her for twenty-five years. He is Vietnamese, his real name being Nguyen That Thanh, but after hiring him and tripping over that name as clumsily as she once tried to drive a car, Kate decreed that henceforth she would be calling him Paco.

She thinks of him as monkeylike in all his small quick brownness, and frankly Paco gives Kate the ethnic creeps, but he alone among the dozens of servants she has employed over the years manages to put up with her moods and lectures and demands without displaying any outward signs of the insolence for which she has fired so many others.

She turns on him with a fierce expression, saying nothing as she points, shakily and accusatorily, at the bicycle's back tire.

Paco's heart sinks. He's tempted to make a joke of it, say something his father used to say, "It's only flat on the bottom," but Paco is acutely aware of Miss Kate's birth defect, born without a sense of humor.

"Well?" she demands.

"Sand spur, thorn," he speculates as he bends to the tire and runs a hand around its circumference. "Patch the tube, pump it up, have you on your way in fifteen minutes or so."

Kate is horrified. "Fifteen minutes or so? *Fifteen minutes or so?* Are you aware, sir, that my meeting begins at ten-thirty, that it takes me fifteen minutes to ride there even if I hurry, that you therefore have only"—she consults her Timex—"*ten* minutes at the very most to repair that tire, *ten minutes*, not fifteen *or so*, as you so glibly put it."

No way, he thinks. Miss Kate doesn't believe in such indulgences as a powered air compressor, so after Paco takes off the back wheel and finds the puncture and patches the tube, he'll have to pump up the tire by hand. His estimate of fifteen minutes was a fudge; in truth the repair will take more like twenty minutes, half an hour. He's not a young man.

"Get to it!"

"Yes, ma'am, but it can't be done in ten minutes."

"Can't? *Can't?* My ancestors didn't build this country on *can't*, surely even an immigrant is aware of America's *can*-do spirit."

Nguyen That Thanh grimaces.

"Proceed, proceed!" she tells him as she glances once more at her practical Timex. "I should leave right at this moment, I wanted to arrive there with sufficient time to go over the speech, freshen up. Now I'll be arriving in a muck-sweat. You don't even have ten minutes. That tire needs to be repaired in *five minutes*. Do you hear me, sir, *five minutes*. I'd like to know what happened to the policy of maintenance. Why aren't these things checked on? Do I have to take personal control of every last . . ."

Paco bows his head and humbly folds in his shoulders as if receiving some sort of negative blessing. Once she launches like this, no telling how long she'll go on. Miss her meeting for sure.

When Kate pauses for breath, Paco offers to put the bike in his station wagon, give her a ride to her meeting, take the bike to the repair shop, then once the tire is fixed Paco will place the bike in the rack outside the church and it'll be waiting there for Kate when she finishes her meeting. Good plan. Paco is smiling.

Kate turns on him with such aggressiveness that he wonders if he's going to be hit. "You, sir, are an idiot! I'm speaking at that meeting in support of a motion to ban motorized vehicles from this island—

and you have the lamebrained audacity to suggest that I arrive at such a meeting *in a car?*"

He sees her point.

Kate is crying and raging simultaneously. "You wish me to be the object of ridicule, is that your aim, sir? Or is it simply that you wish to sabotage the efforts of a lifetime by ensuring I miss that meeting? Which is it, ridicule or sabotage—because those surely are where your suggestions lead, ridicule or sabotage." Her gray eyes are wet and her arms are shaking so severely she can barely read the time from her wristwatch. "You don't even have five minutes now. I require that tire to be fixed *immediately.*"

Immediately is impossible, but Paco can't tell her that. These rich people are so goddamn weird, he thinks. Slightest thing goes wrong, it's a disaster. A woman friend of his worked for a family here on Hambriento for nearly ten years, when she was fired because the master of the house reached out for the toilet paper one morning and found the roll empty. Something like that happens to us regular people, Paco thinks, and we say, "Damn." Then we duck-waddle over to where the toilet paper is kept and get out a new roll. No big deal, minor inconvenience, Life. But these rich people, their lives are arranged so that nothing is ever supposed to go wrong for any reason. When it's hot, they travel to where it's cool. When it's cold, they turn around and go where it's warm. Big houses waiting for them in both places. Weather always perfect. Their food brought to the table and placed in front of them, dirty dishes taken away. Clothes laid out, bills paid, toilet-paper rolls replaced, everything but wipe their butts, but then when they get old and frail we do that for them too. Perfect lives. So that if something *does* go wrong, they have conniption fits. Empty toilet-paper roll, flat tire, for them it's a disaster, a bang-your-head-against-the-wall, tear-your-hair-out, assemble-the-quivering-staff-and-fire-someone, screaming disaster.

Kate Tornsel walks unsteadily to a nearby rain-forest-teak bench and sits there with a collapsing sigh. "I'm ruined."

In spite of himself, Paco feels sorry for her. Looking at his own wristwatch, which cost ten times what Kate's did, he cautiously ventures another suggestion.

"It's ten after. I could drive you and the bike to the repair shop, five minutes. With all the tools they got, another five, six minutes to fix the tire. The shop is just around the corner from the church, you could ride there in two or three minutes. Arrive on time *and* on your bike."

Kate's face has been twisted in contempt while listening to him, but now as she realizes that his proposal could work, she becomes all business. "Fine, then, load the bike, stop dawdling, no time for your *mañana* attitude now."

Then all the way to the repair shop she lectures Paco on how "you people" are like children, everything handed to you, food, housing, salary, days off, medical benefits, Kate concluding that it's hardly surprising that "you people" seldom think beyond your next meal.

It's midnight now, and Kate is sitting on the edge of her bed, her gray hair down and Kmart slippers on her feet. She's wearing a night-gown, no robe. On the cheap fold-out tray in front of her is a huge salad that Kate is wolfing, the first food she's eaten today.

Kate didn't touch the meal that was served at the conclusion of the property owners meeting. She's famous for not eating in public. The sight of others stuffing their faces puts her off. Even people of her own class can be contemptibly crude in their eating habits and if Kate had her way, dining would be treated like elimination, something to be done in complete privacy.

She thinks her speech went well. Although the motion to ban motor vehicles wasn't approved, the executive council did appoint a study committee to examine the feasibility of closing the island to nonemergency, nondelivery vehicles for an experimental period of one week. The study committee, of which Kate Tornsel is a member, will report its findings at next year's annual meeting.

But the big commotion at this year's meeting came after a woman, an arriviste (she's on the executive council but in Kate's view is definitely NOCD, Not Our Class, Dear—probably a chippie who married for money) proposed that the association adopt a charity and then raise money for it by staging theme parties such as Fantasy in White, where everyone dresses completely in white, or a Great Gatsby Ball or maybe an Oscar Night with spotlights and red carpets and an elaborate ceremony during which gag Oscars are given out for best costume, largest donation, and so on.

Everyone thought it was a smashing idea until suggestions were offered for which charity might be adopted. One elderly man spoke passionately in favor of canine cancer research, telling a rambling story about the death of his toy poodle.

But when the woman who made the original proposal said that AIDS should be considered because of what she termed "the Hollywood glamour" attendant to charities supporting the fight against that particular disease, pandemonium reigned in the church hall.

What if we give money to "those people," one wealthy resident asked, and then they want to come here and thank us, are we going to sit down and *eat* with them?

And what if they like what they see here on Hambriento, another asked, and decide to *stay?*

The best way to fight AIDS, an especially indignant property owner insisted, is require that all service people working on the island have a blood test and then fire and ban any of them who are found to "have it."

Kate sat there at the speakers' table not listening to any of this nonsense. She was dreaming of a car-free Hambriento, fantasizing about becoming famous through her anticar, probicycle efforts. Perhaps even an interview on "60 Minutes."

And now it's midnight and she's sitting on her bed tucking into that huge bowl of salad, once again dreaming of becoming famous for her crusades. Oh, wouldn't Daddy be proud! She decides if fame is bestowed on her and then if someone asks for her autograph, why, she'll simply refuse to give it—just as the "other" Kate refuses to give hers. *Don't be ridiculous*, Kate Tornsel will snap at autograph seekers—

Tap, tap.

From the closet.

She stops eating to listen.

Tap, tap.

Must be mice. Have to get Paco in here with some traps, though she

is repulsed by the idea of his little monkey hands rooting around in
her personal effects—

Tap, tap.

Tap, tap.

Tap, tap.

Tap, tap.

FOURTEEN

I awoke around midnight Tuesday and lay in bed listening for noises. How thin this veneer of adulthood, mine so deeply gouged during the last twenty-four hours that here I am, a child again, home from a séance with the Tummelier brothers, lying in bed dreading to hear *in my very own bedroom* the tapping that came from under the "murder table." Dreading to hear it and yet somehow wanting to hear it too. As a child I had only prayer to protect me from tap, tap and other night beasts but now, trying hard to pretend to be an adult, I thought of my father's .357 Magnum, a secret I kept from Marianne, a secret locked away in a wooden box and hidden up in our attic. If I told her I had the pistol, Marianne's fascination with psychological motivations would prompt endless questioning: Didn't I think it bizarre to own the very weapon my father had used to end his life? Did I consider it a token of some sort, a talisman, a symbol of power? And I wouldn't have any good answers, wouldn't be able to explain why I had talked my uncle into giving me the pistol after I was graduated from college or why I held on to it all these years.

But I knew precisely why I wanted it in my hand right now. I felt threatened and having my father's weapon would comfort me.

Lying there in bed I tried to figure out why Peter was doing this. I hated him for it. His friendship was worse than an inconvenience now, I wished him dead.

Then I felt small and mean-spirited for wishing it. He had been more than a friend. At one time Peter was my brother.

For nearly four years, from when we were twelve until I left Hambriento at age sixteen, Peter spent more time with my family than he did with his own: gossiping with my sisters, going out on the boat with Dad and me, eating meals with us. I clued him in on the dorky clothes he wore and went shopping with him to buy new ones. I taught him slang and showed him the insolent posture *de rigueur* for the adolescent male. Together we learned to smoke, we practiced spitting and cussing. But of all the normal teenager things I introduced him to, the one that affected Peter the most was rock and roll. He wasn't allowed to listen to it at his house and knew nothing about which songs were popular, which groups were hot. Listening to rock in my bedroom, the volume cranked, Peter became transfixed.

He liked the old stuff: "Reach Out I'll Be There" by the Four Tops, "Hanky Panky" by Tommy James and the Shondells, Tommy Roe's "Jam Up Jelly Tight," but especially anything by Mary Wells, Martha Reeves and the Vandellas, and the Shangri-Las. He learned all the old songs by heart. The opening line to the Shangri-Las' "Give Him a Great Big Kiss"—"*When I say I'm in love you best believe I'm in love, L-U-V*"—became Peter's signature statement, which he used to compliment everything from my mother's cooking to my sisters' outfits.

Would I have to testify to all of this if Peter went to trial, would I be asked to explain his obsession with me, how we became brothers? Would it come out what happened that one night when I was newly sixteen and came home after a date that consisted of heavy petting, battles over bra straps, moaning and rubbing and promising—but no release? Peter was sleeping over that night and asked me how my date had gone. I complained that I'd soon be suffering from blue balls. Peter didn't know what that was, but after I explained it he said, well, if it's simply a matter of *release,* what are friends for? Would he tell that story to the police, would I have to confirm it?

I wished him, if not dead, then at least gone from my life.

A few days before my father killed himself I overheard Dad and Peter talking: Peter crying and begging my father to adopt him legally, to hire a lawyer and file the papers, saying he had to get away from Richard, my father asking what Richard had done, Peter insisting he couldn't say, he'd be killed if he told.

Which was when my father said he was going to give Peter his word on something and "when Curtis Bird gives his word it's better than any document that any lawyer can draw up, because you can get legal documents changed but no lawyer or courtroom on God's green earth can get me to break my word, never." He said that as of that moment Peter Tummelier was an official member of Curtis Bird's family. "Whatever you need," Dad said, "if I have it, it's yours. Any man crosses you, he crosses me. I'd die for you and if it ever came to it, I'd kill for you. No matter what happens, you can always bring it to me, bring it here, this is your home now, we don't need to file any papers to make it so."

Even though neither of them knew I was listening, I decided that what Dad said went for me too—from then on Peter was blood.

But then Dad killed himself and I never told Peter that I considered him a brother.

I stayed home from work that Tuesday waiting for a call from Florida, for news that Peter had been caught and I was wanted for questioning or news that Peter hadn't been caught and I was wanted for murder.

When Marianne returned from the university late that afternoon she found me doing push-ups in our bedroom. I said I was trying to work off my nervousness but in fact I was thinking about prison, thinking that I'd better start getting in shape if I was to be sent to jail where I might have to defend myself against other men. Marianne didn't believe I'd ever go to jail. When I spoke of it, she said I was being paranoid. Peter was causing trouble, she said, but he wouldn't be able to frame me. That sort of thing didn't happen in real life. Frame-ups were almost impossible to mastermind.

But I thought: *Mastermind*—it fits Peter to a tee.

Marianne and I talked incessantly about last night's phone call to Johnny Laflin, a call that was supposed to put me on record for reporting crimes that might have taken place or were about to take place, a call that was supposed to put me in the clear, set matters straight. But instead it made everything in my life crooked.

And as I lay in bed at midnight listening for tap, tap, I played that telephone conversation over and over in mind.

"Is this John Laflin?"

"Speaking."

"Is this the same Johnny Laflin who fell out of a flatboat trying to pull in a 'cuda he said was five foot long?"

"Who—*Roscoe?*" He spoke my name like a secret.

"Johnny! Twenty years and you're at the same number. I can't believe it. I thought I'd have to go through information and track you down."

"Where're you, you here in Florida?"

"No, I'm calling from Washington, D.C., from my house, *our* house, I'm married six years now."

"That's great, Roscoe," he said without enthusiasm. "How come you're calling me?"

"It's about the Burtons—"

"Oh, Jesus."

"What's wrong?"

Then he said an astonishing thing. "You're going to tell me where their bodies are."

I went cold. "Their bodies?"

"Go on."

"Go on?"

"*The Burtons,*" he whispered dramatically.

"I don't know anything about their bodies." When he didn't reply to that I said, "Johnny?"

Still nothing.

"What's happened to them!" I demanded.

"They turned up missing, been missing since Saturday night. One of our investigative team's been working on it since yesterday, Sunday."

"So what's this about their bodies?"

"The team . . . Jesus, I shouldn't even be talking to you. Have you called anyone else at the department?"

"No, I—"

"The team suspects the Burtons were murdered, their bodies removed from their house and dumped somewhere."

Christ, Peter was telling the truth.

"Roscoe?"

"Why do you think *I* would know anything about their bodies?"

No answer.

"Johnny?" I could feel the cold sweat making my underarms clammy.

"Why're you calling?" he asked.

I took a breath and let it out slowly. "It's about Peter, Peter Tummelier."

"Go on."

I told him everything, Peter gone crazy enough to claim he'd become a vampire, saying he'd killed the Burtons, wanting me to captain a boat and go on a long cruise with him. By the time I finished my throat was so dry it felt like it might stick closed.

Taking a few seconds to absorb everything, Johnny finally said, "Sweet Jesus, that was always one weird family, wasn't it? I could never understand why you and your old man put up with those two boys. You should've called me with this right away."

"I only saw him last night. Hey, Johnny, a guy shows up and starts talking about killing people as a vampire, I'm supposed to take him seriously?"

"You saw him last night in Washington?"

"Yeah."

"Sunday night."

"Yeah."

"And you haven't been back here to Florida?"

"No. The last time I saw Hambriento was when I left there with my mom and sisters, twenty years ago. *You* drove us to the airport."

"All right, I'm going to tell you something, strictly off the record." Then he paused as if debating whether he should do it. "The team found traces of blood and semen in the Burtons' bedroom and like I said before we're treating this as a possible homicide, the bodies removed from the house, dumped somewhere." Laflin hesitated again. "But here's the thing, Roscoe, one of your father's old business cards was found on the bedroom floor."

"Oh, Christ."

"So maybe there's a connection—"

"Of course there's a connection! Peter left that card there! He's trying to implicate me!"

"Hold on—"

"Hold on my ass, I want you to tell me everything—"

"I gotta be careful talking to you. You're a possible suspect—"

"What?"

"Routine. You broke into the Burtons' house that night—"

"Twenty years ago! When I was sixteen, for chrissakes!"

"Hey, just shut up and listen to me. In a homicide case the routine is you look into if anyone ever threatened the victim. It's twenty years ago you broke into their house with a gun but people still remember."

"You remember."

"Meaning?"

"Meaning there was no paperwork on that break-in, no way for your investigative team to look it up, but *you* remembered it, you tipped them off, you told your buddies, 'Check into Roscoe Bird, he threatened to kill the Burtons once,' *right?*"

"Hey, Hambriento's my district. The team comes to me and asks was there anyone ever threatened the Burtons, what am I supposed to say?"

"You're supposed to say some kid threatened the Burtons *twenty years ago* but this kid was under a lot of stress, his father, your best friend, had just killed himself, so it's not the kind of threat you take seriously twenty years later, that's what you're supposed to say."

Johnny didn't speak for a long while.

"You still there?" I asked.

"They're running some checks on you, that's all."

"Checks?"

"Yeah, today they called your office to make sure you hadn't missed work last week, but of course the Burtons disappeared *Saturday* night, so the team is also running some checks with the airlines to see if anyone traveling under your name flew down here this past weekend."

It was like being told I had cancer. *"I'm being investigated as a murder suspect."*

"A routine—"

"Don't keep saying it's routine, it's not fucking routine for me!"

"Hey, Roscoe, you'd better—"

"I *didn't* go down to Florida, the airlines confirmed that, right?"

"That's a matter you should discuss with—"

"Johnny!"

"Your name hasn't come up yet but all the reports aren't in from all the airlines and anyway it's easy enough to travel under another name."

"I don't believe this, I don't fucking believe this. When were you going to let me in on the fact that I was being investigated for murder?"

"I ain't on the investigative team, it ain't my place to let you know jackshit. Besides, the investigation is only a day old. Nobody knows nothing for sure."

"But I'm still under suspicion, right?"

"You'll be fine—you got an alibi for Saturday, some way to prove you were in D.C.?"

"I was with my wife."

"A spouse's testimony ain't exactly iron-clad. Anyone else?"

"Oh, I see."

"See what?"

"Maybe you're hoping they'll put you on the varsity murder team if you're able to use your friendship with me to—"

"You ungrateful little fuck." His tone was quiet but bitter. "How many times I pull your chestnuts out of the fire, huh? Your dad was my best friend and I covered for you, goddamn it. Covered for you when you could've done time for being in the Burtons' house with a pistol. Hell, a year before that I covered for you and your girlfriend when Kate Tornsel was screaming that—"

"Tornsel!"

"Yeah?"

"That's the reason I called you, not just about the Burtons, but to warn you that Peter might be going back down there to kill Kate Tornsel too."

"Jesus, he said that?"

"Not in so many words."

"What *did* he say in so many words?"

"He asked me who I hated enough to kill, asked me if I still hated the Burtons enough to kill them, then he mentioned Tornsel, did I hate *her* enough to want her dead."

"What'd you say?"

"I said I didn't hate anyone enough to want them dead."

"And this was Sunday when you had this conversation with Peter?"

"Yeah, last night."

"You got his address there in Washington?"

"No, I have no idea where he's staying. But I think he's still here. He came to see my wife today while I was at work."

"What'd he say to her?"

"He said he wanted me to captain a boat for him, that he had a way to force me to do it."

"I got to get over to Tornsel's house."

"Wait, where does that leave me?"

"You better be prepared, 'cause all this is going to come out now."

"What do you mean, *come out*?"

"Everything you've told me about Peter, the possible connection between that business card and a revenge motive in the Burton case, a possible threat against Tornsel, *everything*. I'll have to make a full report."

"But what am I supposed to *do?*"

"You think about how you spent the time from when you left work Friday until Sunday morning, everyplace you went, everyone you talked to. Make a list of all the witnesses who can place you in D.C. Friday night, Saturday, Saturday night. Establishing a solid alibi is half the battle."

"*Half* the battle? What's the other half?"

"Proving that you and Peter weren't in on this together."

"Oh, for chrissakes, Johnny. If I was in on it with Peter why would I have called you?"

"I'm just telling you the way the investigators are going to be thinking. And another thing, you'd better adjust your fucking attitude too, decide who's trying to cut you some slack here and who's trying to nail your ass to the wall. I got to get off this line so I can check on Tornsel. I'll be in touch."

"Okay, thank—" But he had already hung up.

And now, exactly twenty-six hours later, I'm in bed worrying about boogeymen from my childhood and being buggered by cell mates from my future, unable to sleep, not tonight, maybe I'll never sleep again.

But of course I did sleep, to be awakened at some dark hour by a tapping noise, voices, *someone in the house*—and when I turned to the right I saw the covers had been thrown back and Marianne was gone from our bed.

FIFTEEN

Midnight Tuesday. Pushing away the folding table that holds her bowl of salad and glass of sparkling water, Kate eases off the bed and takes a step toward the closet, hesitating only briefly before grabbing a poker from a stand near the fireplace. She loves the idea of her native New England, snowy evenings and crackling fires, but detests cold weather, Kate compromising by living in Florida but having superfluous fireplaces installed in several of her mansion's rooms.

She hefts the poker and can just imagine some future interview wherein a reporter asks her about the time she took a poker after an intruder and forced him to flee for his life, Kate forgetting that *two* elements are required for the story to work: that she have sufficient courage to confront the intruder, yes, but also that the intruder have sufficient civility to bow out gracefully, to flee an old woman with a poker rather than kill her.

Halfway to the closet, Kate remembers the visit she had last night from that fat deputy, Laflin. Getting her out of bed to ask about the disappearance of Philip and Diane, wanting to know if she had heard or seen anything suspicious around *her* house or if she had been contacted by Peter Tummelier. "Do you remember him?" Laflin had asked. Of course she remembered, did Laflin think she was senile? He inquired about her security system and said he would put two detectives in a patrol car parked right in front of her house.

"The devil you will!" Kate had told him. "I don't see why you think I should have any information about the Burtons' disappearance but I can take care of myself. I'd like to know where I'd be today if I had to rely on public servants such as *you.*"

When Laflin said he'd have the patrol car park outside her front gate, Kate told him he could waste county money if he wanted but she'd better not see any armed Gestapo on *her* property, or he'd be hearing from her attorneys.

Such nonsense.

And she'd forgotten all about it in the excitement of today's property owners meeting but now, at this hour and hearing that strange noise coming from her closet, *now* Kate isn't so sure that Laflin's concern is nonsense. Maybe she should call him and let *him* open that closet door.

Oh, fiddlesticks, I don't need police protection, I can jolly well take care of myself.

Raising the poker over her head in one hand, she steps briskly to the closet and flings open the door with the other hand. Kate smells rotten fish but sees no one hiding in her closet. Of course not. Intruders aren't *allowed* on Hambriento. A burglar wouldn't dare—

But just as she is lowering her arm he steps out from the back of the closet, from behind hanging clothes, and takes the poker from her hand. Before Kate can speak, the intruder slaps her across the face and tosses the poker across the room.

She's never been struck in her entire life! Daddy certainly never hit her. Kate's never even been threatened with physical violence, and now that it's happened she couldn't be more astonished than if she awoke one morning to find that gravity wasn't working, or that Paco owned the mansion and she was *his* servant, or some other equally outlandishly impossible development.

"Do you remember me, Kate?"

With one hand holding her face, she looks at this small, nicely dressed man, not entirely unattractive with his dark hair and even darker eyes, fine strong features, a feminine mouth. Surely this isn't a burglar.

He asks again if she remembers him.

Something Laflin said to her last night fires off a memory. *That dreadful Tummelier boy.*

"I realize it was twenty years ago."

She remembers.

"Surely when you alter people's lives as radically as you do, surely you remember."

She *remembers:* calling the sheriff's department to report that those dreadful Tummelier brothers were up to something awfully suspicious out on the stretch of beach she can see from her house, the beach she patrols via binoculars. But nothing ever came of—

He speaks in a soft and cultured voice. "Or have you spewed so much bile in your life that you can no longer recall all those whom that bile has stained?"

Summoning courage from her New England bedrock soul, the trembling woman looks dead into his face and says, "I'd advise you to leave before the sheriff's deputies arrive."

"Oh, yes, I saw them parked out there. Drinking coffee."

She turns for the door. "Paco! *Paco!*"

He grabs her stringy gray hair. "Nguyen That Thanh can't hear you," he says quietly. "He lives in a room above the garage, isn't allowed to stay in the big house overnight. Why is that, Kate? Do you find the idea of a man sleeping under the same roof with you too . . . *stimulating?*"

As he pulls her by the hair toward the bed, Kate's head is shaking so severely that it appears as if she is telling the intruder no-no-no-no. Which of course in a way she is.

"I'm here on behalf of Dondo . . ."

Who?

". . . and the Birds," he tells her.

Birds? What birds? She's donated thousands to the Audubon Society. If he is soliciting for wildlife causes, this is hardly the manner—

From a pocket of his sports jacket the intruder removes a roll of wide clear-plastic tape, the kind approved by the post office for securing packages, too tough to tear with your bare hands. From another pocket he takes out a razor blade.

"Please."

Tape in one hand, razor in the other, he pauses a moment to study her. "Kate Tornsel saying please?"

Her head is shaking so severely that tears are thrown from the corners of her eyes to splash in random dots all about her face.

When he strips off a three-foot length of tape, the loud ripping noise causes Kate to flinch.

He presses one end of the tape to her forehead and with surprising gentleness wraps the tape completely around her head, back across her eyes, sticking the free end to her hair just above her left ear. He cuts the tape with a razor. His hands smell terribly of fish.

Beneath the clear plastic Kate's eyes are open and she stares at him with a pleading intensity as he pulls off another three feet of tape, sticking one end over the bridge of her nose, wrapping the tape around her head again, across her nose, securing the free end to her left ear.

With the upper half of her face enclosed in the tough plastic, Kate reaches out with her right hand and places it shakily upon his forearm. "What's to become of me?" she asks.

He rips free another length of tape, cuts it with the razor, and then with the tape dangling from his large right hand, he pauses to consider her question. The intruder had expected her to fight, had expected that someone as strong-willed and scrappy as Kate Tornsel would struggle and scream and throw things. He was ready for that. Fighting with her would've gotten his blood up, energized him— would've made all this easier.

"What's to become of me?" she asks again, not a rhetorical question.

But then what is his answer? He shakes his head.

"I mean heaven," Kate explains as he presses one end of the tape to her right cheek.

"Heaven?" He is smoothing the tape onto her cheek.

"Will I go to heav—"

But then he puts the tape across her mouth.

"It's not for me to say," he tells her, pulling the tape around her head, over her mouth and chin, sticking the free end to the left side of her neck, Kate Tornsel's face now completely encased in plastic, her air cut off.

The tape having caught her in mid-question, it presses against yellowing teeth, securing her thin lips in an opened position. And when the intruder looks down at her, he can see through the clear plastic, past her taped-open lips, right into her mouth.

And it is now, with oxygen denied her, that Kate finally panics. Beneath the tape her nostrils pinch in and flare out, but she can't get any air. Her hands come up to claw at the tape and when he grabs her around the waist she kicks out with her legs, knocking over the tray and spraying salad, spilling sparkling water everywhere.

She tries to scream but she can't of course—can't scream, can't breathe, too terrified to care what he's telling her, something about Dondo and Richard, about Roscoe and Roscoe's father.

Kate drops to the floor and scrambles away on hands and knees until she reaches the door, where she comes to a kneeling position and uses the fingernails of both hands to scratch and pull at the tape.

Aroused, the beast watches. His hunger outweighs his shame, crushes guilt, a hunger too large to make room for anything else.

She's going to throw up—the way blood used to make him vomit in the beginning. Kate grabs the door handle and uses it to stand, trying to will the nausea away even as she suffocates.

Why should it chill him so deeply that her final question was about heaven? Upon reaching one's last moment, even a woman as self-contained and hard-hearted as Kate Tornsel would of course worry about the immortal soul. Will he?

The intruder rushes to Kate and takes her into his arms to insist again, "It's not for me to say."

But then in his mind the intruder hears the casual crystal tinkling of a piano and smiles. He starts to dance with her, turning her around and around as she fights him.

"It's not for me to say," he sings, thinking that if justice held any sway at all, he'd come back someday in some universe as Johnny Mathis. Listen, I can sound just like him. Smiling dreamily, he sings the song.

With Kate struggling like a cat in his arms, he dances her crazily around the bedroom as he continues in a mellow, honeyed voice.

". . . as far as I can seeee, this is heaven . . ."

Her stomach clenches like a fist, squeezing its contents. But she can't vomit, not with the tape across her mouth—can't vomit, can't scream, can't breathe.

He holds her all the closer, seeing through the clear plastic into her taped-open mouth, seeing the brownish yellow liquid carrying bits of lettuce green, carrot orange, radish red, watching her drown in her own bile, hugging her tightly as she twitches with death.

When her head falls back, he quickly slits her throat and buries his mouth into the wound, sucking.

He is at her neck for the longest time, at one point raising her arm to check the Timex on her wrist, and when he finally pulls away, he does so with a violent jerk, spewing a fine red mist.

Holding her in that deadly embrace a moment longer, he finally drops the body to the floor and speaks-sings in a new voice, *"When I say I'm in love you best believe I'm in love, L-U-V."*

SIXTEEN

I looked over at the clock, then out a window: Six A.M., dark. Scrambling from under the bedcovers I wondered if I could make it up to the attic and get Dad's gun before—

Someone running up the steps.

It's Peter, he's come for me, he's killed Marianne downstairs and now he's coming for me. I looked around the room for potential weapons. Nothing, not even a baseball bat, golf club. *Nothing*.

I stood there naked and wanting that pistol in my hand, impotent without it. Whoever was coming for me had topped the steps and I braced myself, both hands tightly fisted, ready for a fight, watching the doorway as Marianne came through it and flipped on the bedroom light. I nearly collapsed from the relief of seeing her.

But then her troubled expression caused me to tense up again. "What is it?"

"Roscoe . . ."

"What?"

"You wouldn't wake up so I went down—"

"Goddamn it, what's going on?"

"Cops. That's who was knocking. Two policemen."

I braced myself again.

"They've come to take you in for questioning," she said.

SEVENTEEN

I kept waiting for them to cuff me, slap me around a little, but the two uniformed officers "taking me in" were nothing if not courteous, *requesting* that I accompany them *voluntarily* (the emphasis was theirs) to be interviewed about a homicide case. No, they replied in answer to my nervous questions, they didn't know what case or who was interviewing me or why the interview had to take place at this dark morning hour. They acted largely uninterested whether or not I agreed to go with them, bored by this assignment. I said I'd go.

Seated in the back of their patrol car I would occasionally lean forward and look between them, toward the front of the car where the headlights were confined, kept in close, by the snow. They chatted amiably between themselves about the traffic problems this snow was going to cause during the morning rush hour, and while I wanted to join in their conversation, every comment I considered making, when I reviewed it mentally, sounded incredibly stupid.

They drove into a tiny parking lot to the side of a station house and I followed them in feeling guilty, feeling as if I should have a coat thrown over my head. But there were no photographers, no hookers in white go-go boots either. Only the interrogation room matched the stereotype I had in mind: small, painted an institutional green and beige, smelling of stale cigarettes, half of one wall devoted to a two-way mirror.

Back at the house, in my rush to get dressed, I hadn't remembered to put on a watch so I didn't know how long I was left alone in that little room but it seemed like an hour. Was the door locked? Should I step into the hall and try to find out if I'd been forgotten? Or was this a ploy to unnerve me for the questioning? Marianne would say my paranoia was acting up again. Then the door opened and in walked a large man I didn't recognize until I heard his voice.

"Roscoe!" He put out his meaty, stubby-fingered hand for me to shake and spoke with an odd and touching formality, the way people do at funerals. "Sorry we have to hold our reunion under these circumstances."

Laflin.

"Johnny, Johnny Laflin, is it really you?" I shook his hand with both of mine.

It had been twenty years since last I saw him but I still couldn't believe how much he'd changed. The Johnny Laflin I knew back on Hambriento was big-shouldered and open-faced with sandy-red hair and small blue eyes that shone with good humor, as if he always had a joke ready to tell as soon as there was a break in the conversation. He had moved down to Florida from New Jersey as a young man, a lifetime ago, but still had Jersey's accent and mannerisms. I remembered him as being not handsome but pleasant and gentle-looking in a Baby Huey, potato-fed sort of way.

But the fifty-year-old man who stood before me now was a wreck.

"Roscoe," he said again.

"Great seeing you, Johnny," I replied.

We were still shaking hands.

His massive gut started below his tits and then curved in just above his crotch, and somehow in the space of twenty years that wonderfully open face of his had eroded, been scorched, turned red, flaked off, turned red again, become spidered with broken veins, been abandoned to the elements, to the bottle, uncared for. His sandy hair had thinned out and gone gray, while in apparent compensation for this topside loss his nose had somehow inflated over the years into a bulblike monstrosity. Four or five hairs stuck right up from the tip of his nose and I was fascinated, wondering, if you looked in the mirror and saw hairs growing like that, why wouldn't you pull them out? His eyes had lost their shine, the whites having turned a milky yellow.

"You look great," I told him.

"Aw."

"No, really . . ."

"You're the one who looks great," he said quietly, still pumping my hands. "Always were the fair-haired boy. I told your old man more than once that anybody as all-American-looking as you should go into politics."

"That would've been a mistake." I kept staring at him. If two decades could ruin Johnny like this, what would the next twenty years do to me? "I hardly recognized you out of uniform."

Laflin looked down at his civilian clothes: cheap blue shirt, striped tie from Kmart, a sport coat that fit him maybe thirty pounds ago, gray polyester slacks, a pair of black brogans that he probably couldn't see because of his stomach. "Spiffy, huh? I shoulda bought a pair of long johns though, this blizzard you got here."

"They're only calling for three to five inches."

"To me, a blizzard." He clasped my shoulders with both hands. "*Good* seeing you again, Roscoe, I mean that."

"So what's the deal, Johnny, what're you doing here in Washington? Why'd you have me hauled down in the middle of the night?"

"You gotta work nights if you're after a vampire."

My expression made him laugh. Then he feigned throwing a punch at me the way he used to do back when I was a kid out on the boat with him and my dad.

"I'm serious, Johnny, how come you didn't come to my house like a friend of the family, meet my wife?"

He raised one shoulder in a sheepish half shrug. "I just got in town myself. I wanted to wait to a decent hour and, like you said, come over to your house, meet your wife and all. But we got to play this one strictly by the book. It'll be better for both of us."

"What do you mean?"

"You were right about Kate Tornsel."

I sat in one of the straight-backed chairs.

"We had a couple deputies out by her front gate, where they could see her bedroom window. A little after midnight they spot something that don't look right, like *two* figures moving around in her bedroom. She lives there alone. The little Vietnamese guy that works for her, he don't stay in the big house, so the deputies drive up and knock on the door, no answer, they get the Vietnamese guy to let them in, go up to the bedroom, no Kate. The crime-scene team is still there. Found some vomit and blood on the carpet, looks like whatever happened to the Burtons happened to Kate too."

"Peter."

"You don't know where he's staying here in Washington?"

"No."

"I gotta find him."

"So you made the team, huh?"

He shrugged. "Not exactly. The homicide investigations team is convinced that whoever done the abductions or killings is still down in Florida. Even if Peter's the one and even if he came up to see you after the Burtons, the team figures he stayed in Florida after doing Tornsel last night. Hambriento is where all the action is. But my information was important enough that I got to come up here and check it out. Which is like a feather in my cap, thirty years breaking up beach parties and pulling over speeders, finally I get assigned, sort of at least, to a homicide investigation."

"I'm happy for you."

He did a quick nod, accepting my congratulations, then caught on that I was being sarcastic. "Remember what I told you before, about figuring out who's your friend, me or Peter Tummelier."

"The way I see it, you'd *both* like to pin a murder on me—Peter so he can get me to do whatever it is he wants me to do and you so you can stick feathers in your cap."

He shook his big head. "These cops here in D.C., they don't care about this case 'cause it ain't theirs. They got enough homicides of their own. But the investigations team down in Florida is hot to crack this before anybody else on Hambriento gets abducted or killed, so you'd better be thinking how you're going to help me. Or else the next guy they send up here ain't going to be a old friend of the family's, it's going to be a guy carrying extradition papers."

I felt something grab in my stomach. *"Extradition?"*

"Yeah 'cause there could be a case made that you're in on this with Peter."

"Based on what?"

Laflin took one of the chairs and turned it around to sit on it backward, facing me across the table. "One, you call me and warn that Kate Tornsel might be next to disappear, and then it turns out she's next to disappear."

"If you think Peter and I are partners in these abductions, then I must be the real stupid partner, the one who calls the police and tells them who our next victim will be."

"Or the real smart one who tries to make sure his partner gets caught."

"Come on, Johnny, you don't believe that." Did he?

"So shut up and listen to me. Number two not in your favor is that someone has been calling airline charter companies here in this area and asking about chartering private flights to Florida, asking if it can be done off the books if the price is right, and the person making those calls has been leaving your name."

"Peter. It's Peter. I told you he intended to implicate me."

"Has he visited you at your office?"

"No, just at the house, twice. Why?"

" 'Cause strike three against you is the fact that someone placed a call to the Burtons' house Monday afternoon and the call came from your office. We'd already set a trace on the Burtons' phone."

I quietly admitted that I had made that call.

"How come you didn't tell me?"

"I didn't think it was important. I wasn't sure if Peter told the truth about killing the Burtons, so I called down there to find out if they were alive."

"But you can see how it don't necessarily look too good for you, how someone could make the case that you're involved, especially when your only explanation for why Peter is doing all this is 'cause he's a vampire."

"I can't help it if he's crazy. Did you want me to lie about what he told me?"

"Of course not. I want you to help me find him. 'Cause while everybody else in the department thinks he's still down in Florida, thinks he's going to keep on abducting people until they catch him, *I* believe *you*, I believe he's trying to get you to run off with him. He always did follow you around like a puppy dog."

I started to say something but he held up a hand. "You always were pretty slick, Roscoe, a big charmer and all that. You liked it the way people always made a fuss over you. Even when I got you off the hook for breaking into the Burtons' house, you acted like it was your due, you know, 'cause everybody loves Roscoe Bird."

Why all this sudden hostility?

"And now you think I'm a stumblebum," he continued, "trying to play at being a homicide detective, but if you'd just get off your high horse and cooperate with me, we got a chance here to help each other. I'm supposed to be in Washington just to collect information but with your help and if Peter comes around to see you again, there's a possibility I can clear up the whole case and get you off the hook to boot."

"I'll help you however I can," I said quietly.

Tired from having been up all night, Johnny rubbed his burnt-red face, then asked an astonishing question. "You ever think there was anything suspicious about your dad's suicide?"

"What do you mean?"

"Tell me what you remember."

"What's this got to do with—"

"Just tell me."

"About the actual day it happened? You were the one who came got me from school. It was all over by the time I—"

"No, I'm more interested in the events that led up to it."

"Well, you know, the trouble with the Burtons began with those charter clients from Montana, that older couple, ranchers, real nice people. We fished tarpon on the morning tide, back at our dock on Hambriento by noon, Mom fixed us all lunch, then the couple left for a drive around the island before the late-afternoon ferry would take them back to the mainland. This couple, I guess they were both in their late fifties, I don't exactly remember, but they walked out on that big pier that belongs to the Burton compound. Philip showed up and demanded that they leave and the way I heard it the couple apologized, said the pier was so large they had just assumed it was a public pier, and then they explained they had gone out fishing with my dad that morning. Trying to be polite about the whole thing.

"Except Philip, asshole that he is, was, he follows them off the pier screaming about tourists on the island, threatening lawsuits and all that shit. But when he grabbed the woman's arm to make a point, the old rancher coldcocked him.

"When Dad heard about it he thought it was hilarious. The rancher and his wife had been fishing with Dad for eight seasons in a row and Dad said the guy was real quiet and dignified but what's right is right and what's wrong is straight through Jack. Dad didn't think it was any big deal getting punched in the nose. Everybody gets decked occasionally."

"Not Philip Burton."

"Yeah, well, I guess that's what Dad didn't realize, that to Burton a punch in the nose was a life-altering experience that was worth starting a war over, a legal war against our charter business. Burton's lawyers called into question whether the business was properly grandfathered in, whether our clients could properly use the private ferries to bring their cars over, even whether Mom's serving lunch to clients constituted the operation of a restaurant. All bullshit, of course, but while Philip is fighting Dad in the courts, his wife and Kate Tornsel came after us through the property owners association. You know the story better than I do, I was only sixteen when it happened, you were Dad's best friend. In the end I guess it just got to be too much for him, he couldn't take the aggravation anymore."

Johnny waited a moment before speaking. "You really think your dad killed himself because of aggravation?"

He made it sound trivial.

"The lawsuits were expensive," Johnny continued, "but the success of your dad's business depended on his reputation, his client list, his referrals. He told me he could operate out of any dock on the mainland and still make a go of it. And you think he'd throw all of that away, three generations of chartering, just because an asshole like Burton was suing him?"

"I don't know, Johnny."

"The most important thing in the world to him was passing on the business to you."

I nodded. Dad was always telling me that he didn't have to get rich, didn't have to build the biggest charter operation in Florida, "only one thing I have to do in my life and that's keep the business together until I can hand it to you in the same shape or better than it was when it was handed to me by my father, who got it from his father—so one day you can hand it to *your* son. This business doesn't belong to me, I'm only taking care of it for you just like you'll do for your kid."

Johnny reached across the table and put a meaty hand on my shoulder. "Sorry for bringing all this up."

I looked away.

"I just wanted to know if you really thought the Burtons were responsible for driving your father to suicide."

"Of course I do! Why in the hell do you think I broke into their house, ready to shoot them for what they'd done to him!"

"Yeah." Johnny stood and stretched. "It was Richard Tummelier who got your dad's pistol from the department lockup so you could use it on the Burtons. He bribed someone—that's what I heard later."

I nodded. "Richard was twenty then, he knew his way around. In fact it was his idea for me to shoot the Burtons."

"It was?"

"Well, I wanted to, I don't mean he talked me into doing something I was dead set against, but Richard was the one who produced the pistol and handed it to me and said if I wanted to get back at the

Burtons why not use the same gun they had forced my dad to use on himself. Then of course they weren't home and I got caught."

"Lucky for you."

"Are you going to explain what you're getting at with all this?"

"Except for Richard giving you the pistol, was there anything else either of the Tummelier brothers did around the time of your father's death that struck you as suspicious?"

I shook my head. "I remember overhearing Peter asking my dad to adopt him."

"When?"

"I don't know, a few days before Dad killed himself."

"Peter's sixteen years old and has his own parents and he wants your dad to adopt him?"

"He was weird, what can I tell you?"

Johnny came around the table and sat right next to me. "None of this might mean anything but it's stuck in my craw for the last twenty years. I just couldn't see any point bringing it up and causing you and your sisters and your mom more grief for no good reason."

"Bringing *what* up?"

"A day or two before your dad's death, Kate Tornsel called me and said the Tummelier boys were up to something suspicious on the beach, that stretch she could see from her house. She said it looked like to her they were playing with a little child, digging up something in the sand, she couldn't say for sure because it was night and she'd been watching them by whatever moonlight there was. I came over on the boat right away. You couldn't ignore Kate. She'd call in a complaint, and if you didn't take action on it, she'd go to your supervisor. I looked at the beach, talked to Kate, next day I talked to both Tummelier boys—nothing came of it. Then a couple days later your dad kills himself. I kept wondering if there was any connection, the Tummelier brothers up to something suspicious, your dad commits suicide, which doesn't strike me as something he would do, Richard being the one who found him—"

"Richard? I never knew that."

"Yeah, said he heard a gunshot, ran to the dock, saw your dad's body in the water. I questioned the hell out of Richard, both about finding your dad's body and about what he was doing on the beach with his brother that night Kate called in her complaint. But I never got anywhere. If there was a child with the Tummeliers on the beach, like Kate thought she saw, you couldn't prove it by me. No child was ever reported missing or anything like that. Then I get a call that you're in the Burtons' house with a gun, then you and your mom and sisters leave Hambriento, then Richard gets sent away to some high-priced loony bin in Europe—and that's that. Except now, twenty years later, people are getting killed and I keep getting this feeling that it's all somehow connected. I ain't told anyone at the department about it, though. I'm hoping that you and me can find Peter and get him to fill in the blanks."

"What do you want me to do?"

"I need to know everything, what kind of car he was driving, if you happened to remember the tags, was it a rental, did he say anything about where he was staying, you see any matchbooks from motels, stuff like that."

"He was driving a black late-model Mercedes with a red interior."

From the inside pocket of his sport coat Johnny took out a cheap spiral notebook with a blue cover, the kind you buy for fifty-nine cents at the drugstore. "Okay, what else?"

"That's it. I don't know where he's staying, where he got the car, if he's going to come see me again, nothing else. What about Richard, is he still in Europe?"

"Last information I got he's in a ritzy sanitarium in Switzerland."

"And you never found out why he was sent away?"

"Hell, Roscoe, you grew up on Hambriento, you know how it is with rich people, you got enough money you can hush up anything. A member of the family gets in trouble and all of a sudden lots of checks get written, lawyers and doctors running around, and us common folk don't end up hearing nothin' about nothin'."

I asked if I could go back home.

Johnny said sure, but something obviously was on his mind. Finally he said, "I'm convinced Peter's going to contact you again. So I was thinking, rather than go through the red tape of getting the D.C. cops to authorize a stakeout of your house, maybe I could come stay with you, then if Peter shows, bingo, we get to the bottom of this. I know it's a imposition—"

"You got a weapon?"

He smiled crookedly. "I ain't exactly authorized to be carrying a weapon here in D.C."

"That's not what I asked you."

"Yeah, I brought a pistol."

"Then you're welcome to stay at my house."

"Good. Hey, I get to meet your wife."

"Yeah, she loves meeting my old friends from Florida."

He stood there smiling, apparently taking my remark at face value.

EIGHTEEN

He lies asleep—or, rather, in a twilight of sleep—on an ugly brown couch in a small construction trailer that has been shuttered against the light. The couch's hardwood frame is broken and springs poke out from the filthy cotton stuffing. He hates this place. Peter is so offended by dirt and disorder that before leaving a hotel room he always tidies up, makes the bed, wipes down all the surfaces in the bathroom. He tolerates this current hovel only because it's temporary. Soon to sea.

Those two deputies down on Hambriento came within minutes of finding him in Kate Tornsel's bedroom. He had to run, carrying her bony body down a back stairway and then around to the skiff. He motored out beyond the pass, chumming for sharks as he went. What beasts they are, roiling the water with their hunger.

Weary from all of that, from the trip back to Washington, Peter lies here waiting for night, when people come out for fun, when their appetites wander. Things go better with night. He told Marianne that his plot was designed like a funnel and that she and Roscoe had better escape with him while they can. Tonight we enter the funnel's mouth.

In the half consciousness of this day sleep he runs a large hand down to cover his swollen stomach. Odd, this hunger. The more you feed it, the more voracious it grows.

Soon to sea. Now that Peter has come into his inheritance he needs someone to watch over him, a daytime guardian, but it's hardly a position you can hire someone to fill because if money is the primary enticement then what's to stop the guardian from driving a stake through his employer's heart at high noon and stealing everything? No, this is an assignment that requires a certain devotion to duty, a friend who wishes to remain mortal but who is dedicated to the role as protector of the beast, warding off daytime intrusions, arranging transportation, seeing to those quotidian details so bothersome to a nocturnal creature in a daylight world.

Roscoe will be perfect for it and the sea will prove bountiful: cruising into an isolated cove where another boat is already anchored, apologizing for the intrusion, inviting the people from the other boat to dinner. Oh, yes, we'd love to have you for dinner. Roscoe could convince anyone to come aboard, so boyishly charming when he wants to be, who wouldn't trust him? Then after dinner we tow their boat out to sea and sink it. None of this tiresome business of being chased by deputies.

In his day sleep Peter smiles to imagine being together with Roscoe like the old days on Hambriento, compatriots, talking for hours on end, playing rock and roll endlessly, re-creating that friendship on a permanent world cruise. Rock-and-Roll Vampires!

But first of course Roscoe has to be convinced to accept the assignment, convinced that he has no other choice.

It's getting to be that time, the beast stirring with anticipation. One of Peter's childhood psychiatrists tried to teach him techniques for controlling his rage, channeling it. Don't hold that anger inside of you, the psychiatrist had explained, because then it will only get bigger and bigger and meaner and meaner. What you have to do is get rid of it. Run until you're exhausted, jump up and down and scream, use exhaustion to release your anger.

But the psychiatrist was wrong. Instead of controlling the rage, you need to feed it. Nurture, cultivate, stoke it. Then *dispense* it.

Hours pass, shadows rise. Comes the night and the beast awakens, hungry.

Tap, tap.

"That's really rude."

Peter turns and looks at the young woman on the barstool next to his. Oh, if only I had the time, he thinks. But as soon as it gets late enough, as soon as Roscoe and Marianne are in bed, he has to perform and can't let himself be distracted by pudgy young women with blouses open to show off their bras. He once again taps a coin on the bar to get the bartender's attention.

"I used to work as a waitress," she says to him, her criticism brightened by an oh-you-devil smile, "and next to someone whistling to get your attention, tapping a coin on the bar is the most irritating—"

"Oh, shut up," he hisses.

She turns away.

She wears her hair in that mop of stringy curls popular among young women except she's not that young. Twenty-nine, a secretary working for a natural-gas lobbyist, Audrey-Eileen has hyphenated her first and middle names in an effort toward panache, to get herself noticed, which is also why she's wearing a black leather miniskirt tonight and no stockings covering her tanning-bed brown legs that are unfortunately a little short, thighs that aren't yet cottage cheese but have become heavy. Red stiletto-heeled shoes match a red blouse unbuttoned to reveal her black bra. Okay, so her mother would say she looks like a whore, a whore so hungry to get fucked that she would come out in six inches of snow to sit at a bar dressed the way she's dressed. But a lot of secretaries dress like this and besides what's a girl to do?

There's this maddening eternal dilemma you're always facing. A man's not interested unless you dress and act provocatively, but then after scoring he's not interested in marrying you if he thinks you've dressed and acted provocatively for too many men before him. And he gets to define how many are too many.

So you try to bait and switch 'em. I'm a whore, I'm a whore—but only until you get to know me, then you'll find out I'm a nice girl after all. It's tough, the technique requiring surrendering your bait then trying to get it back later, and Audrey-Eileen has been fishing like this, losing her bait, ever since she got out of college.

And now at age twenty-nine she wants desperately to be married but keeps running into these goddamn dilemmas. The men who would marry her, plodding low-level executives and blue-collar wage slaves, she doesn't want. And the men she *would* marry, rich men and handsome men and Congress-men, they desire to fuck, not marry, her.

It's like compulsive comparison shopping, unable to afford what she wants and not willing to buy what she can afford, ending up with nothing and living in eternal stupid hope that the perfect purchase is available on the next date.

And now that she's staring hard at thirty, any traces of casualness have evaporated from her endeavors. She meets men at conventions and when they travel into Washington on business. Goes to their hotel rooms and fucks them enthusiastically. But mornings find Audrey-Eileen trying to be the kind of woman she thinks they want to marry, someone witty, interesting to talk to, a good listener, a woman who could look after a household, graciously entertain friends and clients, rear children. Audrey-Eileen wants to convince them she can do all that and *still* fuck with enthusiasm.

A perfect package! So much to offer the right man! Why do they keep leaving her!

Audrey-Eileen's married girlfriends cluck their tongues at her desperate search for Mr. Right, a search they once engaged in rapaciously. They say it's such a cliché, this madonna-whore business. Just relax and concentrate on your own interests. They tell Audrey-Eileen there's a Jack for every Jill, the right man will come along in his own sweet time, you can't rush these things.

Easy enough for them to talk. They've already settled for their boring, $32,500-a-year husbands, living in their cheap townhouses, driving their Jennifers and Marks around on endless child-oriented errands. Or even worse for Audrey-Eileen, some of her friends have lucked out marrying well-to-do husbands, like that self-satisfied bitch who lives on a horse farm in Middleburg, inviting Audrey-Eileen out for weekends to lord it over her. Audrey-Eileen fucked *that* husband just to make it easier for her to bear the smug smiles of a former friend.

It's on toward midnight and Audrey-Eileen is sitting at the bar buying her own drinks and thinking of Donna Rice. When the scandal about her and Gary Hart broke, back when Audrey-Eileen was still in college, it was reported that Donna Rice once speculated with a friend about living in the White House. *Imagine me being the First Lady.* Audrey-Eileen and her college friends howled over that one. How could someone delude herself to that extent? By what convoluted, self-deceiving stretch of hopeful thinking could Donna Rice possibly imagine that Monkey Business Hart would divorce his wife, marry her, win the election, and move her into the White House?

But now Audrey-Eileen understands. Now she no longer laughs at Donna Rice.

Last summer Audrey-Eileen got backstage at a rock concert and met an older man with heavy eyes and a potbelly, a man who said he was a record promoter and who was nice to her when everyone else with the band was ignoring Audrey-Eileen in favor of the teenage groupies. And when this nice older man offered to take her back to the hotel where the band was staying, suddenly Audrey-Eileen was imagining herself married to a rich rock-music promoter, living in a big mansion in L.A., interviewed by *Rolling Stone. Imagine me married to a rich and famous record producer.*

He turned out to be an old roadie who refused to use a rubber, and Audrey-Eileen counted herself lucky that all he gave her was the clap.

It happens all the time now. Some man smiles and says he's from Chicago, offers to buy her a drink, says he owns his own business—and suddenly Audrey-Eileen is scrolling forward to the part where she is living in a fabulous penthouse on Lake Shore Drive, wearing silk dresses and pearl necklaces, winning awards for her work in high society's charitable organizations. And then in his *motel* room, after he's boffed her and now he's standing at the sink washing his dick, that's when she sees brochures from his business: Stanley Steemer, a carpet-cleaning franchise. Under the brochures is a snapshot of his fat wife and ugly dog.

Meanwhile Audrey-Eileen keeps shuffling like tarot cards the possibilities of her life. Maybe the next one or surely the one after that. Next! Come on, who's next for Audrey-Eileen, always an enthusiastic fuck on the first date when every frog is still a potential prince, come on, no waiting, NEXT!

She's a little drunk now. And speaking of frogs, there are those vaginal warts she simply must do something about or Prince Charles will *never* divorce Di and come over here to Washington to marry me. *Imagine me the future Queen of England!* She laughs at herself. Then stops laughing when she remembers that blood test she took last Friday but the results of which she hasn't yet seen. Warts and princes may be the least of her worries. Looking into the mirror behind the bar, Audrey-Eileen raises her glass a few inches and silently toasts the delusions of all the Donna Rices of this world.

"I've always heard that when you start toasting yourself in mirrors, it's time to switch drinks. Here, try mine. It's called a Slow Slide Down a Tall Palm."

She turns on the stool surprised to see that little prick who had told her to shut up earlier in the evening. Audrey-Eileen had been interested in him because of the expensive clothes he's wearing, the homburg. Rich European was her guess. But when he was rude to her she immediately put him out of mind, and now here he comes offering a drink. I'm not going to do it, she thinks, I have my self-respect.

Then she laughs at her self-delusions and gamely takes a sip, expertly suppresses the gag reflex, and announces the drink simply delicious. Which seems to be the answer he was hoping for.

She appraises him with an experienced eye. Early thirties, great suit, that dorky homburg, which somehow looks okay on him, no rings. A little too short for her but she can always slouch. He's not that bad, especially if you go for the severe look. The cutest little mouth. And rich? The possibility activates her salivary glands.

He orders another Slow Slide Down a Tall Palm and directs that it be placed in front of Audrey-Eileen.

"That's by way of apology, for my having been discourteous to you earlier," he says, speaking formally, smiling.

Audrey-Eileen shrugs like maybe she's accepting his apology and maybe she ain't. Play it cool, girl, play it cool.

Before he has a chance to say anything more, the jukebox comes on loud.

"What *is* this dreadful music?"

"Don't you like rock?" she shouts back.

"Rock and roll, yes, *real* rock and roll, but not this noise. Who is it? Guns N' Butter?"

She laughs genuinely, surprising herself; she'd forgotten what it's like not to force a laugh while talking with a man. "Guns N' Roses! But this isn't them."

"Don't tell me who it is, I don't want to know!"

"My name is Audrey-Eileen!"

"I'm Peter Tummelier, nice meeting you! Eileen is your last name?"

She shakes her head to make all those stringy curls sway back and forth across her face. "Second half of my first name! Hyphenated!"

He raises one eyebrow as if partially impressed.

"You live here in Washington, Peter?"

He holds an index finger to his ear. "Let's wait until this dreadful noise is over!"

When the song finishes he tells her he lives here in Washington and lots of other places too. "Hambriento Island off the southwest coast of Florida, in the south of France, the Isle of Man, lots and lots of places. I have houses hither and yon and basically I just travel among them by boat. My fifty-five-foot trawler yacht."

Unable to help herself in these matters, Audrey-Eileen is quickly imagining forward to the time when she is spending three or four months each in different mansions around the world, sending postcards from various ports of call to all of her married and unmarried friends, can you imagine it, Audrey-Eileen rich and living on a yacht.

"What kind of business are you in?"

"Such an *American* question," he says with a sour expression. "What do you *do*, what do you *do*, how much money do you make, what kind of car do you drive, what do you *do*."

In spite of the contempt in his voice, she manages to hold on to her smile. "But you're American, aren't you? I mean, you got a little bit of an accent, but—"

"My dear, I'm a citizen of the world. And to answer your question, I don't *do* anything other than live well. My ancestors were in business. They worked hard so that I wouldn't have to, don't you see?"

She ignores all of that in favor of asking, "Where's your boat?"

"My trawler yacht is in Norfolk being refitted for an extended Caribbean cruise that I'll be starting in a week or so."

Audrey-Eileen smiles broadly.

When another loud song drum-beats its way out of the jukebox, he leans close to her near ear and asks if she wants to come to his place and listen to some *real* rock and roll.

Ah.

She pulls back and looks at his face.

Damn, it's always a tough call, isn't it?

No and maybe he leaves to talk with someone else.

Yes and maybe I get fucked in a way that won't ever put me on a yacht in the Caribbean.

"Hello!" he shouts over the racket. "Anyone home in there, Audrey-hyphen-Eileen? Shall I rephrase the question?"

She forces a laugh and turns all squirmy and coquettish. "What about a midnight dinner? Dinner would be good! Dinner, talk—then *maybe* rock and roll! Do you really have a boat that's going to the Caribbean or are you just pulling my piñata?"

"I have the boat all right and I'm here in Washington rounding up my crew, a man-and-wife team. They'll be handling all the chores."

"I bet your wife appreciates that!"

He laughs at her. "Oh, Audrey-hyphen-Eileen, much too ham-handed! I might have sprung for a midnight dinner . . ." He laughs again. "But you went way overboard on that one, dear!"

Then before she can shout anything that might redeem herself, he is moving down the bar, talking to a long-blonded twenty-two-year-old, causing *her* to force laughter and flash eyes, to look down and smile up at him.

Goddamn it anyway! See, that's exactly the problem, a buyer's market. Audrey-Eileen would *like* to price herself high enough to keep out the riffraff and tire kickers, would *like* to refuse easy sex, would *like* to make 'em hang around until they find out what a great person she really is deep down, but every time she tries going upmarket, some cheap little whore on the next stool starts *giving* it away. Just the way Audrey-Eileen did when *she* was twenty-two.

Pushing away the awful coconut smell of that Slow Slide Down a Tall Palm, Audrey-Eileen orders a Tequila Shooter and watches the asshole in the homburg operating at the end of the bar.

After the second Shooter, Audrey-Eileen decides to walk down there and try feisty. Feisty sometimes goes over when nothing else will. Nasty words out of a sweet mouth, fire in her eyes, I like a woman with spirit, all that bullshit, don't laugh, sometimes it works.

At the glass-bottomed conclusion of Shooter three, Audrey-Eileen marches to where this Peter Tummelier is chatting up the girl with long blond hair. When he finally notices Audrey-Eileen, she speaks loudly enough so that her words aren't lost to music.

"I don't give a rat's ass about your boat or your bank account, I was just trying to have a conversation."

"Sorry, luv," he tells her in a way that says he isn't in the least sorry. "Didn't mean to hurt your feelings."

"The *only* reason I suggested dinner was to get to know you better, certainly not because I was hoping for a free meal, in case that's what you were thinking."

"The thought never crossed my mind, I promise you. I just wanted someone to come home with me and listen to some real rock and roll."

"Well, when I *do* like a man well enough to rock and roll with him, he fucking well knows he's been rocked and rolled!" Then she stares dead hard into the blonde's tinted-contacts-blue eyes. "It's just that I don't like to be mistaken for a common bar pickup."

"I understand what you're saying, understand completely, dear," Peter Tummelier says. But he immediately turns back to the blonde, who shoots Audrey-Eileen a quick get-lost-bitch look before granting Peter her wide-eyed attention once again.

Standing there being pointedly ignored, Audrey-Eileen allows her shoulders to sag.

Then she straightens up, shoulders back, tits out, muttering a soft curse to herself as she pinches a bit of his suit material between her thumb and forefinger, pulling on it and waiting until he turns her way.

"Yes?" he asks in an amused, are-you-still-here voice.

"Come on, cowboy, let's rodeo!" she hollers over the music.

Then Audrey-Eileen turns and walks out the door without trying to make her ass sway, knowing that the tight leather miniskirt and red stiletto heels are doing the job for her, knowing that the hook is set but that the hard part, boating him, hasn't even started yet.

Peter catches up with her halfway down the block. Taking her arm, he says, "I'm hungry."

She smiles and replies, "Me too," in a girlish voice, leaning into him as if they're longtime lovers making up after a spat.

"Beautiful night," he says as they walk arm-in-arm toward his car.

"I love the way the snow hides all the trash."

Hearing this makes Peter so giddy that he feels like breaking out in song but settles for taking a deep breath and telling his new girlfriend, "Ah, you can smell felony in the air."

NINETEEN

Johnny Laflin had some business to take care of with his liaison on the D.C. police force, so after we finished talking at the station house early that Wednesday morning I was driven home by a patrolman to wait for Johnny's call. He planned to check out of the motel he'd booked, then phone me for directions to our house.

Marianne met me at the front door wanting to know what had happened, why hadn't I called, was I all right. I told her everything as we sat in the kitchen with a pot of coffee between us. We talked until the coffee was gone and it was time for Marianne to go to the university. She asked if I was okay, did I want her to stay home from her classes today, but I said I'd be fine, I just had to wait there for Laflin to show up.

After Marianne left I called the office to say I wouldn't be coming in to work today, then I went back to bed but couldn't sleep, too nervous and troubled about everything Johnny had told me. Why was he implying that Peter or Richard had something to do with my father's death, that it wasn't suicide? And what's the connection between all of that and what Peter's doing now?

I got out of bed and wandered around the house, tried watching television, kept looking at the clock. At noon I called the station house but the person I talked to had never heard of a John Laflin from Florida, which worried me until I called a second time and talked to a different person, who said Laflin had been at the station all morning but had just left.

He finally called at three in the afternoon, apologizing for the delay and saying it was going to be several more hours before he could break loose. I gave him directions to the house and said I'd be there the entire time, waiting for him.

Then in those late-afternoon hours, alone in the house, I talked myself into getting my dad's pistol down from the attic.

It was stored in a heavy wooden case among boxes of old college textbooks. I didn't intend to be caught weaponless and impotent as I had been this morning when I thought Peter was coming up the stairs to get me.

I opened the case and stared at the big pistol lying there hard with potential: a .357 Magnum, six-shot, double-action revolver. Dad said that he preferred a revolver over a semiautomatic because with a revolver you always knew if it was loaded or not and didn't have to worry about a forgotten round in the chamber, didn't have to worry about a revolver jamming.

As soon as it was in my hand I felt like a boy playing with something he'd been told not to touch. The pistol had a six-inch barrel with a full shroud beneath and ventilated rib on top, putting a lot of weight toward the muzzle, which helped keep it from raising up on you when firing. Dad explained the pistol's workings and specifications before he ever let me shoot it—he always was a tyrant for mastering detail—and I remembered that although the kick wasn't as severe as you might think, the big pistol sounded like a cannon. In fact when I saw characters in movies shooting these heavy-caliber pistols at each other in a small room or closed-up apartment, I always thought the dialogue following the shoot-out should consist solely of "Huh? What? Huh? What did you say?"

Also in the pistol case was a box of 125-grain semijacketed hollow-point cartridges that would fire at nearly fifteen hundred feet per second, twice the speed of a .38 Special and more umph than the 9mm's most police officers had begun to carry.

Enough power to kill someone who thinks he's a vampire.

Leaving the case in the attic I brought the pistol, which I had loaded, downstairs and then spent half an hour trying out different hiding places. I wanted the pistol close at hand but couldn't let Marianne find it and finally settled for shoving it under my side of the mattress.

I had just done that in fact when Marianne arrived home and as I rushed downstairs to meet her I felt as if I'd been with another woman.

At dinner Marianne and I resumed the conversation we'd begun over our morning coffee: Peter and his plot against us.

She asked me at one point how much influence Richard had over Peter.

A lot, I told her. "Part of it was Richard being four years older but also their parents were gone most of the time, leaving both boys in the care of tutors and servants, so Richard was more responsible for raising Peter than their parents were. Peter hated his father; he said his mother was an alcoholic. I met them but I didn't really know them. Both parents were supposedly descendants of some faded line of European royalty."

"Do you think Richard abused Peter?"

"How do you mean?"

"It's not uncommon for an older sibling to abuse a younger when there's no strong parental presence to intervene. Could be physical abuse, mental abuse, even sexual abuse. When two kids are as isolated as you said Peter and Richard were, the older sibling becomes godlike to the younger one and can basically do whatever strikes his fancy, whatever amuses him or meets his own needs regardless of how twisted they are."

"Richard was twisted all right."

"In what way?"

"Torturing animals, that kind of shit. I wouldn't put up with it. I didn't care if he was older and bigger. I told him if I ever saw him hurting animals I'd bust his chops."

We continued talking until ten that evening, when I called the station house again. Johnny came on and apologized, said he was still tied up.

"I wish he'd get here," I told Marianne after the call. "What if Peter shows up?"

"He won't hurt you," she said. "He's in love with you."

I turned from the sink, where I'd been doing dishes, and stared at her. "What're you talking about?"

"Oh, come on, Roscoe, you must know. I've seen the way he looks at you, half fawning, half predatory. Oh, he's in love with you all right, probably has been since the two of you were kids."

"I . . ."

"Your face is turning red." She laughed. "Just because the two of you might have played sexual games as kids, that's completely normal. Adolescence is a time of sexual experimentation. You grew out of it, Peter didn't. He's still carrying a torch for you."

"Bullshit."

"Which part?" Then she gave me a playful bump with her hip. "Hey, I already told Peter you're mine, he can't have you. And he understood exactly what I was talking about too. Don't worry, I'll protect you."

"I wonder what's keeping Laflin."

Marianne laughed again.

"What?"

"Nothing. Come on, let's sit in the living room, I'm going to hypnotize you."

"You're going to *what* me?"

"Not exactly hypnotism but I'll put you in a frame of mind where you can remember in better detail exactly what happened Sunday night, when you and Peter went out on that toot. Maybe something will come to you about where he's staying or how he gets back and forth to Florida, something that will help your friend Laflin locate him."

We tried her memory-enhancing techniques for nearly an hour, Marianne taking me through the events of that evening, asking me to visualize where Peter and I were sitting, who said what, the expressions on Peter's face, each recalled detail supposedly bringing forth new details from my alcohol-suppressed memory. Marianne took notes but I didn't think there was anything in them that Laflin would find useful.

At midnight Marianne and I both wanted to go to bed, so I called the police station again and was told that Laflin was in a meeting. He'd been at it from before dawn and must be ready to collapse, desperate to break this case and become a hero to the boys back home. I left a message for him to call me just as soon as his meeting ended.

When I returned to the living room Marianne said there was something that occurred to her earlier in the day and she wanted to know what I thought about it. "Maybe we should go ahead and hire a lawyer, just in case this thing goes further than we think it will, in case what Laflin said about extradition turns out to be true."

"Where are we going to get the money for a lawyer? You know how their time adds up. Hell, we spent more on attorney fees than we did paying off Maring when he—"

"Roscoe, what's wrong?"

"*Maring.*"

"And?"

"Sunday night Peter asked me who I hated enough to kill, to want dead, and I said there were certain people I hated but not enough to kill them. He kept pressing me. What about the Burtons? What about Kate Tornsel? And that's when I said, yeah, Daniel Maring, I certainly hate that bastard. I didn't remember until just now that I'd mentioned Maring's name."

"Do you think—"

"I think here we go again, that's what I think. *Fuck.* I was right about the Burtons, about Kate Tornsel, Peter mentioned them Sunday night and now they're missing, so, yeah, maybe he put Maring on the list."

"What are you going to do?"

"I feel like letting Peter kill the bastard."

She waited for me to say something sensible.

"I'll call Johnny again. I'll demand that he be pulled out of that meeting, I'll tell them it's an emergency, I'll tell them I know who's going to be killed next."

TWENTY

She thinks: He's rich.

He thinks: She's going to be easy.

She thinks: Afterward. Afterward she'll show him what a good person she is inside, how sensitive, caring, what an attentive listener, how she's always up, cheerful, a great laugher. Afterward she'll tell him that while she believes in equal pay for equal work and that women should be treated with dignity, she doesn't consider herself a feminist, at least she isn't one of those man-haters who blame men for all their problems. In fact she doesn't really even have any problems. She has lots of interests though, she's not one of those clingy, dependent, whiny women. On the other hand, she absolutely adores cooking for a man, taking care of him—there's dignity in that too. Did she mention she liked to try new things? Afterward. She'll go into all that afterward. First things first.

He thinks: This is stupid. I should just let her off on a street corner, tell her I changed my mind. It's one in the morning, Roscoe and Marianne are asleep, I should be at their house right now, not playing around with this sow. On the other hand she'll be easy and quick, and I'll be well fed for the task at hand.

She thinks: He's the one, I know he is, *I know it.* Look at this Mercedes he's driving, and he's shown me snapshots of his yacht, *R&R Vamp,* and, well, he just *acts* rich. This time I'm not going to be so judgmental, they *all* have flaws, this one is haughty and has a cruel streak, but *afterward* he'll fall in love with me and his meanness will mellow out into kindness, *afterward.* But first things first. Which means that anything Peter Tummelier wants tonight, he gets. Fuck, suck, belts, whistles, swallow, bottom, top, wheelbarrow races and rug burns, back door, front door, in the ear, out the ass—get his attention tonight and then afterward the *real* Audrey-Eileen will be revealed to his ever-loving delight.

"A trailer?" Even to her own ears she sounds shrewish and wishes she had exercised tone control, but really, *a trailer?* She and Peter have traveled through a heavily wooded, isolated section of Rock Creek before turning into a private lane marked by a tree that's been split by lightning. Audrey-Eileen assumed the lane would end up at some tucked-away mansion but instead the dirt road led back into the trees and stopped at what looks to be an old construction trailer.

"What are we doing here?" she asks softly.

"It's a piece of investment property I own. I thought you'd be interested in seeing it."

Investment property? She likes the sound of those words and fast-forwards to a telephone conversation with that smug bitch who lives on the horse farm in Middleburg. *Yes, well, Peter and I are off to Spain this week, checking on some investment property we own there.*

"The value of the investment is in the land," he explains as he gets out of the Mercedes. "The trailer is here for tax purposes. Also a nice deserted place for rock and roll. Come along, dear. In spite of its ratty exterior, it's quite nice inside, much like yourself, I'd wager."

She's game. Wait a second, what did he mean by that?

Inside, the furniture is strictly Goodwill and all the windows are boarded up. Audrey-Eileen warns herself not to start in on the criticism, don't think you can do better next time around, there's already been too many next times around. Smile. Be cooperative. Men don't like sourpusses.

While Peter looks through a collection of CDs, Audrey-Eileen stands in front of a wall of photographs. "Who are all these guys?"

"A friend of mine."

"Friends of yours?" They're all men. Is he queer?

"*Friend.* They're of the same person."

"Who—"

He interrupts to ask if she can dance.

"I manage."

"Oh, I bet you do. After you dance we'll have that midnight dinner."

"Whatever twists your tail, tiger."

When she growls he smiles and asks, "Did you hear about the cannibal who passed his brother in the jungle?"

"Hmm-unh."

"Ah."

"Tell me!"

He just smiles.

I missed something, Audrey-Eileen thinks. Oh, well, *afterward* I'll prove to him what a great sense of humor I have.

"Ready, my dear?"

"Fire up that music box, doll, my motor's running."

As she stands there swaying a little in the shadowed silence, Audrey-Eileen tries to remember everything she was taught in that "Dances of the Sixties" course she took at the community college near where she lives. She hoped to meet older men who were settled in life, but it turned out to be a disaster, because she ended up in bed with a fat fifty-year-old computer wonk who left shit stains on her towels. She wanted to inform him that if only he would wash himself *there* before he left the shower, he wouldn't leave those embarrassing brown skid marks on her Cannons, but she could never quite figure out how to introduce the topic.

The memory of this causes her to stop swaying, to cringe inside with the shame of it. Jesus love me but I've kissed a lot of frogs getting here tonight.

When Peter has all the dials and levels exactly where he wants them but hasn't yet begun playing any music, he stands and turns to her, both of them smiling anticipatorily.

This one's the prince, she concludes.

"I don't have much time . . ." he starts.

Her face falls. Time is the one thing she absolutely requires. If this turns out to be a quickie that means there won't be an *afterward* and she won't be able to work her magic on him, prove to him how he can't possibly continue his life without making her a part of it. For that she needs *time*.

". . . I have to kill someone tonight," he finishes.

Oh, Jesus, please don't let him be a creep, a nut, a weirdo, I could deal with anything except that.

"Exactly what do you mean?" she asks with a perky lilt to her voice.

"I've given this a great deal of thought and I've concluded I provide a service to mankind, fulfill a prophecy of sorts. You see, my dear, pudgy Audrey-hyphen-Eileen, a fear of the night, of what's out there in the night, a beast at the door, it's hard-wired into the human brain from evolutionary history, from a time when the night did contain beasts at the door, at the door of one's cave. So we keep looking out into the dark, expecting monsters, waiting for them, anticipating them, *creating* them through horror tales and ghost stories. Which is where I come in, offering what has been anticipated. *I am* that beast at your door."

"I see." Although in truth she stopped listening to him after he called her pudgy.

"Do you, dear?"

She smiles unsurely.

"I want you to meet my brother."

"Your brother's here?"

"Oh, Dondo!" Peter calls. Then he smiles at Audrey-Eileen. "Must be sleeping, I'll go fetch him. You sit there on the couch." He walks to the other end of the trailer and when Peter comes back he's carrying a big doll.

Looking at its frenzied painted eyes, that blood-red and chipped-tooth mouth, those protruding ears, Audrey-Eileen's lips curl in disgust.

Dondo is wearing blue jammies and tiny bunny slippers with little cottontails at the heels.

Peter places the doll on Audrey-Eileen's lap and instructs her, "Say hello to Dondo."

"Why, hello there, Dondo." She laughs a little. "You know, he's so ugly he's almost cute."

"Ugly?"

"I mean—"

"Dondo, say hello to Audrey-Eileen."

She bounces the doll on her knee and stares into his hard face as if truly waiting for a hello.

"*Dondo*, don't be rude, say hello to the nice young lady."

She laughs again.

"Dondo, goddamn you anyway, I *told* you to—"

She holds the doll up to her ear, cocks her head as if listening, then replaces Dondo on her lap and tells Peter, "Dondo said he was glad to meet me but doesn't like it when you use bad words."

"Don't patronize me, bitch."

"Well." She puts the doll on the couch and stands. "I think it's time for me to go, really."

"Oh, reeelly," he responds, mocking her pronunciation.

Then he kneels in front of the doll and begs, "*Please* say hello." He and Audrey-Eileen both wait. Peter clenches his large hands into fists, squeezes his black eyes closed, and repeats it, "*Please* say hello." They wait. He begins trembling, his small mouth twisted in pain. "Oh, why do you do this to me, why won't you say hello, *please*."

Audrey-Eileen is reminded of that night when she was ten and her little brother had to be rushed to the hospital with a burst appendix,

Audrey-Eileen's mother praying not just with her voice but with her entire body, hands fisted and arms clenched as if bearing up a great weight, praying *hard.*

Which is what this strange little man is doing on his knees in front of that doll, praying hard for it to speak.

She heads for the door. Walking through the snow in these high heels is going to be murder, but—

He grabs her arm. "Where do you think you're going, young lady?"

"I . . ."

"Dondo wants to see you dance, you promised us a dance."

"I have to go."

"I have to go too." His voice softens. "But first a dance. Dance for us and then I'll drive you back."

"Promise?" she asks hopefully.

"Cross my heart and hope to die."

"Okay, *one* song."

"Good." He walks to the console. "This is a tender little tune, soft and sensitive, infused with deeper meaning."

"I like slow dancing."

"You know what I like?"

When he presses the Play button, there's a tinkling of a fake phone ring followed by a booming bass voice. *"Helllooo, baaaby. Yeah this is the Big Bopper speakin'."* Then the world's greatest dirty laugh, deep and lascivious.

Peter points his forearm toward the floor, his index finger turning around and around in quick little circles.

"Chantilly lace and a pretty face . . ."

Audrey-Eileen smiles. I'll give it one more try.

As she bounds around the trailer, short legs pumping and heavy thighs slapping, Peter laughs until tears come to his eyes. He turns the volume all the way up and then collapses on the couch next to the doll. "Oh, look, Dondo, pigs on ice, cows in tutus!"

But out there on the trailer floor, dancing to the Big Bopper's paean to ponytails, wiggles in walks, giggles in talks, and big-eyed girls, Audrey-Eileen perseveres. Hey, she thinks, this could still work, you can't give up on a man just because he's a little . . . *eccentric.* She does the Dirty Dog, the Monkey, she leans forward to milkshake her titties, turns around to shake her tail feathers, making Peter laugh and laugh, marveling that being a rock-and-roll vampire could turn out to be so much *fun.*

He joins her in dancing to the bouncy song and just when the Big Bopper is complaining that he ain't got *no* money, Peter brings up a razor blade, lances her neck, and lowers his face to suck.

But Audrey-Eileen is so startled by the sudden pain that she jumps back, forcing Peter to grab her roughly by the hair and cut her again. He tries to hold on to the woman, to get his mouth down there on one of those flowing wounds, but she's strong, screaming and struggling, keeping him away from her. Blood everywhere. Christ but he's making a mess of it, amateur night all over again.

With her hands held like claws she reaches up and rakes red fingernails down both sides of his face, drawing parallel lines of blood. Then she rushes for the door.

He grabs her just before she gets out, encircling her thick waist with his spider-monkey arms, but she uses an elbow to crack him hard in the mouth. Peter falls back in pain and surprise, enabling Audrey-Eileen to make it out the trailer door.

Never let one escape. Peter's mentor drummed certain admonishments into him: Don't bring attention to what you do, always dispose of the leftovers, and *never* let one escape. Because if you get sloppy and cause a public stir (VAMPIRELIKE KILLER STALKS D.C. VICTIMS), others of your kind will come to silence you, to make an example of you to your peers, and they will employ methods and manners that stand somewhere beyond horror.

Yet here Peter is, looking at the open trailer door, Audrey-Eileen *gone.*

Swift now, he flies after her.

No need for him to worry though. Hobbled by those ridiculous high heels, Audrey-Eileen has managed only a few desperate yards of escape through the snow and within seconds Peter is upon her, wrapping his snaky arms around her shoulders. But there's still tons of fight left in the old girl and she uses her weight to an advantage, collapsing as Peter tries to draw her neck up for another bite, pulling him down into the snow with her, the two of them rolling over and over, leaving the snow trampled and bloody, Peter at one point bashing her face so hard that her partial dental plate is knocked loose and she almost chokes on it before pushing it out of her mouth.

Although she continues resisting, in the end she is subdued by his superior strength, by the terrible feral-animal sounds he makes, all snarl and hiss, and by the loss of that partial plate, all three combining to force her psychological and then physical surrender.

Lifting her in a herculean display of raw power, one of his hands in the front waistband of that black leather miniskirt, his other hand knotted in her stringy locks, Peter brings the struggling woman to a height of three feet before quickly going down to one knee while simultaneously dropping her *hard* across his other knee, breaking her back.

Both of them grunt.

As he drags her back into the trailer, Audrey-Eileen's tongue plays in the gap left by the loss of her partial plate. How odd that naked-wet-hard gum feels, there where her lateral incisor, canine, and first premolar should be. Her father wanted to get rid of the horse, but of course it wasn't Beauty's fault, a bunny rabbit had spooked him, and when Beauty went right, Audrey (she hadn't hyphenated her names yet, she was only thirteen) went left, thrown from Beauty's back and, as bad luck would have it, landing face-first on a protruding rock.

Peter has her inside now, laid out on the trailer's floor. Audrey-Eileen is paralyzed from the waist down but she's still trying to push him away, scratching at his face as he tries to lick up what has spilled onto her clavicle before he goes for the biggest of the wounds he's made, finding with his tongue a loose artery that's spurting like a tiny garden hose. Peter sucks hard and tastes something that's not right.

Her upper body alternately stiffens and trembles in a grand-mal type of seizure. Peter knows he should stop, because something is definitely wrong here, he can taste the wrongness, but he's not going to let her go to waste after all they've been through together. And besides, this is the best part, when the meal stiffens and trembles, it's like what you feel at the onset of an orgasm, that fine preclench clench deep in the base of your genitals, and you can't stop, you *choose* not to stop, not at this point, not when the vessel containing your orgasm is tipping and just about to spill, un-uh, no way.

Fuck it. Peter swallows, too late to stop now, eyes glazed in ecstasy, sucking and swallowing, ejaculating into his trousers, belly filling, rage feeding itself fat.

While Audrey-Eileen is dying peacefully. It is well documented in the literature that after attacks by that class of major predators powerfully clawed and heavily jawed—lions and tigers and bears—survivors have reported that while they were being mauled, during what they believed to be their final few moments of life, they experienced the sudden onset of an eerily pleasant serenity. The brain, having accepted death, opts to go out in peace, flooding itself with painkillers and mood softeners of massive potency, apparently stockpiled for this particular possibility, death by exquisite trauma. In fact she seems to have all the time in the world to scroll through an eclectic collection of thoughts and memories.

There was that time when she just turned eleven and Daddy took her out to a farm on the edge of town and showed her a black horse with a white blaze on its forehead and asked her what she would think of a little girl who owned a horse like that, and Audrey said such a girl would be the luckiest girl in the whole wide world, and Daddy said, well, I guess you're the luckiest girl in the whole wide world because that's your horse, honey, I bought it for you last week, happy birthday.

You go through another eighteen years of life, as Audrey-Eileen just has, and you never match the happiness of a moment like that.

She thinks of the afternoon her parents came home from the hospital with her brand-new baby brother.

She remembers how she felt getting ready for her high school prom, the newest of her partial plates fully installed and appearing totally natural. Audrey stood in front of the full-length mirror attached to her closet door and as she examined that laced and taffeted image looking back at her, turning this way and that, trying out different kinds of smiles, she thought, *I'm beautiful.* And then immediately regretted it, as if thinking such a thing was morally wrong and might well jinx her.

Now she questions how in God's name did she end up like this when all she ever wanted was what she had as a child—a nice family, a nice family of her own. She should've married that boy from college, kind of goofy-looking, but a nice guy—and now she can't even find voice to call out his name.

In six seconds she'll be dead.

As she feels this pervert sucking and swallowing at her neck, Audrey-Eileen thinks, Well, at least *my* suck-and-swallow days are over.

Three seconds.

She recalls this past Friday's unread blood test.

One second.

And hopes it's positive because then, *afterward,* this asshole will discover what the real Audrey-Eileen is all about.

With her tongue feeling where teeth should be, she dies.

Peter finally pulls away from her neck and atomizes a crimson spray into the air before gulping for breath as he staggers back from the body. He is choking and spitting up blood, looking at the doll and trying to speak-sing, *"When I say I'm in love you best believe—"*

But he gags and can't finish.

Meanwhile, over there on that ratty couch, little Dondo sits watching in implacable judgment.

TWENTY-ONE

"Roscoe?"

"Johnny!"

"So what's up? Has Peter contacted you?"

"No—"

"So what's the emergency, I'm swamped here."

"I just remembered—"

"Where Peter is staying?"

"Johnny, will you shut up so I can tell you!"

"Sorry, I'm running on nothing but black coffee and adrenaline."

"Sunday night when Peter and I went out drinking, I remember another name being mentioned, along with the Burtons and Kate Tornsel—"

"Who?"

"Daniel Maring."

"Maring? From Hambriento?"

"No." I explained who Maring was, how his name came up, and why he might be Peter's next target.

"You got an address?"

I gave it to him.

"I'll jump right on it. This should get these D.C. guys moving, now that the next victim might be hit on their own turf. I'll have 'em send a car over to Maring's place."

"Peter could show up *here,* you know."

"Okay, I'll have them send a car to your place too."

"When are *you* coming?" I whined.

"Hey, the shit's really hit the fan down in Florida, and I haven't had a chance to—"

"What do you mean, the shit's hit the fan?"

"They found a body."

"Whose?"

He didn't tell me.

"Johnny?"

"You'd better get yourself a lawyer. I think the boys in Florida are about ready to name you."

"What are you talking about?"

"I can't really say other than—"

"Johnny! Come on, whose body was found, one of the Burtons?"

"No."

"Kate Tornsel?"

No answer.

"Oh, for chrissakes—"

"I shouldn't be telling you any of this but I will." He gave a weary laugh. "And you ain't going to believe this, Roscoe, you ain't fucking going to believe it."

TWENTY-TWO

Coupla guys down from Queens to kill sharks. That's how they put it, too, not going to Florida to fish or going to Florida to catch sharks, naw, they tell their buddies in Queens, "We're going down to Florida to kill sharks." Not bad guys, just ignorant. Shark population reduced, a whole system getting fucked up when its major predators are eliminated, have just as much fun catch-and-release—but by God these two guys from Queens want to go down to Florida and *kill sharks*. Call 'em Mutt and Jeff.

Anyways, Mutt and Jeff both just turned fifty and they're treating themselves to this shark-killing birthday trip. They find themselves a captain who specializes, or so he says, in fishing sharks. While they're negotiating a price with the old salt, Mutt and Jeff trip over themselves calling him Captain. The plan is to go out at midnight 'cause that's when the predators feed of course, *at night.*

Except our heroes here, they ain't too bright about how they prepare for this seafaring safari, because what they do is, they hit the bar at the Holiday Inn where they're staying and tell old fraternity stories and start downing boilermakers like they did in their college days and they're loud and they're tipping big and they're eyeing all this young cooze come into the Holiday Inn for some action, Mutt and Jeff nudging each other in the ribs and nodding their heads knowingly like, see that one, yeah, that long tall drink of water over there, I could get a little of that, nooo problemo, señor.

Midnight rolls around and while they ain't exactly shit-faced, they've been soberer. Captain spots them weaving and pitching there on the dock like the dock is already under way and his mouth tightens, while the mate, his heart sinks 'cause all he's thinking is, Assholes going to puke and I'm the one cleans it up.

So now the boat is way the hell out in the ocean somewhere, and sure enough Mutt and Jeff have *mal de mer*'d themselves sober, keep apologizing to the mate and keep telling Captain they don't understand it, never been seasick before, must've been something they ate, fucking cheesy hors'deavors at the Holiday Inn. Captain says, "Don't worry, boys, happens to the best of us." Then when the mate begins chumming putrid fish guts and horsemeat over the transom, Mutt and Jeff start in with wanna-die cases of the dry heaves.

Coupla hours and a gallon of coffee later and they're almost righteous, hooking sharks right and left, bringing some of them to the boat, where the guy who isn't reeling the shark in gets to shoot it with Captain's semiautomatic 30-30.

Kill maybe a dozen sharks, shooting them in the water and letting their compadres feed on the bodies, when Mutt hooks a beauty. Fucking monster twelve-footer that'll grow another eight feet by the time they get back to Queens. Hammerhead. Takes Mutt a solid hour to land the sucker. Jeff shoots it something like fifteen times.

Captain says, "Wanna bring that one in, boys? Measure it, weigh it, get your picture took?"

Hell, yes.

So it's half an hour getting the monster aboard, Captain telling them about a dozen times to stay away from it, these babies ain't dead till they're rotted.

Mutt and Jeff are amazed by the size of it. That wide shovel head with those weird fucking eyes stuck out at the ends, head must be four foot across, but it'll be wider by the time they get back to Queens.

Then all the way in, Mutt and Jeff sit up on the flying bridge with the Captain to hear shark stories.

Like the time this guy hooks Old Hitler, which the Captain explains is a hammerhead's been around these here waters since the end of W-W-2, make *your* shark look like a minnow, Old Hitler mean as a snake and with a taste for human flesh, too, 'cause he was always showing up at shipwrecks, first in line for the survivors, bites off their legs and leaves the top parts still floating in their life jackets.

Mutt and Jeff are both reminded of that sick joke about what do you call a armless, legless guy in a swimming pool—*Bob*—but they don't interrupt Captain to tell it.

Anyway Old Hitler took up residence around these waters after the war and everybody was trying to catch him but he'd break your line or ram your boat, there was no catching him. Until this one guy gets the bright idea he's going to fish Old Hitler on a quarter-inch steel cable that he has rigged to the winch on the front of his Jeep, which he has parked on a pier. Going to winch that sucker in. A week of night fishing and finally Old Hitler strikes. Gets hooked. Tries the usual tricks, rolling over and over to wrap the line around his body and break it except now it ain't line it's quarter-inch steel cable, and then sounding and then running but nothing works 'cause Old Hitler's got a stainless-steel grappling hook in his mouth and the other end is attached to a Jeep.

So the fisherman hits the Go button on the winch and starts winding Old Hitler in. Rolls up a hundred feet of cable, hell, the guy's already practicing his bragging rights, then Old Hitler kind of comes up to the surface real slowlike, coming up like a big 'gator, like a fucking redwood log, and that head of his, ten foot across, eyes on either end, he's checking out the situation. Sharks'll do that, you know. Come up to the surface and see what's what in the world of air. Then, *like he knew exactly what he was doing*, Old Hitler turns his ass end to the dock and starts pulling like a Missouri mule.

The winch holds but it won't turn, not enough power. Standoff.

Then the *whole Jeep* starts moving, getting pulled along that pier, toward the water.

Guy can't believe it. Well, fuck this, he locks the hubs, jumps in the Jeep, straps himself into the driving harness, fires up the engine, puts the Jeep in four-wheel, throws the transmission in reverse, and starts backing up.

That works for about fifteen feet but the pier is all wooden planking and the tires lose their grip, start spinning front and back, and Old Hitler gets down and *pulls,* and there goes that Jeep, tires smoking, guy in the driver's seat panicking, jamming the pedal to the metal, transmission screaming, but *still* that Jeep is getting pulled toward the end of the pier.

Mutt and Jeff, big-eyed like a coupla Boy Scouts, listening to this shit.

Captain says, Our hero in the Jeep panics big time, can't get out of that harness and sure enough the Jeep gets pulled off into the water with him still in it. Coupla other guys get to the pier just then and last they see, the driver is still behind the wheel and the Jeep is sinking but not straight down, sinking off at a angle because Old Hitler is still pulling it.

Damn, Mutt and Jeff say in unison.

Then Captain lobs 'em the punchline: "Still to this day if the water is clear enough and if you're in the right place at the right time, you can look down and spot this old Jeep being pulled through the water behind a couple hundred foot of cable, the Jeep all rusted and barnacle encrusted, streaming along underwater, ten miles an hour, being 'driven' by this human skeleton with its bony hands still gripping that steering wheel."

Overhearing this down in the cockpit, the mate moves his right wrist back and forth—Captain jacking off the paying customers again.

So Mutt and Jeff, Captain and mate, and the shark Mutt and Jeff killed, they all get back to the dock just as the sun is coming up. Mutt and Jeff are tired, hung over, sick, but all goosey with excitement too, they can't wait to hit Queens and start telling all the stories of their

adventures on the high seas, killing sharks. That's the whole point of
the trip, you come back with stories.

Mutt and Jeff are standing on the dock admiring their shark, which
is hanging by its tail but still looking dangerous. Jeff says he thinks
Spielberg should've made the shark in *Jaws* a hammerhead 'cause
while the great white is a deadly enough hunting machine, for out-
and-out evil looks, ain't nothing worse than this hammerhead. Mutt
says, "You mean *Benchley* should've made it a hammerhead, 'cause
Benchley's the one wrote the book." Jeff says, "Whatever."

Captain comes around and explains there's a tradition to shark
hunting, you cut 'em open and see what they've been feeding on, it
helps you understand the species. This makes Mutt and Jeff feel
righteous and by the time they get back to Queens it's going to sound
like they were on an oceanographic expedition, taking sharks purely
for scientific reasons like they're a couple bona-fide Jacques "Man iz
zee only animal zat keels for sport" Cousteaus.

Captain produces this huge Arkansas Toothpick and proceeds to
cut open the shark's soft underbelly so that eventually all kinds of shit,
guts, and partially digested fish, come pouring out in a stinking heap
that almost causes our heroes to commence ralphing all over again.

Captain says he's going to go get a hose and wash everything off, see
exactly what we got here, Mutt and Jeff meanwhile holding their
breath and kicking through the shit, expecting to find license plates
and stuff, like that scene from *Jaws*.

It's still not quite fully light yet, so when Jeff kicks something loose,
he's not sure it is what he thinks it is. *Can't be.*

Then Mutt sees it too and both of them bend down for a better look.

A human arm.

No doubt about it. From right above the elbow all the way down to
the hand. Even got a wristwatch on. Timex.

Mutt and Jeff lean *real* close.

Jeff checks out the wristwatch and sees the goddamn thing is still
running, so he glances over at Mutt and says—

No actually that ain't the way it really happened. What *really* happened was, soon as Mutt and Jeff realize it's a human arm they

immediately back off and start shouting, "Captain! Captain!" while repeatedly taking the Lord's name in vain.

But the way they tell the story for the rest of their lives in Queens, see, they're both leaning down for a close look, Jeff spots the Timex, notes the second hand is still moving, so he turns to his partner and says, "Takes a licking . . ."

Without missing a beat Mutt finishes it for him. ". . . and keeps on ticking."

TWENTY-THREE

Awakened by a noise, I sat up in bed and looked over at the digital clock—*3:03 a.m. Thu. Mar 17.* What now? A downstairs door, its handle being rattled. Maybe the patrolman Johnny said he would send to guard us had finally arrived and was going around the house to make sure the doors were locked. Whatever it was, oddly enough I felt less frightened than irritated. I wanted all this to be over with, I wanted my regular life back, I wanted Marianne and me to be able to discuss nothing more abnormal than paying off the rest of our debts and whose turn it was to cook dinner and whether we should go to a doctor and find out why we weren't having babies. I was weary of remembering Hambriento, reliving those awful days following my father's death, talking about vampires, thinking about lawyers, worrying if I would be arrested and extradited to Florida. I wanted to get up in the morning and face nothing more exciting than—

A voice. Our bedroom was right over the kitchen and I definitely heard someone down there.

I checked on Marianne, who was deeply asleep and then, worried that whoever was in the kitchen might hear my footsteps, I *eased* out of bed and over to a front window. A patrol car was parked across the street, I could see the cop behind the wheel, could see the glow of his cigarette in the darkened car. I wanted a cigarette too. I felt if I could just sit down and smoke a cigarette, this three A.M. opportunity would pass.

Having no tobacco products in the house I slipped on a pair of jeans but didn't bother with a shirt before retrieving the .357 Magnum from under the mattress. I stepped onto the landing, to the top of the stairs, standing there listening, hearing nothing.

What's the smart thing to do? Come on, Roscoe, what's the *smart* thing to do? Go back and open my bedroom window, call out to the cop parked across the street, "I think someone's in the house . . . and can I bum a smoke?" But I was already creeping down the steps, emboldened by the heavy pistol, tired of waiting around for the next thing to happen *to* me.

At the bottom of the steps (the kitchen was down the hall, then to my right) I stopped to listen again.

Nothing.

The noise that awakened me, the voice I thought I heard, were they only my imagination, the residue of a bad dream?

About to straighten up from the crouch I had unconsciously assumed, I heard the outside kitchen door being opened.

Quickly making my way down the hallway, I looked around the corner, then stepped toward the swinging door that would open onto the kitchen. I felt cold air blowing under the door onto my bare feet, and my mind perversely summoned up stories I'd read or programs I'd seen on television in which people, recalling their encounters with ghosts, described how the air always went frigid whenever these spirits were about. Will a .357 Magnum kill a vampire? When the furnace kicked on down in the basement I twitched.

Get a grip, I told myself. I raised the pistol and pushed the door open in front of me.

Moonlight reflecting off snow illuminated the kitchen well enough that I didn't need to turn on the overheads to see no one was there.

But the kitchen door leading to our backyard was wide open, letting in the frigid night air. Snow had been tracked in.

I crossed the tiled floor, feeling a shivering chill when my feet squished into some of that tracked-in snow, and, standing at the opened door, I saw in the otherwise unmarked snow of our backyard fresh footsteps leading from the kitchen, across the yard, and to the chain-link fence marking the back of our property.

I turned around and did a quick check of the kitchen, trying to figure out what might have been taken or what Peter (I assumed it was Peter, who else?) was looking for. Then, turning again to the opened door, I saw him.

He stood on the far side of the chain-link fence, looking right at me. How had I missed him before, he was so startlingly obvious now—his black overcoat, black homburg—against the night-white snow.

Just as I was about to call out he took off running, his coat billowing behind him like a cape.

I didn't debate, I just pulled on a pair of rubber boots sitting there by the door, grabbed a down vest from a nearby hook, and gave chase.

As I ran, my feet kept trying to pull out of the boots and although the vest warmed my torso I could already feel my bare arms and hands (especially the right, gripping that pistol) turning cold. But after climbing over the chain-link fence and seeing Peter turning left at the end of our alley, I didn't hesitate to follow.

I was armed.

Armed but stupid, because I had no idea what I'd do if I caught up with him. Hold him for the police? *Shoot him?* To my father's way of thinking, not knowing what you would do in an emergency was unforgivable. He told me that if I took action in an emergency and it turned out to be wrong, that kind of error in judgment could be overcome with experience. But to have no idea what to do, to be at a loss, to dither, these failures to think straight hinted at a dangerous flaw in character that no amount of instruction could correct. On a charter boat you have to be prepared for any contingency, a plan of action always in mind, making sure beforehand that you've brought along the requisite spare parts, adequate fuel, that all your systems are operating properly, your backup batteries charged, freshwater tanks

checked and tested, radio working, emergency gear double-checked—
on and on he preached this to me like a catechism. And now, chasing
Peter, I could hear my father's rebuke: What're you going to do when
you catch him? I don't know, Dad. Then why are you chasing him?
I don't know. Yet on I ran, actually grinning with the thrill of it, coming
to the end of the alley, turning left and seeing Peter halfway down the
next block. I wasn't worried.

I had a gun.

I recognized this brand of confidence from my barroom days, confidence edged with an attitude that was hot-blooded and foolhardy
and all-male. Don't fuck with me, Peter, I'm tired of your games. I felt
this dangerous attitude in the way I was running, an aggressive bounce
to my stride in spite of the clumsy rubber boots, aware of my shoulders, my concentration focused, my predator's binocular vision locked
like radar on the fleeing prey.

In fact when I saw two young black men on the sidewalk up ahead
of me (they were wearing letter jackets and had their shoulders
hunched high against the night's cold), I didn't experience the usual
defensive-alert mode that kicks in for D.C. residents, even the most
politically correct of them, when encountering young black men after
dark. I didn't go around them, didn't keep my eyes averted. Instead
I ran right between the two startled young men and made eye contact
with the one who had to step toward the street, his sneakered feet
sinking into deep snow, to avoid me. I even slowed my pace a little
to hear if they were going to say something behind my back, challenge
me. But they didn't of course. Whatever they were doing out at three
in the morning, this crazy white guy running through the snow with
bare arms and holding a big pistol, he was obviously up to something
worse.

On an intellectual level I knew it was dangerous and unnecessarily
provocative to have a handgun with me out here on the streets, but on
a lower level, in the gut, in the testes, I felt potent, lion-hearted,
holding in my hand God's power, life and death, which made me
unafraid, a fucking colossus in rubber boots. Being armed was like
having talent.

I followed Peter out of our residential neighborhood and into a commercial area leading toward Connecticut Avenue. Although the running had warmed me into a sweat, my feet were freezing in those thin rubber boots and my pace soon became so painful and plodding that I was sure Peter could have lost me if he'd tried. Yet every corner I turned, there he was, a block away.

Belatedly I thought about tucking the pistol into the waistband of my jeans, trying to cover it with the vest, because if a cop drove by and saw me running with this big Magnum in my hand, I'd be arrested. How would I explain myself: *Chasing a vampire, officer, and while I can see by the expression on your face that you don't think vampires exist, I want you to consider this, if a person* believes *he is a vampire and if he acts upon that belief to the extent of killing—*

But I didn't get the chance to hide the pistol because when Peter crossed Connecticut Avenue he ran in front of a 1970 Chevy Malibu that hit its brakes and went into a sideways slide down the middle of the snow-slick street, traveling about twenty yards like that before being broadsided by a Jeep.

Heaving to catch my breath, I stood there on the corner and witnessed the accident as if watching it on television.

After the crash I ran into the middle of Connecticut and looked in on the driver's side of the Malibu. A blond kid in his early twenties, wearing dress pants and a brand-new jeans jacket, was leaning back from the steering wheel and his forehead was bleeding, the blood already leaking down into his eyes as he glanced up at me. I tried to pull open his door but it had been crushed shut by the impact with the Jeep, which had careened over and embedded itself nose-first in the piled-up snow at the far curb. The kid in the Malibu kept blinking because of the blood in his eyes.

When he saw the pistol in my hand his expression evolved from pain and confusion to fear and panic: first this little man in a homburg runs right in front of him, then his Malibu gets broadsided, and now this crazy guy with a gun is trying to pull open the door. Poor kid must've wondered whose nightmare this was.

Dazed, he began scooting away from me, toward the front passenger door. I was just about to go around and help him get out when

I saw Peter standing on the far side of the car, looking over the roof at me. *Where had he come from?* He wasn't winded from the run and his face showed no discernible expression.

I leaned down and banged on the driver's window with the pistol butt, hollering to the confused kid, "Stay there, lock your door!"

But Peter already had the other door open, pulling the young man out and laying him there in the slush of Connecticut Avenue.

By the time I got around the back of the car—slipping once to my knees and grabbing the bumper to get up again—Peter had knelt down and was holding the kid's head with both hands, furiously licking blood from his face.

"Christ," I muttered as I ran over and kicked Peter in the side. But those thin rubber boots allowed more damage to be done to my toes than to Peter's rib cage and the kick didn't stop him from licking. It was repulsive, Peter holding the young man by the hair, keeping his head pushed down into the slush, ignoring the kid's screams and fists, lying half over him and making long fast swipes with his tongue across the kid's forehead and eyebrows and down the sides of his face, wherever blood showed.

I leaned low and placed the pistol's muzzle at Peter's temple, just below the brim of his homburg. "Get away from him."

Peter slowly turned until the muzzle pointed right at his blood-smeared mouth. When I cocked the hammer and again told Peter to back off, he released the young man and grabbed the pistol with both hands, shoving the first few inches of the barrel into his mouth and using his big hands to move the barrel in and out, his head bobbing back and forth with the rhythm of it.

I was so mesmerized with disgust that I only faintly heard the young man's voice, speaking from directly beneath where Peter was performing this obscenity, the kid pleading with me in a hey-stupid voice, "Pull the fucking trigger."

Peter, the barrel still in his mouth, nodded in eager agreement, causing the pistol to jerk up and down in my hand.

But instead of shooting him I put my right boot on his shoulder and shoved him backward as hard as I could.

Peter rolled over and over in the street slush, traveling much farther than my shove should've propelled him, laughing as he went.

I bent down to the young man and asked him if he was okay, offering to help him sit up, but he knocked my hand away and wisely scurried under his car.

Which was when I heard a scream and saw Peter dragging someone out of the Jeep stuck over in that snowbank.

"Peter!"

Ignoring me, he had the driver of the Jeep—a young woman with dark hair and wearing a leather jacket over a short wool skirt—down in the snow, one hand grasping the front of her jacket, the other hand holding on to her hair, pulling her head back, exposing her neck, ignoring the blows she kept landing on his face.

"Peter!"

He looked away from the young woman to watch my approach. But he wasn't smirking in his usual manner, he just stared at me, at the pistol I held on him, the hammer still cocked.

He opened his mouth as if in a silent scream, then kept it open as he slowly turned back to the struggling woman.

"Peter, goddamn it, I'll shoot you!"

I brought my left hand up to help steady the pistol. But at this distance and shaking the way I was, I knew I'd have as much chance of hitting the young woman as I would of killing Peter.

So I ran closer, watching Peter put his face to her neck, the woman shrieking, hitting her fists on the back of Peter's head, kicking out with both feet. Her skirt had risen up to her hips, showing a pair of red underpants that contrasted starkly with the dirty snow. There was an awful eroticism to the tableau in that snowbank, and I was shamed by how deeply it tugged at me, how vividly I recorded the details, tufts of very black curlies peeking out from the sides of those red underpants, how I was tempted to do nothing, to let it continue, a voyeur sweating for the next scene, for Peter to open her jacket, lift her sweater—

I fired. And I saw where it hit, making a hole in Peter's slush-stained overcoat just below his right armpit.

He jerked back from the woman and reached around with his left hand to slap at the wound, as if being stung there by a yellow jacket. Then, abruptly, he tumbled over onto his side and lay still.

The dark-haired young woman immediately scrambled up from the snowbank and took off at a dead run down the middle of Connecticut Avenue. She was almost hit by a cab, which veered off to miss her and in doing so ended up plowing into the undamaged side of the old Malibu. I worried that the Malibu's driver was still hiding under the car, but then I saw him across the street, holding his forehead and watching all this unfold, a horror show he was glad to have escaped but had to know how it would end. The driver of the Jeep ran to him and through the clear cold night air I could hear their excited voices.

Having stopped trembling as soon as the pistol fired, I felt unnaturally calm, even taking time to speculate idly that these two kids, the driver of the Malibu and the driver of the Jeep, might start dating, get married, and for the rest of their lives describe in wonderment the amazing way they met. I watched the pissed-off cabbie get out, grab his door with both hands, and slam it shut. He was marching over to the young couple, intending to bawl them out, when they began pointing at me. The cabdriver stopped and turned.

I had to get out of there. . . .

No, wait, they weren't pointing at me, the two kids were pointing off to my right, motioning for me to look. I whirled around. Peter was gone. But over there where they were pointing I saw him just turning the corner of a building, lurching into a small alleyway.

Three more cars had stopped at the accident site and these newly arrived drivers and their passengers joined the young man and woman and the cabbie to form a community of sorts, all of them on one side of the street, me on the other. They were talking together, staring, pointing. The two kids who had been in the original accident were blurting out their fantastic stories. I heard one voice say, "He's got a gun." Then another ask, "Has anybody called the cops?"

I had to get home. I'd telephone the police from my house, let them arrest me *there*, after I had dressed properly, had warmed my frozen feet, had put the pistol away. I wanted a chance to explain everything to Marianne, I didn't want her hearing it from the cops.

I ran. The direction toward home led past that alley Peter had ducked into and while I didn't intend to pursue him, when I got to the alley's entrance I couldn't help looking in.

The alley was narrow, barely a car's width, and the snow was marked by one set of tire tracks, one set of footprints. Fifty yards away, under a weak yellowish light that made the alley snow look peed upon, stood Peter, beckoning me.

TWENTY-FOUR

I decided to end it here in this alley, here where I can make sure Peter doesn't get away, where if he's hurt, if he's in there dying from my having shot him, where I can wait with him while he dies, I owe him that much.

He spoke when I was about twenty yards away, his voice burred with pain. "Are you ready to captain that boat yet?"

He had braced himself against the brick wall of the building to my right, trying for a casual posture, but I knew he was leaning there for support. I had shot him, *I saw where the bullet hit.*

I told Peter we were going to wait for the police and an ambulance to show up.

He grimaced. "I won't press charges if you won't."

I walked another ten yards through the snow.

"You've ruined my coat," he said, brushing off some of the slush.

I came closer.

"We've already bought the boat, registered it in your name. We're ready when you are."

"We?"

"Dondo and—"

"Who's Dondo?"

He smiled, speaking dreamily. "Just the four of us, rock-and-roll vampires cruising the seven seas. Well, *two* of us get to be vampires, you and Marianne get to be the crew. She doesn't like old-time rock and roll?"

"Hates it."

"Pity."

"Are you hurt bad?"

He laughed a little. "I'm dying."

I felt myself sag internally. "I'm sorry, Peter. I had to . . . I thought you were going to kill that girl."

"Oh, I *was*."

"Why are you doing these thi—"

"But I'm not dying from what *you* did to me, it's something I ate, that's what's killing me, someone I ate, and the only thing that can save me now is massive transfusions of new blood, good blood, *untainted* blood. Care to donate?"

"Why don't you sit down. See that piece of cardboard there? I'm sure someone has called the police, an ambulance."

"Will the ambulance bring blood? I need blood. A gallon should do it. I could easily extract that from a couple . . . donors. Either of those two robust young people out there on the street would've set me on the road to recovery, then one other late snack I have scheduled for tonight, *voilà*, I would've been all better. But you . . . shot me."

"Peter—"

"The least you could do is donate a spare pint or two, *I vant to zuck your blud.*"

"I'm sick of this vampire shit."

"I've already tasted you once, dear friend."

I glared. "You son of a bitch."

"Indeed."

"I ought to—"

"Don't you remember asking me what it tastes like?"

"Shut up."

"And I asked if you hadn't ever tasted your own—I thought every-one did—but you were horrified—"

"*Shut up!*"

"God, how we laughed that night, don't you remember?"

"You're going to jail for those murders in Florida. They've found a body."

"No, they haven't."

"Oh, yes, they have—an arm. You'll probably fry. Tell me, Peter, will the electric chair kill a vampire?"

He laughed, then winced at the pain caused by laughing. "It tastes like thick clam juice, mainly it tastes salty. Shall I compare thee to blood?"

"If I thought you and your fucked-up brother had anything to do with my father's death I'd kill you right now, I wouldn't wait for the state of Florida to do it."

Surprised by this, Peter pushed off from the wall and stepped toward me. "What are you talking about?"

I raised the pistol. "Johnny Laflin told me—"

"That overgrown Boy Scout—"

"What do you know about my father's death?"

"Only what *you* know, that he killed himself because the Burtons were trying to drive him out of business—"

"You and Richard were up to something."

When Peter took two more staggering steps toward me, I shouted, "Stop! I'll fucking kill you!"

He held out a hand in my direction. "You can't believe I could in any way be responsible for your father's death, you can't believe that, you know how I worshiped him."

"What were you and Richard doing on the beach right before Dad died, burying something, digging something up, and you had a—"

"I visited your father's grave this past Friday, I spent nearly an hour there, pulling weeds, planting flowers. You know what else I did? I collected a jar of seawater from along the shore near where your house was, on Hambriento, and I took it to the cemetery . . ."

I lowered the pistol.

". . . and I poured the seawater over his tombstone. Do you remember the inscription? 'Curtis Bird. Seafarer, Home from the Sea.' "

I felt as if my soul were leaking out.

"Have you been to his grave?"

I shook my head.

"I don't know what you're implying about my being involved in your dad's death," Peter said softly, "but if you even remotely believe that such a thing is possible, you don't have to shoot me again, you've already killed me."

He collapsed, first to his knees, then falling onto his side in the snow.

"Peter?" I started for him.

"I'm cold, God help me but I'm cold. Roscoe?"

Just before I reached Peter I heard a commotion behind me and, turning toward the entrance to the alley, I saw a dozen people standing silhouetted against the streetlights. "Call an ambulance!" I screamed. No one moved.

When I heard music I twisted back around to where Peter had been. He was gone.

And Martha Reeves and the Vandellas were singing.

"Nowhere to run to baby, nowhere to hide, got nowhere to run to baby, nowhere to hide . . ."

Holding the pistol in front of me, I crouched and pointed it at one side of the alley, then the other, but I felt stupid doing this because there was no place for him to be, no Dumpsters to hide behind, no footprints leading away from where he'd been, nothing disturbing the snow beyond where I stood except those tire tracks that went out the far end of the alley. Peter must've walked in those tracks, that's why he hadn't left any footprints.

"It's not love I'm a-running from, it's a heartache I know is come . . ."

The music bounced loudly between the walls of the alley, and I wondered if Peter had stuck a small cassette player down in the snow where he had collapsed, stuck it there and turned it on, then followed a tire track out of the alley—could he have done all that in the time it took me to holler at the crowd of onlookers? And with a bullet in him?

"*. . . Each night as I sleep, into my heart you creep . . .*"

Suddenly Connecticut Avenue was screaming with sirens and I thought only of escape, getting to my house, going home to Marianne.

TWENTY-FIVE

Retracing the same route Peter and I had taken during our chase, except this time the pistol was tucked in my waistband and covered with the vest, I kept waiting for a patrol car to come screaming up behind me, beefy cops piling out, throwing me facedown into the snow. Handcuffs, verbal abuse. God knows I deserved it. But I walked home unmolested.

I went in the back way because I didn't want the cop who was supposedly guarding our house to see me. I'd left the kitchen door open and the place was freezing, the furnace going full blast down in the basement. The clock above the refrigerator said it was four in the morning.

I got a broom and swept out the snow that Peter, and now I, had tracked in, then went down on hands and knees to wipe up the water with paper towels. After that I struggled to extract my frozen feet from those rubber boots. Adjusting the kitchen tap until it ran tepid, I raised one foot and then the other into the warm flow. As my feet thawed they stung with a thousand dancing needles. I could've cried it hurt so bad.

With aching feet thankful for carpeting I walked down the center hallway and looked out one of the two narrow windows flanking our front door. The patrol car was still there and I wondered, when the truth finally came out about what had taken place during the past hour, would the patrolman in that car be demoted.

Not until I was halfway up the steps did the full impact of that past hour hit me. Like a fist in the stomach when you're not expecting it. I actually had to reach for the railing. I couldn't get my breath. *Oh, sweet Christ.* The police were going to come for me: I shot a man, I shot a man, then ran away.

Down on both knees, still holding that railing for support, I was so scared I wanted to puke. I'm going to be arrested, lose my job, I'm going to have to hire lawyers with what precious little money we've saved since being sued by Maring, and Marianne will have to drop out of her studies a second time, she'll be devastated, I've humiliated her all over again, she'll leave me.

Kneeling there on the steps paralyzed by wretchedness, I suffered through several more self-pitying minutes before my survival instincts kicked in. What are the possibilities here? I must've just barely wounded Peter, his heavy overcoat probably deflected the bullet, otherwise he couldn't have escaped that alley so quickly. He's not going to die. The only person who got a look at my face was that young man in the Malibu, and he was so shaken by the accident, so terrified by what Peter was doing to him, no way could he make an identification. Maybe none of this will come back on me.

I went the rest of the way up the stairs, turning right into our bedroom and experiencing an instant, liquid warmth of relief to see Marianne there in bed, sleeping peacefully just as I had left her.

Don't admit to anything, I instructed myself. Don't tell anyone, not even Marianne.

I walked around to my side, took off the vest, slipped the pistol out of my jeans, and tucked it back under the mattress. After Marianne leaves for the university in the morning I'll clean the pistol and return it to that box in our attic.

I dropped my pants and got naked into bed with her, into that fevered cocoon she had created there under the covers. I wanted to put my arms around her and draw close but I knew the coldness of my body would shock her awake so I reluctantly stayed on my half.

"Roscoe?" she asked sleepily.

"You were expecting someone else?"

She reached around to pat my leg. "You're freezing."

"I went downstairs, I was thirsty."

"Next time put on your robe," she murmured.

"I will."

TWENTY-SIX

Tap, tap.

Tap, tap.

Tap, tap.

Tap, tap.

Colonel Daniel Callahan Maring, U.S. Army Quartermaster Corps, retired, finally awakens.

Tap, tap.

Tap, tap.

And although it's five in the morning, Maring's not overly worried, he has a pretty good idea what this is about. In fact earlier in the evening he called various friends and bragged that he was under police protection. That Bird character again, Maring told his friends. Seems Bird has an old buddy who's completely nutso, going around threatening to kill Bird's old enemies, so guess who comes up on the hit list, yours truly. No, hell, I ain't afraid, there's a patrol car parked right outside, but I did send the wife away to stay the night with her sister.

Tap, tap.

Yeah, yeah, I'm coming. Maring dresses in a pair of gray slacks and a blue oxford shirt, which he tucks in and buttons all the way up, no excuse for sloppy appearance, not even when you're being roused from bed at five in the morning. Although he's a business executive now, Maring wears his blue suits the way he once wore his army uniform: clean, sharply pressed, squared away, worn with pride. He's six feet tall and at age sixty still carries himself like a West Point cadet.

Tap, tap.

Maring wants to put on his wingtips but settles for a pair of leather slippers before hurrying downstairs. At the front door he checks the peephole and confirms that it is indeed a uniformed patrolman there on his doorstep. Must have some information about Bird's crazy friend, Maring thinks as he opens the door.

"Patrick O'Malley O'Brien O'Ryan at your service, sor," the little cop says, clicking his heels and bowing.

Damnedest-looking police officer Maring has ever seen—and what did he say his name was? The cop is about five and a half feet tall, wearing a uniform that must be three sizes too large for him, he's even had to roll up the cuffs, and the patrolman's hat is so big that it sits comically low on his ears.

"O'Ryan?" Maring asks.

"That it is, sor, that it is," the cop replies in a brogue so heavy it must be faked.

Maring can't believe they'd let a police officer go on duty looking as this one does. If one of his junior officers had ever shown up for duty dressed the way this little cop is, Maring would have put the officer on report in a heartbeat. No standards these days, none at all.

"Well, what is it, O'Ryan? You've apprehended Bird's friend?"

"Beggin' yur pardon, sor, I was hopin' fer a wee drink of water, I'm feelin' a little liverish, so I am. Somthin' I et."

Maring can't believe this shit. "You got me out of bed at five in the morning for a drink of water?"

"Well, y'see, sor, it's—"

"It's outrageous, that's what it is, Patrolman. What's your supervisor's name?"

"Richard, sor."

"His full name!"

The little cop makes a comical attempt at coming to attention. "Sergeant Colonel Captain Richard the Third, sor!"

He must be drunk, Maring thinks. "You're a disgrace to your uniform."

"Thank you, Colonel, sor," the cop says as he looks down at the front of his jacket and rubs at a dark stain there where the tunic is ripped. "Hot fudge sundae, and aren't I the slob entirely." Then he looks back up into the stern blue eyes of Colonel Daniel Maring. "About that water, sor?"

Maring sniffs and has half a mind to slam the door on him but of course there's still the matter of being stalked by Roscoe Bird's psycho friend, still the matter of needing police protection. "Come in," he offers reluctantly, "the kitchen is to your right."

Watching the little cop from behind, Maring notes how his uniform bags at the seat, how the rolled cuffs drag the floor. He's walking stiffly, holding his right elbow close to his side, in fact he looks as if he's about ready to collapse.

When they're in the kitchen, Maring gets a glass down, places it on the counter, then nods toward the cold-water tap. "You're favoring your right side."

"Shot in the line of duty, sor."

This softens Maring's opinion. The guy's probably in great pain, taking heavy-duty medicine that's affecting his judgment and personality, no way in hell he should've been allowed to go out on duty in his condition. "Get your drink, son, and then I think you should call in and ask for a replacement."

But the cop just stands there looking at Maring, making no move toward the sink.

"What is it?"

"I woos just wonderin', sor, when I awooke you with me tap, tappin', were you dreamin', sor, dreamin' of soome sweet Irish Colleen, were you now, sor?"

"Don't push your luck, O'Ryan." But as a matter of fact, Maring often dreams of a nameless young Irish woman. He has never been to Ireland but his mother was born there and when Maring was a boy his maternal uncles spoke fondly to him of Ireland's young women. How beautiful. How innocent. How they would break your heart with their shyness, their downcast eyes, their rosy complexions that colored bright scarlet with the embarrassment of being in close proximity to a man. Green eyes and red hair. Girls like girls nowhere else on God's earth.

Maring's own dear wife is meek enough but she's Greek, not Irish. And she's dark, both in complexion and in mood, a woman who prefers the shades down and the house quiet. He married her because her compliant nature appealed to the bully in him and because he found her black hair and dark eyes and olive skin powerfully erotic, but over the years and with all the kids grown up and moved away, his wife's compliancy has come to bore him and the darkness of both her looks and moods has given rise in Colonel Maring to a kind of intimate disgust, the way he felt about his own body when it began its betrayal of aging, thickening, sagging, embarrassing him. The Greek has grown a mustache.

Not that he would ever divorce her, not even if she sported a full beard. Maring is old-school Irish, pre-Vatican II Catholic, and divorcing the mother of his six children simply is not an option.

But he can dream. You can't be held responsible for what you dream of, and what Colonel Daniel Maring dreams of is Irish girls.

Tap, tap. The little cop is rapping his knuckles against the refrigerator door to get Maring's attention. "Hullo there, sor. Woolgatherin', were you? Thinkin' of that Irish Colleen agin, her milky white titties, that tiny toft of red between her coltish legs."

"O'Ryan—"

"And how she giggles when you tip her oonder the chin and how she goes all blotchy and blushy when the colonel's feelin' randy and proposes a little o' the slap and tickle, heh?"

"Get your water and then get the hell out of my house."

"I have a friend who says you're inordinately proud of being Irish," the cop says, having abruptly dropped the brogue. "What exactly did you *do* to become Irish."

"Forget the water, get the hell out *now!*"

"But I can't leave until I complete my assignment."

"What assignment?"

"I've been assigned by my supervisor to fellate you."

Maring figures he hasn't heard him right. "What did you say?"

The little cop smiles shyly. "I'm here to fellate you."

Maring turns red, veins swelling to the surface on his neck and across his forehead as he sputters with outrage, "I don't know if you're drunk, on dope, or if you're out of your mind on some kind of prescription medicine—but before the week is out I *will* have your badge."

"Oh why wait a week, you can have it now," the cop says, pulling the badge from his shirt and limping over to give it to an astonished Daniel Maring.

"You're crazy."

"*Now* may I fellate you?"

Maring holds out his hand. "I'll have your sidearm too, mister." And then is surprised again when the cop hands it over without protest. "I'm going to call in and demand that someone come by and collect you."

"But I haven't fellated you yet!" the cop screeches, dropping to his knees and throwing both arms around Maring's legs.

The colonel has become so angry at this stupid, filthy farce that he slaps the cop across the top of his head, sending the oversized hat rolling.

But the little cop holds on and begins singing, *"Oh Danny Boy, the pipes, the pipes are calling, from glen to glen and down the mountain side . . ."*

Although it's a fine Irish tenor, Maring is not placated.

". . . the summer's gone and all the flowers are dying, 'tis you, 'tis you must go and I must bide . . ."

The cop releases his hold, leans back to look up at Maring, then quickly runs a hand high to the inside of the colonel's right leg.

Maring hits him again. "You fucking creep."

"... *in sunshine or in shadow ...,*" the cop sings, getting painfully to his feet. As he stands he unfastens a button of his tunic, reaches in, withdraws a long, thin-bladed knife, and uses it to slash Maring across the neck.

"There's been a terrible misunderstanding," Peter says as the suddenly wide-eyed Maring drops the pistol to raise both hands and cover that bloody neck wound.

The blade flashes again and again, drawing deep red lines across Maring's forehead and nose, the colonel howling with pain, raising his arms to protect his face, getting those arms slashed.

"I misspoke myself," Peter says calmly. "My assignment is to *fillet* you." With Maring's arms crossed over his face, Peter is able to use the knife on the colonel's belly, laying him open all the way to his green-veined intestines.

In pain and panic, Maring throws himself around the kitchen, crashing over chairs, knocking blenders and toasters from the counters, painting the room red, choking on his own blood.

Meanwhile Peter is opening drawers. "Where do you keep the silverware?" Too late for blood to save him now but he still has a taste for it.

Maring bulls into the refrigerator, grabbing the handle and nearly pulling the huge appliance over on him when he finally collapses to the blood-slicked floor.

"Such a waste," Peter says, having found a tablespoon that he holds at the colonel's leaking neck. Waiting for the spoon to fill, Peter mumbles, "*Fillet* you, not fellate you, there *is* a difference."

TWENTY-SEVEN

Sometime before dawn our bedroom filled with an eerie bright-white light and I awoke thinking Jesus had come for me. But then an electronically amplified bullhorn sounded, and I knew it probably wasn't Jesus.

"ROSCOE BIRD! THIS IS THE POLICE! COME OUT WITH YOUR HANDS UP!"

The craziest thoughts ran through my mind: that policemen yelling through bullhorns really do say come out with your hands up; that the neighbors will be fascinated; that I should give careful consideration to how I dress.

"What's happening?" Marianne asked, huddling close to me in bed.

There was no way I could quickly explain the events of Connecticut Avenue. "I guess the police want to question me again."

"Using a bullhorn?" She wasn't making a joke.

"I'll go down and find out what they want. You stay here. And for God's sake don't go near any of the windows."

"Roscoe, I'm scared."

"Me too." I was just putting on my shirt and pants when the bull-horn addressed me by name once again.

"ROSCOE BIRD! YOU HAVE THIRTY SECONDS TO SHOW YOURSELF, THEN WE'RE FIRING TEAR GAS!"

"Roscoe!"

"I know, I know!" I hurriedly finished dressing. "Listen to me, after I'm taken away I want you to contact a lawyer, call the guy we used when Maring sued us, get him to recommend a criminal lawyer—"

"FIFTEEN SECONDS!"

"Roscoe!" she pleaded.

"I'm going!" I rushed from the bedroom and ran down the steps to our front door, which had a spotlight trained on it too, filling the windows that flanked the door with a screaming brightness that promised to blind me when I stepped out into it.

As soon as I opened the door a cautious foot or two, the bullhorn barked. "BOTH HANDS, BIRD! HOLD 'EM OUT, FINGERS SPREAD! STEP TO THE PORCH! DO IT! NOW!"

I pushed the door the rest of the way open and stood there, caught in that overpowering light, too petrified to move.

"HANDS UP, OUT ONTO THE PORCH, OR WE OPEN FIRE!"

Hesitating, I heard a familiar voice: "Roscoe, *do it,* they're going to cut you down!"

It was Laflin. *"Johnny!"*

"Just put your hands up and come out on the porch, you'll be fine."

"Shut up, Laflin," I heard a voice say.

But Johnny was still talking to me. "Come on, Roscoe, *come on* before you get shot!"

As soon as I had taken three tentative steps out onto the porch I was jumped by two figures dressed entirely in black. They had been wait-ing on either side of the porch and when I instinctively brought up my hands to protect myself, one of the SWAT cops hit me across the face while the other buckled my knees.

Even though I wasn't resisting, was in fact doing my damnedest *not* to resist, they wrestled me to the ground and pressed my face into the snow while jerking both hands behind me, cuffing them. There was a lot of angry shouting and no one was in a hurry to get my face out of the snow.

Why were they so mad at me? I had shot Peter and then run away but that didn't seem reason enough for their hostility, like they could barely contain themselves from stomping very hard on my head.

Suddenly I was being hauled upright, someone reading me my rights, all these uniformed officers closing in around me, their black and white faces absolutely livid with hatred.

As I was being shoved toward a patrol car I heard Johnny Laflin trying to speak to me but I couldn't make out what he was saying and they wouldn't let him get close. In the background, piercing through all the masculine voices, Marianne called my name.

I was put into the backseat of a patrol car, a plainclothes detective on either side of me. Both back doors were still open, the two detectives—one black, one white—talking to various people, orders being passed back and forth. When Laflin appeared in one of those open doorways I hollered for him. "Johnny, you got to help me!"

"I can't help you now, Roscoe, it's one of their own's been killed."

"Shut up, Laflin!" the detectives flanking me both shouted. Then they closed the doors and the patrol car began making its way through the crowd of cops and neighbors that had filled the street outside my house.

"Am I being arrested?"

The white detective on my right laughed bitterly while the one sitting to my left, the black man, said, "You're under arrest for killing a police officer."

"A police officer?"

"That's right, a police officer," the white detective said. "Not to mention your old boss, Daniel Maring."

"But I didn't kill them, I swear to God I didn't."

"Just keep your mouth shut until we get to the station."

"Didn't Johnny tell you about Peter, Peter Tummelier?"

The white detective smacked me in the forehead with the butt of his palm. "I told you to shut the fuck up, didn't I?"

We rode on in silence for a few more minutes before the black detective asked, "What's your father's name?"

"Curtis. Curtis Bird."

"Yep, that's what it said on the knife all right."

"What knife?"

"The knife we found sticking in Maring's neck," the black detective said.

"The same knife you used on the police officer who was stationed outside Maring's house," the other detective added. "Any of this ringing a bell, asshole?"

No, none of it rang any bells at all.

Standing in the living room biting her nails, an old habit she broke years ago but has given in to wholeheartedly in the past few minutes, Marianne telephones for the third time but all she gets is the attorney's answering machine. No one's at his office of course, not at five-forty A.M., and Marianne doesn't have the home number. All she can do is keep calling until someone answers at the office.

None of the police officers will tell her what this is about, what Roscoe is being charged with, they just say she'll have to check with the detectives down at the station.

After the last of the cops have left, Marianne tries the number again, but it's barely six A.M. and no one's at the lawyer's office yet.

"We have to hurry."

She drops the phone and whirls around to face the voice. It's another cop, a short cop in a baggy uniform, his hat low over his eyes.

"I thought you had all gone," Marianne says nervously.

"Come along," he tells her as he raises the hat's brim. "The sun will be up soon."

"*Peter.*"

"Dondo wants to meet you."

"Who?"

"Hurry, *I'm dying.*"

TWENTY-EIGHT

I was innocent. No, that wasn't exactly true, I did track Peter through the snow and put a bullet in him, but the detectives who'd been questioning me hadn't even mentioned that episode. I'd been arrested for killing Maring and the police officer who was assigned to guard him—and of those crimes not only was I innocent, I was ignorant.

I'd been placed in a small square room, eight by eight, sheeted with plywood on all four walls and across the ceiling, scuffed linoleum on the floor. The cops called it the holding cell but in fact there were no bars, just those unbroken expanses of plywood and linoleum. No furniture, no sink, no commode. When I wanted to go to the bathroom I had to call someone to take me to a real holding cell, one with bars and metal beds covered with thin mattresses, a cell that held prisoners. And there I was directed to stand in front of a steel commode while a police officer uncuffed me and waited. The three men being held in that cell waited for me too and with such an intent audience watching I found it difficult to perform, all the more so when the cop standing behind me jammed my ribs and told me to hurry up. It finally came out in fits and spurts, the three prisoners snickering. And when I asked my jailor if I could wash my hands, he laughed too. The answer was no.

Back within those plywood walls I read the graffiti of men who'd been there before me. Their themes ran to the love of God and the desire to have their cocks sucked. I felt friendless, abandoned, and with a sense that the worst was yet to come. I was a dog nailed paw and tail to a vivisectionist's table. Won't someone offer me a hand to lick?

Being brought out for a third round of questioning at noon (confirming the time by a hallway clock), I found an older white detective waiting for me in the interrogation room. I'd been questioned by good cops, bad cops, black cops, white cops, one Hispanic cop, cops my age, and cops younger than I. Now this old guy, in his early sixties. I wondered what approach he'd take, the kindly old gent or the avenging Jehovah? They all had their own approaches, but lurking shallowly beneath these performances of interrogation was raw anger. They believed I had knifed one of their brothers—and now I was compounding that sin by refusing confession.

The old detective motioned to a chair and told me his name, Jim-something, I no longer tried to keep track of my inquisitors' identities. He went through the usual preliminaries about my rights and the details of time and place, doing this for benefit of the video camera that had been set up in one corner, its lens trained on my chair.

"Where'd you put the uniform?"

At least this was a new question. "What uniform?"

Jim-something, who had white hair and acne scars, didn't take my question kindly, though he did explain: "The uniform you stripped off that police officer after you knifed him, the uniform you then wore to get into Maring's house."

"Maring *knows* me, a uniform wouldn't get me into his house."

"He knows you because you used to work for him, he fired you, you assaulted him, he sued you, you paid him a settlement, he cleaned out your assets, you wanted him dead."

"I didn't kill Maring or that police officer."

Jim-something sucked air through his teeth. "How do you explain that your knife, your father's knife, was found in Daniel Maring's neck? We know it's your knife 'cause not only does it have your father's name on it, Laflin identified it."

"Where is he, I want to talk to him."

"Laflin ain't on this case anymore, your ass is ours now."

"Johnny could tell you about the Tummelier family—"

"How do you explain fresh tracks that led across the snow in your backyard? How do you explain a pair of rubber boots that were still wet when your house was checked after you were arrested?"

"I *explain* all of that," I replied, getting testy even though I knew I shouldn't, "by saying that Peter Tummelier took the knife from our kitchen tonight and then went over and killed Maring exactly as he indicated to me that he would, *exactly* as I told Johnny Laflin, which is why there was a cop out in front of Maring's house in the first place! I'd have to be pretty stupid or awfully goddamn rash to warn the police about a murder and then go ahead and commit that murder."

"Which is it?"

"Which is what?"

"You stupid or rash?"

"Neither."

He sat across the table just staring at me, occasionally breaking the silence by sucking at his teeth. I resisted the temptation to tell him it was an irritating habit.

"How'd you get that black eye?"

Another new tack. "I wasn't aware that my eye was black, I haven't seen a mirror, but I assume it happened when I was arrested outside my house."

"You were struck because you were resisting arrest, because you didn't follow the officers' orders to come out and stand on your porch with your hands up."

I couldn't tell if it was a question or a statement but I answered anyway. "I'm not sure why I was struck, I certainly wasn't resisting arrest."

"But the officer who struck you could have been under the *impression* you were about to resist, you raised your hands—"

"Look, I'll concede he could've been under that impression but I'm telling you, I wasn't resisting anyone. You're asking about this because you're afraid of a lawsuit?"

"Are you afraid of going to prison?"

"*Yes*—afraid of going to prison for something I didn't do."

"Where's Peter Tummelier?"

"I have no idea. But if you find him, all your questions will be answered, he's the one who did these killings or arranged for them to be done."

"You know what I'm thinking, Roscoe?"

"No, what's that, Jim?" I immediately regretted the sarcasm.

"I'm thinking you and Pete cooked up this murder spree together. He kills some people in Florida, you get to be the good citizen by reporting this to your old buddy Laflin, then you kill your ex-boss here in D.C. figuring that the heat will still be on Pete but meanwhile he's never left Florida or has run off out of the country someplace. He takes the blame for *all* the killings, you get off scot-free."

"That's not true. Do you know anything about me? If you knew anything about me you'd know I wasn't a killer. I work for an education association, I'm a—"

"I know you broke into that couple's house down in Florida, I know you had a gun, threatened to kill them, I know *that* about you."

"Twenty years ago! I was sixteen, for chrissakes, my father had just committed suicide."

None of which had any effect on Jim-something. "If your friend Peter isn't in Florida or out of the country, where is he?"

"For the hundredth time, I . . . don't . . . know." But what I did know about Peter, that he had attacked two people on Connecticut Avenue, that I had in fact shot him, none of this had I told any of the detectives, because I wasn't sure how they would take it. They might conclude my violent act against Peter made me *more* likely to be guilty of killing Maring and that police officer. Before I said anything about any of that I wanted to talk to a lawyer, but Marianne still hadn't produced one and when I had been allowed to call home earlier in the day she didn't answer the phone.

"So your friend Pete's a vampire, huh?"

"He told me he believes he's a vampire. Why? Was there blood missing from the victims' bodies?"

Jim-something rose so quickly from his chair that he knocked it over backward. "You think that's funny, you think this vampire shit you've come up with is *funny*?"

Convinced he was about to hit me, I flicked my eyes over at the video camera as the old detective leaned across the table to give me a close-up of his acne scars and a breathy sample of the beer and pizza he'd had for lunch. "What would you say if I told you the camera ain't on, asshole."

"I want to talk to an attorney."

He leaned back. "That's your right, we offered to supply an attorney but you said you were hiring your own, where is he?"

"My wife's arranging it."

"So?"

"So what's taking her so long?"

He didn't know of course, and neither did I.

TWENTY-NINE

A two-foot doll dressed in red fuzzy pajamas imprinted with little blue unicorns is trampolining on Marianne's chest. She's on the floor, lying on a tarp, bound hand and foot, a piece of clear plastic tape across her mouth. The doll's hard bisque face is monstrous in its intensity.

"When do we eat! When do we eat!" the voice screeches.

As the doll's heavy wooden body pounds harder and harder on her ribs, porcelain limbs clanking, the voice calling her the most wickedly obscene names, threatening to kill her, to eat her, Marianne begins weeping tears that flow from the outside corners of her brown eyes to make tiny salt streams down her temples.

"Crybaby! Crybaby!" the voice shrieks as slim fingers reach from behind the doll to pull at the tape until it can be gently removed from Marianne's mouth.

Lifting the doll from her chest, the man carries it over to a simple, sturdy pine table that is stained all across its top. Then he returns and helps Marianne sit up.

Tall and eccentrically elegant, the man is dressed in velvety black trousers and a creamy-white shirt, wearing red slippers; his beard is blond, and his sad gray eyes are frighteningly large.

Marianne wonders who he is, a friend of Peter's? And yet this man, confident and calmly self-assured, is so unlike Peter with all his scurrying mania.

Marianne chooses her words carefully. "Thank you for taking off that tape, it was very kind of you."

He walks behind her, puts his hands under her arms, and lifts her to her feet. Then he drags her to a chair next to the doll. Marianne's hands are tied in front of her. He arranges them on her lap, straightens her sweater, and brushes off the front of her jeans.

When she says, "Thank you," he replies, "Don't mention it." After an idle moment's silence Marianne asks him if he's going with Peter on the world cruise. She sounds casual, careful to give him no excuse for turning violent.

Not answering her but seemingly fascinated by her presence here, he strokes his short, neatly trimmed beard.

"You're a vampire too?" she asks as if it were the most normal of questions.

He smiles slyly.

"Peter didn't mention you."

He clears his throat. "I think dear Peter is in way over his head. Of course when you're as sawed off as that little runt is, getting in over your head is rather a way of life, wouldn't you say?"

She nods and waits, then says, "Vampires fascinate me."

"*Ah.*"

"I've begun a study of the phenomenon."

"Really, now. Do you think you can get me Anne Rice's autograph?"

Marianne smiles in a way that brightens her entire face.

"I *like* you," he says, feigning shyness.

"So. What happens next?" she asks, holding hard to that winning smile of hers.

"If the leprechaun pulls off this plot of his, we all go a-sailing."

"*All* meaning you, me, Roscoe, and Peter?"

"And Dondo of course," he adds, nodding toward the doll.

She looks over at the doll, then back at the tall, thin man standing before her. "How long have you known Peter?"

"All his *short* life." He pauses. "Get it, his *short* life." When Marianne still doesn't laugh, the man tells her, "It's going to be a long cruise, dearie, wise to pace yourself."

"If you hurt me," she blurts out, "Roscoe will never agree to be your captain."

Raising his chin he scratches under his neck with languid, backward flicks of his long fingers. "The ocean is full of boat captains."

"But if you interest me," she continues in a softer voice, "I might convince Roscoe he should do it, that we should go along on this world tour, it would be a unique opportunity to study vampirism."

He reaches out and strokes the side of her face. "Such a beautiful little pixie. I wonder if I'm going to be able to resist your warm salty charms."

It suddenly comes to her: "You're Peter's brother, you're Richard."

Momentarily surprised, he quickly composes himself and quietly applauds her, tapping the fingertips of his right hand against the palm of his left, the way a queen might politely acknowledge some royal performance given solely for her benefit. Then he bows. "Richard Tummelier, at your service, mum. I'm not insane."

Marianne nods as if she's taking that assertion under consideration. "Who's Dondo belong to?"

"Belong to? What a rude question. To whom do *you* belong, Maid Marianne?"

"You know what I mean."

He goes over and picks up the doll, holding it carefully in the crook of his arm, as you would a sleeping child. "Dondo is our brother."

"Your brother?"

Raising the doll until they are face-to-face, the tips of their noses an inch apart, Richard opens his eyes so wide that they bulge outward past the vertical plane of his face. "Little Donald is in there *someplace.*"

THIRTY

Like a pilot shot down over enemy territory that has had its schools and hospitals bombed, I was constantly being paraded out of my plywood box for all the survivors to see. They weren't interested in hearing they had the wrong man, what they needed was to look at my face, to stare the beast in the eye.

By mid-afternoon that Thursday I became frantic that Marianne still hadn't shown up with a lawyer and asked, *demanded,* that a car be sent over to my house to check on her. After all, Peter, the real killer, was out and about, though apparently both the D.C. police and the sheriff's department in Florida remained convinced that Peter had stayed in Florida and I, in evil alliance with him, was the one doing the killings here in Washington. The detectives interrogating me said they would check on Marianne if I gave them Peter's address in Florida. But he's here in Washington, I insisted. *Where* in Washington? I didn't know. Who else has seen him in Washington besides you? My wife.

Where is she? *I don't know*, that's why I've been asking you to send a patrol car to our house and find out what's happened to her. But the detectives said that since I was being so uncooperative, they felt under no obligation to run my errands, find out where my wife was, why she hadn't shown up with a lawyer. Maybe she's bailed out on you, they taunted, maybe she's run off with a lover, with this Tummelier character, why don't you tell us where he is, we'll see if she's with him. When I pointed out that I couldn't tell them what I didn't know, they returned me to my plywood room.

Wandering around that little space feeling battered and abandoned, I finally decided that even without the benefit of counsel and even if it made me appear to be a violent man entirely capable of homicide, I had to confess what had happened on Connecticut Avenue.

When I banged on the door and announced that I had something to say, I was immediately ushered to the interrogation room, where half a dozen detectives awaited me. They wanted a confession the way starving men want meat, and I could only hope they wouldn't be disappointed in what I was about to serve up.

I told the story quickly and without artifice, and then passionately argued that my story proved Peter was still in Washington, it explained how he got the knife out of my kitchen, and best of all I told them, the story can be checked out because police were called to the scene on Connecticut Avenue, statements must've been taken, all they had to do was examine their records.

They were outraged. They called it a stupid, fucking story. They said it insulted their intelligence. They slapped their hands on the table and banged chairs about and said my "new" story was almost as bad as my vampire story. Why not just come clean, they asked. Tell us you killed that police officer and then went in and sliced up Maring. Confess, be a man. But I stuck to my story and they roughly hustled me back to the eight-by-eight room and told me not to bother them again until I had something reasonable to say.

As the day wore on I was fed and watered and taken on toilet trips, but my questions went unanswered: had anyone verified my Connecticut Avenue story, where's my wife, where's my lawyer, where's Johnny Laflin?

At six-thirty that evening, my thirteenth hour of captivity, I was escorted again to the interrogation room, where the older detective, Jim-something with the white hair and acne scars, waited for me. By now familiar with the routine, I sat in the chair on which the video camera was trained and waited to be spoken to.

"You're in a world of shit, Mr. Bird."

"My story checked out, didn't it?"

"You're going to end up doing time, I give you my solemn promise on that. Illegal possession of a firearm, discharging a firearm, felonious assault, endangering the lives of others, leaving the scene of a crime, withholding evidence—one or all of them will stick and you're going to end up in prison, chump. The only way you can cut yourself some slack is to tell us where we can find Peter Tummelier."

I couldn't believe he was still asking me that. "If I knew where Peter was I would've told you."

"You held out on us, waited all day before saying anything about that business on Connecticut, what else you holding out?"

"Nothing."

"Where's the pistol?"

"I thought you searched my house."

"We weren't—"

Just then the door opened.

"Johnny!"

Still wearing the same cheap clothes he'd had on when I first saw him, with his shirttail now hanging out over his belly like a maternity top, Johnny looked worse than I felt. Had he slept at all? His eyes were bloodshot, his scorched face puffed out as if beestung, and even from across the small room I could smell his greasy sweat.

Deeply unpleased with this interruption, Jim-something said, "How many times you been told to stay out of this, Laflin? You got no jurisdiction here—"

Johnny cut him off by dropping a sheaf of papers on the table. "Bird's coming to Florida in my custody."

"Bullshit he is!"

Johnny nudged the papers with one big paw. "Read 'em and weep, Lieutenant."

As Lieutenant Jim-something quickly flipped through the papers, I kept trying to catch Johnny's eye but he refused to look in my direction.

"You ain't going nowhere with him," the lieutenant said as he tried to hand the papers back. "Not till I go talk to the idiots that signed off on this."

"Bird ain't killed nobody," Johnny said. "You knew that as soon as his story about shooting Tummelier checked out."

"We're charging him with illegal possession of—"

"Listen to me, Lieutenant, you got your homicide victims in the morgue, we're still looking for two of ours down in Florida, and Bird has vital information on where those bodies can be found."

I did? In fact I had no idea what Johnny was talking about but didn't intend to contradict him because after thirteen hours with these angry police officers, extradition to Florida struck me as an excellent idea.

"He ain't going nowhere," the lieutenant insisted. "Not until we find Tummelier."

But Johnny had already walked around behind me, pulled me to my feet, and was cuffing my hands behind my back. "Those are your copies of the order," he told the detective. "If you stop me from removing Mr. Bird, we all take a trip to the judge's chambers."

"You stupid fuck."

Johnny looked up at the video camera. "I'm conducting myself here as a professional law enforcement officer carrying out my duly authorized orders and I'd like the record to show my fellow officer's lack of courtesy."

Which impressed the lieutenant only into modifying his previous statement, "You stupid *fat* fuck."

We left in a hurry and I kept my mouth shut until we were in Johnny's rental car. "What information do I have about bodies?"

"None that I know of."

"But you said—"

"That was the only way I could get the papers through."

"The extradition?"

"No, it's just an order authorizing me to transport a material witness for forty-eight hours, but we ain't going to Florida."

"We're not? Where, then?"

"First of all away from here," he said, starting the car.

"We have to stop by my house."

"No time, Roscoe."

"We *have* to, Marianne's disappeared."

"What do you mean, disappeared?"

"I mean she hasn't answered the phone, she hasn't shown up with a lawyer, and I think Peter has something to do with it, maybe he's kidnapped her to get at me, but those cops back there didn't want to hear any of that."

"All right, we'll swing by your house, then we're going over to Virginia, Fairfax County."

"What's there?"

"Richard."

"Richard Tummelier?"

"None other. He's in a very exclusive, very expensive private asylum called the Evergreen."

"How do you know?"

"Hey, I'm a detective."

No, I thought, you're an overweight, small-time deputy sheriff from Florida, hoping to break your first and only homicide case.

"See, I figured as close as those two brothers were," Johnny was saying, "no way would Peter plan this murder spree and then go on the lam for the rest of his life without making some provisions for Richard. And I don't mean just making sure his monthly nuthouse bill in Europe was paid for either, I mean taking him along on the boat trip. We'd already checked on mental institutions in Florida so I start calling around to see if there's an expensive loony bin in *this* area, only the best for the Tummeliers. The Evergreen fit the bill but they won't tell me if a Richard Tummelier is enrolled there, doesn't matter that I'm the law, it takes a court order just to see their patient roster.

Except when I call back and say I'm Peter Tummelier and want to talk to my brother, the receptionist almost puts me through, like it's something she's been doing routinely, and only at the last minute does she remember to ask me for the patient's identification number, which you got to know before they'll confirm the patient is even there, much less let you talk to him. I say I forgot the number, which is when she gets suspicious but by then the damage is already done, I pretty much know that Richard Tummelier is in residence."

"You *are* a detective."

"Fucking-a."

Johnny stopped at a 7-Eleven and took off my cuffs. "Don't need cuffs to transport a witness," he explained. "I put 'em on you for the lieutenant's benefit. How's your eye?"

I touched it and looked in the rearview mirror. A real shiner. "This is the first I've seen it."

"You okay?"

"Worried about Marianne."

"Well, I got to go in and get some coffee, Christ, Roscoe, when I finally come down from all this caffeine it's going to be the crash of the century. You want something?"

"Marianne."

"Be back in thirty seconds."

But when we finally arrived at my house we found it empty, no note from Marianne, no indication where she might be. I called everyone I could think of from the university but Marianne hadn't been to any of her classes that day, no one had seen her. Then I called the lawyer we used when Maring sued me and although he'd already left for the day, another lawyer working in his office insisted that no one there had heard from my wife or been contacted about my arrest.

I told Johnny we had to get the D.C. police involved in this, get their help in searching for Marianne.

"Don't be stupid. Finding Peter is the key to finding Marianne, and the cops here are already doing all they can to find Peter. He killed one of their own, you understand what that means, you understand the weight that carries? The fact that Peter might also have kidnapped

Marianne ain't going to make them look for him any harder than they already are."

"But they could stake out this place where Richard is staying."

"That's where you and me are going, buddy. It's the whole entire reason I got you out instead of doing this on my own. If anybody can get Richard to talk, it's you. If he knows where his brother is he'll tell you. Not me, not the D.C. detectives, *you.*"

THIRTY-ONE

Light comes in under the closet door, illuminating the doll's face from below: hideous and yet so strangely hypnotic that Marianne can't stop staring. She's miserable. No, it's worse than that, she's wretched with pain and fear, with a growing sense of hopelessness. If Marianne believed in the immortal soul, she would now be thinking about the final disposition of hers.

Tied hand and foot, loosely gagged with a black silk cloth, she's been left alone all day in this walk-in closet, her mind wandering among the possibilities: that Richard will hold her captive until Peter can return here and kill her, that Roscoe and the police will rescue her, and most improbably of all, that the Tummeliers and Birds will end up on a boat together. She's determined not to wait passively upon her fate, however, and considers how she might seduce Richard, not seduce him sexually but win over his emotions, use him as protection against Peter. And to do that she has to learn more about Richard, why he was institutionalized initially, what makes him tick. But as Marianne tries to think this through logically, she keeps getting sidetracked by the doll there at her feet: eyes that stare at her with a living intensity, mouth that seems about to open and let loose that screeching voice Richard uses, arms that appear to move ever so slightly, about to reach for her. To avoid this warping of reality, Marianne must close her eyes and employ relaxation techniques, the gag forcing her to breathe carefully through her nose.

"Now isn't *that* a picture for the family album!"

She squints against the flood of light coming in from the opened closet door. Richard stands there beaming at her and at Dondo, who has somehow ended up snugly beside her on the closet floor. Richard carries the doll over to a chair at the pine table, then does the same for Marianne. She looks around at the room and realizes how messy it is, what a slob Richard must be under his gentlemanly facade. When he removes the gag, she works her jaws and stretches her mouth. "I fell asleep," she tells him, apropos of nothing.

"Slept the day away, just as I do."

"If I promise not to call out," she asks, "can you please not gag me again? It's uncomfortable, I can hardly breathe. And I'd like to have the ropes off too, they're making my hands and feet numb."

"My, my, aren't we irascible. Tell me, Maid Marianne, is it *that* time of the month? I certainly hope not, I can't be held responsible for what might happen if I scent blood."

Hurting from being tied up and left in the closet, exhausted from fear, Marianne speaks rashly: "Why do you feel compelled to put a trivially obscene twist on everything you say?"

And then she's surprised when Richard, instead of reacting angrily, looks chastised.

She presses her advantage: "Untie me."

"I've already loosened the ropes once, when you went to the loo," he says quietly.

"Loosen them again."

Turning from her to caress the doll, he screeches, "Loosen them again, loosen them again! Get me something to drink, get me something to eat, change the channel, you never bring me flowers, get a job you lazy bum, my mother was right I shoulda never married you!"

Richard lifts the doll around and thrusts it at Marianne.

Marianne looks directly into the doll's white eye spots and calmly says, "Fuck you, Dondo."

As Richard leaps to his feet she braces for a slap. But he's laughing, holding one hand over his mouth like a child who's not supposed to be laughing in church but can't help himself, his protruding gray eyes mirth-filled. He lowers his hand to whisper, "Fuck you, Dondo" as if experimenting with the naughtiness of it, then immediately covers his mouth and laughs again.

How like children these Tummelier brothers are, Marianne thinks: selfish, self-indulgent, deadly children.

After loosening the ropes and gently rubbing her wrists and ankles, Richard brings a tray over to the table and asks Marianne if she would care for something to eat.

"I'm hungry but I'm afraid I couldn't keep anything down."

"Oh I know *that* feeling."

She nods toward a glass of orange juice on the tray. "Is it medicated?"

"No, dear. Peter has made special arrangements for his older brother here at the Evergreen, arrangements that include no medications, no disturbances during the daylight hours. You pay a thousand dollars a day and you'd be surprised at how generously you are accommodated. Here."

He holds the glass to her mouth and after Marianne has sipped the juice, Richard daintily wipes her lips with a linen napkin and asks if she's sure she wouldn't care for something to eat.

"No thank you."

He turns to the doll. "How about you, Dondo?" Then answers himself with a shrieking, *"Fuck you, Richard!"* And laughs as he carries the food tray into the bathroom, where he cleans the plates into the toilet and flushes everything away. "Do you have to potty again?" he calls to Marianne.

"No."

"How about you, Dondo?"

Richard comes out of the bathroom chuckling. "Oh I *do* think I'm going to enjoy your company on this cruise," he tells Marianne. "*If* the little munchkin ever gets us on the boat. Tell me, sweetie pie, how did Peter look to you?"

"He looked sick."

"That's what I thought."

"You do know what Peter has been doing, don't you, Richard? Peter's plot? It's not a fantasy, it's not some game he's playing. Peter has murdered people."

"I know and I'm worried. There's an ocean of blood-borne diseases out there and although one learns to detect them at first sip, little bubba is still new at all this."

She stares at him a moment, then asks, "You became a vampire first?"

He raises his blond eyebrows.

"No, really, I'm interested."

"I was first at everything."

"How'd it happen?"

"Well." Richard grabs the doll rudely by one arm and lays it on the table so he can sit next to Marianne. "I was 'attending' this charming little institution in Switzerland where this faggy old vampire had been ensconced for God knows how long. He was probably the subject of one of those case histories you've been studying. Anyway. Years go by, I get bored, and the old vampire begins seducing me with these stories about The Life, so eventually I partake of the forbidden fruit and the old fag and I end up noshing on a couple of fat Swiss attendants.

"Peter, bless his loyal little heart, he moves me to another institution, pays big bucks to ensure my nocturnal living arrangements, and even brings me the occasional snack, if you catch my meaning. But mostly we are *very* discreet. Don't want to keep getting kicked out of institutions, eventually you run out of the better ones.

"Then Petey becomes envious. My own fault. I kept bragging up The Life, how exciting it was, the power, the *immortality,* and without a by-your-leave he digs up a vampire somewhere and partakes. Well, didn't *that* throw a monkey wrench in the old coffin. He could no longer be my guardian, because suddenly we *both* needed a daytime protector.

"Which is when Peter tells me he's been working on this grandiose plan, cruising the world on a big boat that your own dear Roscoe would captain. Peter thought Roscoe would *leap* at the chance to captain a boat in a permanent all-expense-paid cruise, but if Roscoe didn't leap, the plot was for Peter to nudge him along by snuffing out certain of Roscoe's old enemies in a way that would put the blame on Roscoe and leave him no alternative but to flee prosecution and come with us. You see, I know all about what my brother is up to."

"It's—"

"Ludicrous? Undoubtedly. But I indulge my little Napoleonic sibling. I agreed to return here to the States and move into the Evergreen and await the boarding call. Except Petey keeps catching his pantaloons on various snags. One snag being that Roscoe has gotten himself married to a beautiful and delightful woman and wants nothing more than to live out his life in her tender arms. A sentiment that, having met you, I can certainly understand, believe me. But it does play havoc with Peter's plot."

Marianne brings up her bound hands to brush at hair that has fallen across her forehead. "Why were you institutionalized in the first place?"

"Oh you must be bored silly with my stories, with the very sound of my voice."

"No, I'm fascinated."

Richard glances over at the doll, which he takes from the table and places on his knee.

"When do we eat, I'm starving!" the voice screeches.

"Now, Dondo, I've explained this all to you. We have to wait for Peter."

He turns the doll around so that it faces Marianne. "Let's eat the bitch, let's eat Audrey Hepburn!"

Richard raises his face over the doll's shoulder. "Dondo agrees with Peter," he says shyly. "That you look remarkably like the young Miss Hepburn."

"Why do you feel it necessary to speak through a doll?"

He puts Dondo down. "I've never met anyone quite like you, dear—anyone so *unafraid.*"

"I'm terrified."

"Truly?" he asks as if she has just paid him a compliment.

"But intrigued too."

"I don't have to speak through anyone to tell you what I feel for you in my heart of hearts."

She wonders if he's joking.

"I've never been able to talk so freely, so easily with anyone, usually it's all such a *performance.* But with you . . ." Richard interrupts himself by grabbing Dondo and shrieking, "No fool like an old fool! You want to get in her pants, I know you do, peeking through the keyhole when she was peeing, you want to get in her pants but all she wants is to escape, that's why she's being nice to you, you twit!"

He stares at Marianne, his eyes large and wet. "I would like to apologize for Dondo's rudeness. And I can assure you I most certainly did not peek through any keyhole."

Richard bounces the doll up and down on his lap. "Did too! Did too! Did too!"

"I didn't."

"Did! Did! Got a boner too!"

Richard reaches around and puts his hand over the doll's face.

"Dondo and I are both under a great deal of stress," he softly explains to Marianne. "Peter said he'd be back with Roscoe at dusk and we'd all leave for the boat immediately. Well, he's not here. And being alone with you is a most poignant agony."

She arches her brows.

"At first . . ." He seems embarrassed. "At first I wanted to gobble you up but now, now I'd like to touch you . . . as a man touches a woman." Richard sighs dramatically. "I just *know* little bubba Peter has gotten into some bad blood, I recognized the signs."

"I was wondering, someone with your financial resources, why can't you arrange for bottled blood, then you could avoid the risky business of—"

"I suppose you mortals could live on pureed liver and I.V. drips too, but would you *want* to? Peter and I do in fact keep an emergency supply of refrigerated whole blood but nothing quite matches the *thrill*, the heart-thumping excitement of hot blood fresh from the source, that feel of your victim squirming beneath you, that warm salty gush of a severed artery."

He jumps the doll up and down on his lap and shrieks, "You get off on it, you get off on it, you come in your pants!"

Richard gives Marianne a pained look, as if there's nothing he can do about Dondo's abysmal behavior.

"Why were you institutionalized originally?" she presses.

"That takes some telling."

"I'm not going anywhere," Marianne says, raising her bound wrists.

"It doesn't look as if any of us is going anywhere. I truly am worried about Peter."

"Tell me what happened. Why were you sent to Switzerland?"

"Persistent pussy, aren't you? Shall I lie on the couch so you can analyze me?"

"Richard, I'm serious—about being fascinated by you."

"Fascinated enough to want to join me in The Life?"

"What?"

"Become a vampire, dear, I could arrange it, we could do it right now."

She has to fight down the fear as if it is vomit rising in her throat. "I want to learn more about you, why you were institutionalized originally. *Please*, Richard, tell me."

"Oh who could refuse those big brown eyes? Let's start with Mother, then. She was addicted to pills and alcohol and this delusion that she was the most desirable woman ever to slither down a stairway in an evening gown. She told me once . . . This is embarrassing. But you *are* my analyst and I suppose one shouldn't keep secrets from one's analyst."

"Go on."

"Mother told me once that whenever she was having a party, right before she went down to meet her guests, she would . . . how to put it delicately . . . she would *finger* herself. Then she would greet her male guests by kissing them lightly on the cheek and would apologize for getting lipstick on them. She would wipe the lipstick from their faces and in the process would run her fingers across their upper lips. She claimed this made men follow her around like so many puppy dogs, though they themselves didn't know exactly why they found her so alluring, didn't realize she had scented them. Now, can you imagine a mother telling this to her adolescent son?"

"She must've been a troubled woman."

"You don't prepare to meet men by performing such a vulgarity, do you?"

She shakes her head.

"I would hope not. And Father? He had his own peculiarities, including a most bizarre sense of humor. I bet you can never guess in a thousand years what he wanted to name me, what he actually wrote on the birth certificate."

"What?"

"Herbaceous Borders." Richard waits for her to laugh but when she doesn't, he continues bitterly, "Actually wrote it on the birth certificate, *Herbaceous Borders Tummelier.* My mother had to get it changed and Daddy always did refer to me as Herbie. Oh yes, Father had a withering sense of humor. When Peter was born, Father gave me a corgi, dreadful little dog, and my job was to bring the dog in of an evening. Keep in mind this was when I was four and five years old. Sometimes I had to wander all around the island searching for the foul little creature, hollering for it at the top of my lungs, shouting out its name. Caused quite a stir, I was always being escorted home."

"Why?"

"Daddy had named the dog Help. Hilarious, hm?"

Marianne shakes her head.

"This little boy wandering around at dark screaming, 'Help! Help! Help!' People rushing out from their houses, asking me what was wrong, 'rescuing' me, taking me home. Father thought it was hilarious."

"I'm sorry, Richard."

"Be sorry for Help, the poor pathetic creature was eaten by a hammerhead shark."

"Really? That's awful."

"It was, rather. Took twenty pounds of calf livers to chum them in. Of course by then the corgi was ancient, could barely swim. And you know what I said when Mr. Hammerhead came up for his corgi snackingtons? I whispered, 'Help. Help. Help.' Care to hear more about my childhood?"

She looks down at her bound hands resting in her lap.

Richard continues. "Father owned something called a Volter, which was an antique carnival attraction, back from the time when electricity was still largely a novelty. It was a big cast-iron affair, with a slot for a nickel, a set of handles, and a large dial. The idea was, you inserted your nickel and turned the dial to whatever setting of electricity you wanted, from the barely discernible tingle you got on *One* all the way through the quite painful shocks that occurred when the dial was on *Eight* or *Nine*. It seems odd, I realize, that a carnival-goer would pay to see how much of an electrical shock he could tolerate but, as I said, electricity was a novelty back then and I suppose it's no different than paying to be frightened on a roller coaster.

"Father introduced Peter and me to the Volter when we were toddlers. He'd berate us if we let go of the handle too soon, reward us if we could hold on until Three or Four, then he'd give us a jar full of nickels and tell us to keep practicing. Can you imagine? I remember spending hour after hour in Father's trophy room, Peter and I feeding nickels into that Volter. Anticipating the shock was the worst part. You see, the Volter didn't put out a steady current, the shock would suddenly pulse—which I suppose was the fun at a carnival, watching the rubes holding that handle and waiting to see them jump when they got shocked. But it wasn't fun for Peter or me, we were desperate for our father's approval and we'd push the dial up to *Five, Six, Seven,* standing there gripping that handle, waiting for the shock to pulse, it was quite torturous, we would shock ourselves until it seemed that our entire nervous systems were affected. Headaches, nervousness, uncontrolled blinking . . . I would *dream* of the Volter and then twitch and jerk in my sleep.

"Whenever we were able to reach a new level of these self-inflicted shocks we'd tell Father and he'd come to watch, laughing at us. I finally wised up around age eight but not Peter. Poor Peter would've sat in the electric chair if he thought that would win our father's approval, and he kept working the Volter until he burned his hands with the shocks. I finally disabled the damn thing."

Genuinely affected by what he's told her, Marianne says, "I don't understand how it is that parents do the things they do to their children. I've read the books, I've read the psychological explanations, but I don't *understand*."

"It was a long time ago, dear," he replies. "Our parents were gone most of the time in any case, and Peter and I bonded much more closely than most brothers ever do. The only time we ever felt sorry for ourselves, in fact, was when we met Roscoe and his family. They were so normal, they treated one another so decently—Peter and I never realized this was an option, to be treated decently within one's family. Roscoe introduced us to rock and roll, did he tell you that? Though Peter was much more taken with the music than I was. I adored Curtis, Roscoe's father, and Peter had this mad crush on Roscoe. It was all quite pathetic I assure you, how wretchedly vulnerable we were to the smallest gestures of kindness." Richard gets up from the table and checks out a window. "Where *is* that brother of mine?"

When he returns to Marianne he bends down and touches his thumb to the outside corner of her right eye. "I've made you weep."

Emotionally tough and ruthlessly rational on most topics, Marianne has always been vulnerable to the pain of children. She can't abide even hearing about cruelty to children, couldn't bring herself to study the phenomenon from a clinical point of view. She originally wanted to specialize in child psychology but reading the case histories of abused children unsettled her, made it impossible for her to do the work.

And when Richard leans down and gently hugs her, Marianne sobs out loud.

"Oh now stop it," he tells her, "or you'll get *me* bawling."

Richard has to turn away to hide his tears. "Time for Dondo's nap," he says in a choked voice, lifting the doll carefully into his arms and taking it over to the bed. After tucking the doll under the covers, Richard leans down to kiss it, whispering as he does, "The cunt's mine."

THIRTY-TWO

Evergreen. Richly displaying burnished brass letters on a black slate background, the sign was mounted on a two-foot-by-three-foot metal frame and stood laconically to the left of the winding lane that Johnny Laflin and I had just entered. You wouldn't know unless you knew. As Johnny drove, I looked out through the snowy forest of spruce and cedar trees, the occasional massive red oak. The grounds comprised a collection of tidy red-brick buildings, some of them as small as one-bedroom cottages, others large enough to hold gymnasiums. The Evergreen gave the appearance of an exclusive, richly endowed liberal arts college, except that at nine this particular evening no "students" were out walking in the snow.

When we were a hundred yards from the administration building a man stepped out from a small white gatehouse. He wore a blue overcoat and carried a clipboard.

Johnny rolled down his window.

"Visiting hours are over, gentlemen," the man said.

"Police business," Johnny countered, flipping his badge. "I need to talk to whatever administrator is on duty tonight."

"That would be Ms. Allfrey," the guard replied. "I'll call there and announce—"

But Johnny was already rolling up the window, driving forward. "We're going to bull our way in there, son," he told me. "I'll leave the keys in the car in case one of us has to make a quick getaway."

"What are you talking about?"

" 'Homicide investigation.' 'Killer on the loose.' 'Probable cause.' " Johnny was hyped. " 'Police emergency.' You throw those terms around, civilians go blank, they'll let us see Richard all right, don't you worry."

He hadn't counted on the formidable Ms. Allfrey, however. Johnny's bluff got us past the receptionist, who explained the situation via an intercom and then escorted us into the administrator's office—paneled walnut on two walls, floor-to-ceiling bookshelves on the other two, thick rich carpeting, antique globe—where Ms. Allfrey waited leaning against the front of her solid-cherry desk.

"Gentlemen," she said curtly, stepping forward to shake our hands the way a man would. "I'm Tanya Allfrey, deputy administrator of the Evergreen."

Tanya. Yes indeed. Her heart-shaped face, pretty blue eyes, and pointy chin reminded me of Julie Andrews in *The Sound of Music*—Julie Andrews showing a bit of the dominatrix, however: patent leather high heels, a black skirt slit fetchingly too high for office attire, a white blouse that strained intriguingly, and a floppy black bow tied a little too tightly at her creamy neck. In spite of what I'd been through with the police and in spite of my concern about Marianne, I felt a viscerally naughty tug in Ms. Allfrey's direction.

She was all business. "You've shown up on my watch, so it's my responsibility to ensure everything is conducted properly. I'd like to see your credentials and whatever court orders you have."

After handing over his deputy's badge and another set of the papers authorizing him to transport me to Florida as a material witness, hoping these items would look sufficiently official to cower Ms. All-frey, Johnny started in on his caffeine-cranked spiel about being in the middle of a homicide investigation, having probable cause to check the Evergreen's patient roster. "Don't give me any trouble, miss, this is a police emergency and we can either do it the nice and quiet way or I can have a dozen squad cars here in twenty minutes."

Tanya wasn't impressed. *"This,"* she said, handing the deputy's badge back to Laflin, "gives you no jurisdiction here, and *this,*" she said, returning the papers, "authorizes you to transport a witness to Florida. None of which has anything to do with the Evergreen. So please do call your squad cars. In the twenty minutes it takes them to arrive I shall have an equally impressive fleet of lawyers waiting to greet them."

Johnny blinked nervously before resuming his attack. And as he and Ms. Allfrey went at each other, escalating threats, I could see Johnny was hopelessly outclassed. Back at the house I had shaved and taken a quick shower before dressing in a reasonably presentable pair of slacks, blue oxford shirt, Harris-tweed sport coat, but Johnny still wore that dirty, wrinkled polyester outfit, his thinning hair was greasy, and he was so wild-eyed with nervous exhaustion that he looked less like a police officer than a patient ripe for commitment to the Evergreen.

Which gave me an idea.

"I've heard enough," Tanya finally said, cutting off Johnny's in-creasingly strident arguments about why he needed to see the patient roster. "You gentlemen can leave or you can wait in the reception area until our attorneys arrive. If you attempt to enter the grounds, I'll call the state police. Have I made myself clear?"

As Johnny kept sputtering about the critical nature of his investiga-tion, Ms. Allfrey turned to me, looked questioningly at my black eye, and asked, "And exactly who are you?"

I took a breath and went for it: "My name is Roscoe Bird and I'm an attorney representing Mr. Laflin's family. We wish to commit Mr. Laflin to your care here at the Evergreen."

For the first time since we'd arrived in her office, Tanya was unsure of herself. She looked at Johnny. "Mr. Laflin?"

Johnny looked at me.

"It's best this way, Mr. Laflin," I told him.

Before he could reply, Ms. Allfrey said, "Surely you know, Mr. Bird, there is a specific procedure that must be adhered to if we are to admit a patient. We must have referrals, we must—"

"What I know, Ms. Allfrey, is that during two commitment hearings held at the request of the Laflin family, Mr. Laflin managed to appear completely sane. And then immediately following those commitment hearings Mr. Laflin repeatedly displayed behavior that was markedly *not* sane, endangering himself and others. *He* gave me this shiner. I thought it was important that you see one of these episodes for your-self—Mr. Laflin pretending to be a deputy sheriff in the middle of a homicide investigation." I turned to Johnny, who stared at me as if I was the one who should be committed. "Is it true, Mr. Laflin," I asked in a patronizing tone, "that the killer you're looking for is a vampire?"

"Well, yeah, he—"

I interrupted him by throwing a knowing look in Tanya's direction and telling her, "Last month he acquired some phony credentials and showed up at the White House claiming he was a fire marshal with orders to shut the White House down as a firetrap. There was a scuffle, perhaps you read about it in the *Post*."

"No, I—"

"And now he thinks he's a deputy sheriff looking for a vampire."

"Well—"

"Mr. Laflin's family is quite well-to-do," I continued, "and the family is willing to pay whatever is necessary to ensure Mr. Laflin receives the best care possible."

"Now wait a goddamn second, Roscoe—"

"*Please*, Mr. Laflin," I told him, "you agreed to sign yourself into this facility so we wouldn't have to go through another of those unpleasant competency hearings."

Johnny just stared, the upright hairs on the end of his red, bulbous nose twitching. He knew what I was up to, of course, but was still trying to decide if he should go along with it.

"What about the papers, his badge?" Tanya asked.

"Oh, our Mr. Laflin is quite resourceful in acquiring the outward trappings of whatever persona he adopts."

But Ms. Allfrey wasn't convinced. "We don't take in patients off the street, Mr. Bird. Not even those willing to sign themselves in. There's a *process* that must be adhered to."

"I understand what you're saying but perhaps you'll want to bypass the normal process this evening because if Mr. Laflin's current delusionary episode follows the usual pattern, he'll soon be convulsing, swallowing his tongue, vomiting on your lovely carpet."

We both turned to Johnny, who shot me a murderous look before capitulating and going into his act: rolling his eyes, making apelike sounds, flapping his arms as if attempting to get his two hundred and fifty pounds aloft. He grabbed a pencil off Tanya's desk and stuck the eraser end in his ear. It was a pathetic performance and in truth Johnny appeared more authentically unbalanced back when he was trying to convince Ms. Allfrey to open her patient roster to him than he did now, trying to act crazy but in fact coming across as terminally silly.

"I don't know what the two of you are up to," she said, "but—"

Tanya was interrupted when Johnny dropped to the floor and went into his version of convulsions.

I headed for the door.

"Mr. Bird!" she called. "What's the name of your law firm? You'll be hearing from our attorneys about this, I promise you!"

But by then Johnny was faking a bad case of the dry heaves and in the confusion of attendants being called, Tanya shouting orders, the receptionist rushing in to help her boss—I was able to slip out through a rear door of the administration building and onto the grounds.

I knew what to look for. If Richard Tummelier was here, he'd be in the most expensive, most isolated cottage that the Evergreen offered, the search made all the easier when I noticed nameplates on some of the cottages' doors.

Running now among pathways plowed through the snow, wondering how long it would be before the severe Ms. Allfrey would sic her attendants on me, I went deeper into the campuslike setting, back to where the brick cottages were set farther apart, to a cottage all by itself at the end of a cul-de-sac.

Mr. Tummelier.

Looking at that nameplate, stomping snow off my shoes, trying to catch my breath, I reached up and tapped on the door.

THIRTY-THREE

His heartbreaking stories of a ruined childhood have touched her and Marianne believes that under different circumstances she could help Richard—all of which makes her feel guilty for the way she is so consciously manipulating him. Although Marianne has never had the personality for flirting, she knows of course how it's done: listening intently to a man's opinions no matter how dumb they might be, leaning close so that he feels you against him, laughing even when nothing truly funny has been said, smiling, pouting, judiciously crying, acting impressed. She hates seeing a woman do it, Marianne preferring to be straightforward, blunt if necessary. But this is different. She needs an ally in the event Peter shows up. Her life is at stake.

"We will have such great fun on the boat," Richard says happily at one point, as if discussing a long-awaited vacation with his girlfriend. He tells Marianne that talking to her relaxes him even when the subject is painful, as are memories of his parents. He says he's almost ready to tell her about Donald. But mainly he speaks of the cruise. "Peter and I have already purchased the boat, it's being surveyed this week. In fact we registered it in Roscoe's name. I remember with such fondness the times I spent on Mr. Bird's boat. Roscoe's father was a wonderful man."

"His suicide must've affected you terribly."

"Yes." He looks away.

"After Mr. Bird's death, after Roscoe and his family left Hambriento, that's when you were sent away, wasn't it?"

"Yes."

"Why?"

He sighs. "It was shortly *before* Mr. Bird's tragic death that my parents returned to Hambriento from one of their frequent trips to Europe, returning home this particular time to announce rather grandly to Peter and me that they had adopted a child."

"Adopted a child?"

"Oh yes, apparently damaging their two biological sons didn't sufficiently satisfy their desire for wreaking havoc on the next generation. They wanted to convey their particular madness to a brand-new baby. Baby Donald."

"Where is he now?"

Richard runs a hand down the back of the doll, which lies prone on the table next to where he and Marianne are sitting. "Dondo here is all we have of our little adopted brother."

"I don't understand."

Richard stands and walks to a back window. "Where *is* that Peter? I can't call him, he doesn't have a phone in his lair, and I fear—"

"His lair? Where is that?"

Richard turns from the window to face Marianne. "If Peter got a dose of bad blood, the progression of the disease might take only hours in him, not weeks or months or years, mere *hours*. And the only antidote is good blood. But how do I get blood to him?" Richard taps a finger to his bearded chin. "Perhaps I could order up a pizza to be delivered to Peter and he could nosh on the delivery boy."

"There's another option."

He raises one blond brow.

"You and Peter could come in from the cold," Marianne ventures.

"What a charming way of putting it."

"I know people at the university who'd love the opportunity to speak to both of you, sophisticated people who would take you and Peter seriously."

"And put us in therapy? Like trying to 'cure' homosexuals, oh I've heard about that. Show some poor trembling queen a photograph of a delicious hunk and then give the queen a rude shock. Aversion therapy, isn't that what you call it? What would you do with Peter and me, show us photographs of neck wounds and then try to shock us into being averse to the very idea of sipping blood? I'm afraid it doesn't work that way, my dear."

"I didn't mean anything as crude as that. I'm talking about *studying* you and Peter."

"Lab vampires?"

"No—"

He quickly glides across the room to kneel at her chair. "If Peter has died, who will watch over me? Will you, dear Maid Marianne, will you watch over me?"

She forces a coquettish smile and says, "Yes," in a little girl's voice.

He acts both surprised and thrilled. "Truly?"

"I'd watch over you, yes."

"Oh *darling!*" He places one of his hands over Marianne's bound wrists. "You're troubled, aren't you? Your scientific training rejects the possibility that vampires really exist, but you're troubled because being with me is starting to convince you that I am what I say I am. You're drawn to my power, intrigued."

"Yes," she lies.

"I could tell you such stories of The Life, stories of the hunt."

"I want to hear them."

He rests his head in her lap. "Loneliness is The Life's drawback, its crippler. What's the point of being the richest man on earth if you're the only man on earth? And what's the point of being the beast, possessing this power, if there's no one to witness your terrible greatness, no one with whom to discuss and share The Life? Which is why Peter and I pledged to stay together. I hadn't actually considered the possibility of sharing anything other than blood with *a woman*."

Worrying that her flirtation has been too effective, she lifts her tied hands and rests them on the back of Richard's head before telling him, "It's important that we stick with Peter's original plan, all four of us together on the boat."

"But if Peter's dead and you've agreed to watch over me, why do we need Roscoe?"

"He has to captain the boat, silly."

Richard looks up from her lap. "Do you love him?"

She's tempted to lie but doesn't. "Yes."

"Ah." He smiles. "But now *I've* fallen in love with you. And I couldn't bear to awaken at sea some quiet evening and hear the two of you thumping away at each other in the next cabin. I would feel . . . betrayed." He stands. "Never cuckold a vampire."

There's something familiar about that. Marianne searches her memory and realizes it's what Peter mumbled when they were drinking tea in the kitchen, when she told him that he couldn't have Roscoe, that Roscoe belonged to her. She thought she heard "never cut a cold empire" but actually he said exactly what Richard just said, "Never cuckold a vampire."

"Marianne?"

"Tell me what happened to your adopted brother. Donald."

"Oh we're beyond discussing little Donald's fate, I need to know your intentions, need to know who will reside forever in here," Richard says as he leans close to Marianne and taps a finger on her sternum. "Roscoe's a nice man I'm sure, I certainly remember him as a dear boy, but when *I* make love to you I will seduce your very soul, I will lay you raw then heal you up again, I will hand you the world, I will give you immortality."

When he kisses her on the mouth she smells rot on his beard and can't bring herself to kiss back, not even to save her life.

Tap, tap, tap.

Startled, Richard grabs a handful of hair at the back of her head and presses her close to whisper, "Betray me now and you will die most horribly, I promise you." Holding a hand over her mouth he drags her into the closet, tightens the ropes around her wrists and ankles, and tears off a length of clear plastic tape.

"Please don't, I can't bear to have that tape on me again," she pleads. "It's worse than the gag, I can't even breathe—"

Tap-tap-tap-tap.

"Do you love me?" he asks hurriedly. "In the hours we've been together, have you fallen deeply enough in love with me that I can trust you?"

Glancing at that tape he's holding, then back up at his monstrous eyes, Marianne whispers, *"Yes."*

"Oh but aren't you the sly boots," he says with a breathy chuckle as he puts the tape over her mouth anyway, closes the closet, then hurries into the next room.

Tap-tap-tap.

Standing there at the door, Richard takes a moment to compose himself before opening it.

THIRTY-FOUR

I'm not sure I would've known it was Richard. The last time I saw him he was twenty years old, a willowy young man, and now here he stood as an elegant forty-year-old dressed in black trousers, a white shirt, red leather slippers. He had close-cropped blond hair and a neatly trimmed blond beard, and it was only his large gray eyes that I remembered from Hambriento.

Apparently not recognizing me, he smiled sadly and offered a limp hand. "I'm not insane."

"That's a great opening line, Richard."

As soon as I spoke, his big eyes bulged even more in surprise and delight. "Roscoe!" he exclaimed, tightening his grip on my hand. "Dear, dear Roscoe Bird, oh please do come in."

I entered the small living room and asked Richard how he was.

"I'm *not* insane. I keep saying that for the record, but after twenty years of asserting it I still haven't found anyone to believe me."

"I believe you."

"Oh *do* you?"

"Sure. I never thought there was anything wrong with you." It was ham-handed but I didn't have time to dance.

Richard reached out and touched the side of my face, leaving his hand there until I removed it and said, "I need to find Peter."

"Yes, I understand we're all about to embark on an extended cruise."

"Do you know what Peter has been doing, how he's been trying to convince me to go on this cruise with you?"

"I would assume you didn't need any convincing, that you would jump at a chance to captain a boat as your father did, as you were meant to."

I decided to bypass the details. What I needed from Richard was how to find Peter—and presumably Marianne with him. "Where's your brother staying?"

Richard walked over and sat in a wing-backed chair, crossing his legs at the knee. The casual elegance of his manner put me in mind of a documentary film I'd seen on Noel Coward. "Please," he said, tossing a hand toward the chair next to his. "Sit down, let's visit, we have so much catching up to do."

I glanced back toward the door I'd entered and wondered how long it would be before Ms. Allfrey and a squad of determined attendants would show up here to collect me. "I desperately need to know where Peter—"

"They locked up the wrong brother, are you aware of that?"

Although Laflin had planted a suspicion in me that Richard and Peter knew something about my father's death, I couldn't go into any of that now. "Where's Peter?"

"Why are you so *desperate* to find my brother?"

"My wife is with him and—"

"Uh-oh." He flashed his eyes and grinned. "Someone is being cuckolded and I can guess who."

"Do you know where your brother is?"

"But of course."

My heart jumped. "Where?"

"I don't think I should tell you because—" He was interrupted by a thumping noise coming from the next room.

"What's that?" I asked.

Richard sighed and trailed a languid hand across his beard. "My suite mate. Oh yes even with all the money we're bestowing on the Evergreen I still have a suite mate. It's not a matter of economy but of *therapy*. The psychiatrists here don't think it's healthy for their wards to live alone."

Now in addition to the thumping I heard a muffled voice.

Richard stood and walked over to the wall, which he hit several times with the flat of his hand. "Quiet, Ralph, I have a guest!"

I went to the room's interior door and listened.

"If you intend to open that door," Richard told me, "please give me a chance to get out of range first."

"Out of range?"

He laughed. "Ralph has the rather *blistering* habit of tossing his feces at the unwary."

I put my ear to the door but by that time both the thumping and the muffled voice had stopped. I tried the handle, which was locked.

"Oh I forgot, it's kept locked after hours. Here, let me call the administrator's office, someone will run down with a key."

"No—"

"I insist. Meeting Ralph is an education." He went to the phone, held the receiver to his ear, and smiled at me as he waited to be connected.

"Richard—"

He held up a finger and spoke into the phone, "Yes, this is Richard Tummelier. I have a visitor, Mr. Roscoe Bird, and—What's that you say?" The longer he listened, the higher his eyebrows rose. After he put the phone down he looked at me with the queerest expression. "Ms. Allfrey herself will be right over. Apparently she is quite upset with you. What *have* you done?"

"Tell me where Peter is, *please.*"

He relaxed his shoulders. "On one condition."

"Name it."

"That you go see Peter alone. If he's done something naughty you can alert the authorities *after* you meet with Peter by yourself. I fear he's in a bad way but maybe seeing you, just you alone, will cure him. If you promise me that, I'll give you directions to his . . . I'll give you a map."

"I promise."

He went over to a small desk and took out a sheet of paper that he folded into fourths. Holding the paper out to me, Richard said, "We did have great fun on Hambriento, you and Peter and I, didn't we?"

"Yes," I replied, reaching for the paper just as Richard withdrew it.

"I teased you two younger boys mercilessly, didn't I?" he asked, again holding the paper in my direction.

"Yes you did." And when I reached for it a second time, once more Richard lifted the folded paper out of my grasp. No patience left, I shouted at him as a child would, *"Give it to me!"*

"Yes of course." He handed it over. "And do hurry. Your therapeutic presence may well be Peter's last chance for survival."

There came a frantic pounding at the cottage's front door.

"Out the back," Richard whispered, taking my arm. "Where's your car parked?"

"At the administration building."

"After you leave here circle around to your right until you come to a service road, it'll take you to the far side of the administration building."

"Thank you." I shook his hand. "I'll do what I can to help Peter."

"Oh I'm sure you will."

Once out the back door I took off running through the snow. The only other time in my life I could remember experiencing this particular brand of intoxication, exhilaration laced with terror, was when I broke into the Burtons' house intending to shoot them. Except now I was out to save a life. Marianne would be with Peter, I was sure of it. As I ran, the night's craziness fed on itself, blocking out rational thought, creating a certain internal logic. What are you doing, Roscoe Bird? I'm running through the snow-covered grounds of an insane asylum, on the way to save my wife from a vampire.

THIRTY-FIVE

I drove off the Evergreen's property shortly before ten P.M., leaving
Johnny Laflin detained either as a potential mental patient or as a law
enforcement officer who'd overstepped his authority. It wasn't until I
had gone several miles that I stopped the rental car to look at the
paper Richard had given me. His directions led to a spot marked with
an *X* and labeled *Peter's lair,* the route taking me down Rock Creek
Parkway and close enough to my house that I could stop there to see
if Marianne had shown up.

She hadn't. I left her a note, which I'd meant to do earlier, and then
on an impulse went upstairs to see if the pistol was still under my side
of the mattress.

It was. You'd think that after the trouble it got me into the last time
I carried it, I'd have the good sense to leave it home this time. But
you'd be wrong. I replaced the spent cartridge and took the pistol with
me because the neatly lettered words on the map said it all: *Peter's lair.*

I put on a pair of boots and brought along a flashlight, then drove back to the parkway and, following the map's directions, turned onto that maze of lonely tree-tunneled lanes along Rock Creek. Houses here were isolated, set back from the roads, which were poorly signed, and after traveling for more than an hour I was sure I was lost. Then I saw one of the map's landmarks, took the turn, and continued searching for the "lightning-split oak tree" that apparently marked the entrance to the private lane leading to Peter—and Marianne.

I went past it, hit the brakes, backed up, and drove down the lane until my headlights shone on a dilapidated trailer.

Not a mobile home but a *trailer,* one of those old-fashioned, pseudostreamlined, one-axle jobs I saw on highways back when I was a kid living in Florida, tourists pulling them behind their Oldsmobiles and camping out of the trailers during one-week vacations. But no one lived in them permanently, they weren't meant for that.

This one had been used hard: dented, fire-scorched, bulletholed, its front window covered with plywood, its frame low on rotting tires so flat they couldn't even remember what it was like to be round and airtight. The trailer was snow covered but that didn't help its appearance.

I had to make sure Peter knew it was me and that I was alone, I didn't want him to panic and hurt Marianne. I tucked the big pistol in my belt, under my jacket, and got out of the car to holler. "Peter! It's me! Roscoe! I'm by myself and I'm coming in."

Approaching the trailer I saw that trash had been piled under the plywood-covered window, which was to my right of the door, the trash piled there as if Peter had simply slipped his garbage out from beneath the plywood to let it fall on the ground. Very unlike him. Maybe it *wasn't* him, maybe Peter hadn't returned to the trailer with Marianne, maybe this wasn't even the right place.

I looked down at my watch, a little past eleven. When I raised my head again I saw rats.

Living in D.C. you get used to them but usually only as wall-hugging alley-creeping shadows moving from one Dumpster to the next. These moonlit rats, however, went openly about the snowy trash pile, in and out of holes, moving with impunity.

I remained standing there, fascinated at how the rats moved, with a kind of fluid insinuation, entering and exiting the maze of holes they had Swiss-cheesed into the small volcano of garbage. When I finally shone my flashlight there, rats slipped like brown plasma into their various burrows.

I waited to make sure they weren't going to come out again and then continued for the trailer, immediately stopping when I heard the plywood being pushed away from the window. I shone the light and saw something being lowered—something rats had been waiting for because even with my flashlight still on the trash pile they began making their reappearances, cautiously at first, snouts sniffing, then a head showing, eyes reflecting red, until some sort of signal was passed along and rats came out by platoon and company, looking up at what was being lowered from the trailer's window, scaly tails whipping with excitement.

I couldn't figure out what it was, a plum-sized piece of meat or fleshlike plastic, brown and red, hooked to a steel leader that was fastened to what looked like fishing line being fed out by someone hiding behind the plywood—presumably Peter.

He must've seen my headlights, must've heard me call. Peter was doing this for my benefit.

I trained the flashlight on one rat who worked his way to the top of the pile, first in line for the bait. In his impatience he turned to the garbage around him and began sniffing at and then pulling on what looked to be soiled diapers. Bracing front paws like a dog he unfolded the diapers, revealing to my flashlight a stomach-turning palette of stains, your basic earth tones, red and yellow and brown, upon which the rat commenced to feed with manic eagerness.

But he also kept taking breaks to look up at the bait descending his way with maddening slowness.

I continued holding the flashlight on this drama until the plum-sized bait finally reached the rat, which sat back on his haunches like a cat. He wanted it but was afraid to touch it and this approach-avoidance dilemma frustrated him into several frantic bouts of grooming. When two other rats joined him at the top of the heap, he chased one away with squeals and a curious boxing stance, then mounted the other intruder and pumped ass until this interloper also fled.

Now he was alone with what he wanted but could not bring himself to touch. He circled it with a rabbitlike hopping, then stretched out his neck to sniff, to touch it with his nose. He pulled back. He came forward. And when he finally couldn't stand it anymore, the rat lunged and took the entire bait in his mouth, immediately turning to scurry away with his prize.

Except he descended only eighteen inches or so of the trash pile before the line leading up into the trailer's window jerked taut, pulling the rat short, hooking him.

Squealing, the rat immediately flipped over on his back and used all four paws in a desperate attempt to divest his mouth of the bait and its hidden barb, keeping his mouth open as he came back over on all fours, twisting his head violently from side to side, jumping straight up and down like an angel-dusted kangaroo, then using his front paws to dig frantically in the trash trying to create a burrow into which he could pour himself.

Nothing worked, he was caught.

And then pulled, lifted by the mouth. It must've hurt worse than anything in his rat experience; the high-pitched screaming took on an eerily human sound.

Dragged up the side of the trailer, the rat twisted and fought, squealed and screamed, tail whipping, paws paddling against the trailer's rusted and pocked skin, turning around and around as if to tie his body into a knot, fighting like a two-pound hunk of boneless, hotly firing muscle, resisting right up to the moment he was jerked inside the window.

I heard one muffled thump, like a stomped foot, then all was quiet.

When I directed the flashlight back at the trash pile—rats gone—the beam flickered then went out. After hitting it several times against the palm of my left hand, the flashlight managed a weak and yellowish beam.

"If you wa-a-ant . . . something to play with, go and find yourself a to-oy. Baby my time is too expensi-ive, and I'm NOT a little boy-oy."

A cappella, the softly pleading voice came muffled from within the trailer.

"If you are serious . . . don't play with my heart, it makes me furious, but if you want me to love you-ou, then baby I wi-ill, baby you know I will."

Like a soul caught inside there, pleading its release, giving me gooseflesh.

"Don't be ashamed, let your conscience be your guide."

Reminding me of what a sad, wanting child Peter had been.

"But I-I-I-I-I know that deep down inside me I believe you love me, forget your foolish pri-i-i-i-i-de."

Then silence.

I waited but there was no more singing.

"Peter!"

What's he doing in there?

"Peter Tummelier!" I called.

"No," he replied hoarsely, "Aaron Neville."

THIRTY-SIX

When the trailer door opened I took pistol in hand and used its high-caliber courage to cover my approach. A few feet in front of the trailer I stopped where the snow had been trampled and stained. Shining my yellowing light around this area I saw the glint of something metallic and was just about to reach down and pick it up when I realized what was attached to the metal device: human teeth.

"Too weak to kill," came Peter's voice from somewhere inside.

"Is Marianne with you?" I called back, stepping carefully around what looked to be a dental plate before rushing to the trailer's opened door, peering in at nothing but darkness.

"I see you're armed again," he said. "But this time I'm too weak to kill."

The flashlight chose that moment to go out completely.

"Roscoe?"

"I'm right here."

"Come in, I need you."

"Turn on a light first," I said, tossing the useless flashlight into the snow. "Peter?"

When he coughed I heard something gurgle disgustingly in his chest.

"Peter, what's wrong?"

No answer.

"Turn on a light so I can come in."

Still no reply.

"Peter, is Marianne in there?"

"I think you'd prefer to . . ." Another coughing spell. "Prefer to remain in the dark."

About Marianne?

I'd seen electric lines leading to the trailer and assumed it had been wired for lights. Pistol in my right hand, I reached around the door-jamb with my left. "I got the switch here, Peter, watch your eyes, I'm turning it on."

"Don't. Please."

"Why?"

"I'm ashamed, you were never meant to see this place. Nor do I want you to see me, not like this."

"You're sick?" It was the bullet wound, he was dying because I'd shot him. "I can't do anything for you unless I come in and I'm not coming in without a light on."

"You're not going to like what you see."

"Watch your eyes."

"Wait!"

I heard the rustling of material, then Peter's muffled voice. "Okay, I'm ready."

I flipped the light switch but stayed in the doorway. Peter was in a large overstuffed chair in the middle of the trailer's interior, or at least I assumed it was him, because the figure in that chair was completely covered in a dingy sheet, as if he and the chair were being protected from dust in a house that had been closed for the season.

"Peter?"

"Yes," came his voice from beneath that sheet.

"What have you done with Marianne?"

"She's safe."

Thank God. "Safe *where?*"

"Do you remember what you used to say about that Aaron Neville song?"

"Peter, take off the goddamn sheet." He was trying to scare me.

But Peter didn't remove the sheet and it was then, when I finally stepped into the trailer, that I was assaulted by a stench so overpoweringly bad that I immediately pulled out a handkerchief and covered my nose and mouth.

"Back when we were rock-and-roll teenagers," he said from beneath the sheet, "you told me that 'Tell It Like It Is' was your most potent seduction song. You said that when you played this song for a girl and lowered your eyelids and gave her that James Dean, sad-hurt little-boy lost-puppy wounded-poet look of yours, the girl was powerless to resist. Remember?"

But I wasn't listening, I was looking around the trailer for any signs that Marianne might have been here. The trailer's interior was an open rectangle, kitchen area at one end, to my left, with a couch at the other end and that overstuffed chair in the middle. No place to hide. One entire wall was covered with photographs that struck me with an instant familiarity, but it wasn't until I stepped closer to the wall that I realized all the pictures were of me: as a baby, obviously before I'd met Peter—he must've gotten the photographs from my mother; as a boy; as a teenager; photographs of me and my dad, of Peter and me and my dad; me on our boat; me holding up a string of fish, mugging for the camera. Pictures in which whoever was with me had been cut out; blurry snapshots and formal high school graduation photos. There must've been fifty of them crowding that trailer wall.

If it was my shrine, I felt less flattered than creepy. My skin went clammy.

"Is this where you've been living?" I asked the sheet-covered figure, who didn't answer.

It was a sty. Rubbish (papers and clothing, CDs and cassettes, soiled bandages) scattered the floor. Winter-hatched flies, encouraged to life

by the trailer's incredible stench, polka-dotted the walls while on the
floor light-fearless cockroaches commuted busily from one pile of
trash to the next. Plates left out on various counters were covered with
mold and with colonies of ants, while armies of centipedes marched
on something brown lying on the floor in front of the small dead
refrigerator.

But the filth I could see was minor compared with what I smelled:
decay and rot, feces and urine, big meat that had gone bad—an odor
seemingly strong enough to yellow the air, penetrating the weave of
my handkerchief and clasping with a vomity pastelike hold on to the
back of my throat.

I walked around to the front of the chair. "Peter?"

No movement from under that dirty sheet.

"Peter, what's happened to you?"

"It would be better," came his weakened voice, "if you turned out
the light."

"I want to see you."

"Are you sure?"

I wasn't but I said I was.

"You won't run away and leave me alone?"

"Of course not."

"You'll stay with me while I die, I'd like that."

"Yes."

Two hands emerged from either side of the sheet. They were Peter's,
I was sure of it, large and long-fingered, but I had never seen him with
dirty hands before—dirty in that ground-in permanent way you see on
homeless street people, as if the very pigment of the skin had been
irrevocably stained. His normally well-manicured fingernails were
broken, three of them missing completely as if torn off in an injury
that had healed badly.

And then after another moment's hesitation, he pulled the sheet
down to reveal his head and bare shoulders.

The man was a corpse. Since I'd last seen him, less than twenty-four
hours ago, Peter had been transformed into a wizened living cadaver,
so dried out and shrunken as to be lost in that overstuffed chair.

He reminded me of photographs taken by Allied troops liberating

Nazi death camps, the survivors only barely clinging to life, only a few hours, a few hundred calories, from drawing into that final fetal position assumed by the starved.

But more than starvation had ravaged Peter, something far worse than a gunshot wound too.

Suppurating sores pocked his face and shoulders, some of those sores almost perfectly round while others had spread over his skin like a red-encrusted moss. One especially putrid ulcer bloomed outward from the far corner of his right eye and was the apparent cause of the eye having turned milky white, perhaps blind. Scary images from an old sex education film I saw in college came to mind, *tertiary syphilis.* Except whatever Peter had was worse.

Both of his cheeks carried long parallel gouges of proud flesh.

What little hair he had left stuck out in clumps like miniature fright wigs pasted randomly over his crusty skull.

Had I come upon him elsewhere, in a cave perhaps, not only wouldn't I have recognized Peter as my friend, I would've doubted he was a member of my own species.

His once-proud nose had deflated like the tires on this trailer, the tip of that nose hanging so far down that it appeared he could touch it by sticking his tongue straight out.

All over his upper lip and around both nostrils was what I assumed to be snot, some of it dried like fish scales showing a dull gloss against his skin and some of it repellingly fresh.

Peter's mouth hung open as if from exhaustion and though I stood several feet back from him and even with the trailer's orchestra of competing stenches, when he breathed out to speak, his flesh-rot breath stirred my nausea like a stick.

"Care for something to eat?" he asked, suddenly holding up the dead rat that he had hidden in the folds of his sheet.

Vomit gulped up in my throat so quickly that I barely had time to bend over and chuck it away from my clothing, throwing up right there on the floor eventually to attract a column of cockroaches eager for an offering so warm and fresh, followed by a Luftwaffe of flies and later the slow but inevitable march of ants and that rolling-legged troupe of centipedes.

I kept spitting, kept wiping my tongue with the handkerchief, but nothing would remove the taste from my mouth.

When I finally looked Peter's way again I could tell that even in his deathly state he was pleased with the effect his little joke had produced.

"Jesus, Peter, what's happened to you?"

His ulcerated lips pulled down as if he was about to cry. Peter turned his head toward a corner of the chair, ashamed of himself.

"I told you, I'm dying."

I didn't doubt it.

"You can get me something," he said.

"What?"

He didn't answer.

"Peter? What can I get you?"

When he turned my way those terrible lips held a grisly smile.

"What?" I asked.

"A small white child?"

What stuck in my mind was the *way* he phrased it, giving equal weight to the two adjectives, as if saying, "A large blue Buick?"

I told him it wasn't funny.

"A girl wearing her first training bra?"

"Shut the fuck up or I'm leaving." Though of course I couldn't go, not without learning what he'd done to Marianne.

"Valentino."

"What?"

"Valentino."

"Peter, what're you talking about?"

He had closed his eyes.

"Pe—"

"When I was a boy that's who friends of my parents said I looked like, a miniature Valentino."

Then he fell asleep or passed out or died, it could've been any of the three.

I was just starting in his direction to check for a pulse, dreading the idea of touching him, when he opened his eyes, surprised that I stood there before him. "Roscoe?"

"Yes."

"*Roscoe*, dear friend."

"Listen to me, Peter, as soon as I'm sure Marianne is okay I'll get you to a hospital. Tell me where I can find her or where the police can find her, then I'll—"

"I've been infected."

"By *what?*"

"By *whom.* By Audrey-hyphen-Eileen, willing enough but no moves, bad blood." He closed his eyes to picture her.

I had no idea to whom he was referring or even if he knew what he was saying and when it seemed that he had passed out again I went over and kicked lightly at his chair. "Peter, wake up! Where's Marianne!"

He opened his eyes but didn't look at me as he stroked the little brown carcass in his lap. "Did you know that male rats on occasion will fuck a female to death? It's true. When several males are fighting to mount a single female, sometimes the competition and sexual frenzy become so exquisitely *singular* that the males will fuck the female hundreds of times, one after another, traumatizing her unto death. Then you know what the males do? They keep on copulating with the corpse. Poor little guys can't help themselves." He looked up at me. "Marianne is fine."

"You sonofabitch!" I raised the pistol to his ruined face. "If you've hurt her I'll blow your fucking head off."

"I'll be dead by morning regardless of what you do to me."

He was right. What could I threaten him with? Shooting Peter in his current condition would only be an act of mercy.

"You'll stay with me until I die, won't you, Roscoe?"

"I could save you. Tell me where Marianne is and I'll take you to an emergency room."

"You can save me but not by taking me to a hospital."

Sensing the hopelessness of getting any useful information out of him, I went over and sat heavily on the couch.

Peter seemed to be sleeping again but after a minute or so his eyelids fluttered and he looked nervously about the room until he located me. "I thought it was a dream, that I had only dreamed you were here. But you're real, aren't you?"

"Yes," I replied wearily, "I'm real."

He spoke haltingly as if it hurt to use his voice. "As I lay dying these past hours I imagined your arrival here, the door opening, you rushing in, horrified by my condition but saddened by it too, throwing your arms around me, weeping in grief." He rested for a full minute before continuing in a stronger, angrier voice: "I must say however that in none of these fevered imaginings did I picture you arriving *armed*."

I glanced down at the pistol. "You've killed people, you've kidnapped my wife, what do you expect? And if you've hurt her, then you can rot in hell for all I care."

As I spoke these words Peter's balding death's head was turned in my direction but he said nothing, showed no reaction, sitting there sheet-covered and wasted, yet somehow serene, like an awful parody of Gandhi except without the reputation for nonviolence.

Peter wept. "That's your father's pistol, isn't it? The gun you used to shoot me last night, and now you've come to kill me with it, it's the very same weapon your father used to end his life. Isn't it! Oh you cold-hearted bastard." He was sobbing. "The time I spent with you and your family was the only sanity I've had in my life, when your father died the better part of me died with him, and now you've come to kill me with the gun that ended his life? Why not dig up his grave and use his bones to beat me to death! And *I'm* the vampire? No, you're the *monster*." Choking on tears, he was prevented from saying more.

We sat there in our individual and mutual horror until Peter sobbed out a plea: "You can save my life!"

"What do you mean?"

He wiped tears and pus from his eyes and begged me to listen. "If someone from today were somehow transported to medieval times and if he took with him certain modern gadgets, a Polaroid camera, a battery-operated VCR, a tape recorder, and if he claimed he was a wizard and then as proof of his magic he demonstrated these gadgets, what do you think would happen to him in the king's court?"

I shrugged

"I'll be dead in a few fucking hours, can't you please humor me this one last time!"

"Tell me where Marianne is and I'll—"

"Well, the answer is, the ancients would *not* celebrate this modern man and his modern gadgets, they'd challenge him to levitate and conjure, to make good on his claim of being a wizard, but of course he'd be unable to perform any authentic magic, because with the onset of the modern era we traded in our magic for gadgets, and he would be put to death as an imposter who happened to possess some fascinating trinkets."

"I don't understand what this has to do with—"

"The magic still exists! Certain individuals have held it in trust during the awful age of rationality, they have passed it on. Vampires exist, I'm one of them, and—"

"Oh for chrissakes."

"I could make you one too. Your becoming a vampire tonight would save my life and then the two of us could—"

"Seeing you like this hardly makes me want to join up."

"Don't be an idiot, I made a mistake, I knew something was wrong with that blood but I swallowed it anyway. I didn't care, I didn't care if I died. This whole effort of trying to convince or force you to come with me on the boat, it has turned out to be such a farce, I can't *force* you to love me, protect me, but you have a chance tonight . . . Roscoe? Listen to me. You have a chance not only to save my life but to enter upon an adventure of such power and potency, such thrill, such intensity that you will awaken every evening with my name on your lips, thanking me."

I shook my head, saying no to him and expressing my pity at the same time.

"Roscoe, you're being stupid, petulant—"

"Even if what you're saying about vampires was true I wouldn't do it, not at the cost of my soul."

"But if you never die, you never have to forfeit your soul, that's the beauty of it."

"*You're* dying."

He slumped in frustration, shrugging me off as a lost cause.

"Just tell me you haven't hurt Marianne."

"I haven't hurt Marianne," he replied by rote.

"Where is she?"

"She's safe."

I stood and told Peter I wished I'd never met him.

"Don't say that." He began crying again. *"I love you!"*

"I'm leaving, I'm finding a phone and calling the police, let them deal with you."

"Roscoe, please."

"Adios, motherfucker."

"You're always leaving me!"

I continued for the door.

"Because of your father!"

That stopped me. "What do you mean?"

"He left you in the worst possible way anyone can leave anyone, so subconsciously you use that as the ultimate threat—*I'm leaving you!*"

"Bullshit."

I crossed in front of him and was just at the trailer's door when Peter screamed, *"Rattus norvegicus!"*

Turning I saw he was holding the dead rat triumphantly by its scaly gray tail. But this time I wasn't shocked. "I've seen your rat act."

"But have you seen *this!*" He put an index finger behind his right earlobe—or what was left of it, a remnant of angry chewed flesh.

"Fair's fair, Roscoe! They eat me, I eat them. Do you *see* what they've done to my ears, how they've already started on me, didn't even have the decency to wait until I croaked. You know of course that they go for the soft parts first, earlobes and lips. Eyes. They bite holes in your cheeks to get at your tongue, that's the part they prize above all else."

"Put the rat down, Peter."

He held it up even higher and mocked me with a whiny voice. *"Put the rat down, Peter.* Oh I've put 'em down all right, I've put a dozen of 'em down in the last twenty hours. You have any idea what rat's blood tastes like?"

"I'm going."

"At least the little fuckers kept me alive. Not that it matters to you, *you* would've preferred to come here and find me dead already, isn't that right?"

"If you aren't going to tell me where Marianne is, what you've done with her, then, yes, I would've preferred to find you dead rather than listen to your filth."

He had begun to swing the rat back and forth like a metronome. "Takes a clever man to hook a rat, Roscoe. You have any idea how suspicious they are? I had to feed them for hours before they became trusting enough to take the bait. Fussy eaters too. About the only part they found irresistible was her nipples."

I rushed over and whipped the pistol's muzzle across the top of his skull.

"Yes, yes!" he screeched. "Kill me! Kill me!"

I hit him again.

Then he stood. My God he was quick, leaping animallike upon me, the terror threatening to explode my heart, Peter *upon me,* one wasted but powerful arm around my neck, his other hand pushing that rat against my face—and now I was the one who screeched.

It suddenly came to me: He was after my blood.

With a power I could neither understand nor resist he got me to the floor. I had dropped the pistol. Peter locked me in a grip I couldn't break, holding the rat against my mouth like an older boy overpowering and torturing his kid brother except a thousand times worse, rubbing that awful carcass across my mouth as he talked so maniacally fast that I could barely understand him. "*Rattus norvegicus* breeds at three months up to seven litters a year as many as twenty pups in a litter plentiful supply if you can stomach them Chinese served live newborn rat pups as a delicacy called them table deer quite the treat to pour out a bowl of newborn rats all pink and hairless mewling little inch-long blind fetal pups snapping them up with your chopsticks click click click click yum yum yum the bones so soft you can crunch 'em like popcorn."

"Please," I begged.

And then just as suddenly as the attack began, it was over. Peter rolled away from me to lie over on the floor, on his back, arms spread, the bloody sheet about his emaciated body like a profane imitation of the shroud of Christ.

I got up wiping at my mouth obsessively with both hands, still tasting rat. *You bastard.* Where is that pistol! I watched Peter's chest but didn't see it rise or fall. Had he died? I nudged his side with the toe of my boot.

And in response he spoke without moving, without opening his eyes. "Oh, loveheart, don't you see, I could've taken you any time I wished."

Believing him, believing that he might still do it, I looked around until I found the revolver.

Eyes still closed, Peter held a hand in my direction. "Help me over to the cóuch."

"I'll kill you!" I screamed, still shaken from the attack.

"Don't worry, I'm not going to make you a vampire against your will, even though I could, even though I *should,* to save my life and *give* you The Life. But I won't, not against your will. And you're obviously too pigheaded to accept what I offer. Which leaves only dying, bowing out gracefully. Just don't let me die on the floor, help me to the couch. That's all I ask."

When he raised his hand a second time, I took it.

"Help me up."

There didn't seem to be any portion of his body uninfected with sores, which I was determined not to touch, rendering ineffective my efforts to help him stand.

"You won't become one by *touching* me," he said disdainfully.

He finally got to his feet largely on his own; upright he was even more pathetic, this bent stick figure who looked and acted a thousand years old.

On the way to the couch Peter tried to keep the sheet around him but it slipped to reveal the entire right side of his body where the flesh was puckered and purpled as if from a severe acid burn. Had the bullet wound I gave him done that? I tucked the pistol away, no longer having the heart to hurt him more than he was already hurt.

After he lay upon the couch I arranged the sheet over his wasted body and said I would go out and find a pay phone, call an ambulance.

He shook his head. "Sit here with me until I'm gone. Marianne's safe, I promise you. I left her with someone who's under the strictest orders not to harm her."

"Who?"

"After I die she'll be released, there will no longer be a reason to hold her ransom, now sit here next to me."

When I did, Peter immediately grasped my hand. "The pain is . . . quite incredible."

"I'm sorry."

"I know. It just didn't work out, did it?"

I shook my head.

He pressed my hand against his bony chest where that racking liquid cough threatened to strangle him, bringing tears and blood to the corners of his dark eyes. On his nearly hairless skull new blood oozed thickly from where I'd hit him with the pistol. The crying had produced fresh snot, which migrated down his upper lip before slipping over to a corner of his small delicate mouth. I still couldn't look at Peter without experiencing a revulsion so soul-deep that only by force of will did I stop myself from running out of that trailer.

He was shaking his head, telling me no about something, and then I realized he wanted me to release his hand so he could turn over and face away, so I wouldn't have to look at him. When I let his hand go I saw in the middle of his palm, centered within a triangle made by life and love lines, a tiny but beautifully detailed bird.

After his back was to me I asked, "When did you get that tattoo?"

No answer.

"Peter?"

"Hasn't your God promised to hold you in the palm of His hand?"

"How long have you had it, I never noticed it before."

"With sufficient vigilance you can keep almost anything hidden, even the obvious."

"Let me see it again."

Without turning to face me he held up his opened hand. The bird, tattoo blue, had been rendered in flight.

"What do you call it," he asked, still holding his hand open, "when you're out on the water at night and the moon casts a line of light across the water's surface and the reflection points right at you and no matter where you go, how fast you travel, that reflected line of light keeps pointing nowhere else except right at you, what's that called?"

"Moonglade."

He was silent for a long time. When I touched his shoulder he didn't move.

THIRTY-SEVEN

"Peter, did you hear me, it's called a moonglade."

He shuddered, then wept again.

And I was at a loss what to do. It had been a ruinous night and Peter's condition left me with no sane rationale because if the impossible—a vampire corrupted by bad blood—didn't explain Peter's unnaturally swift descent into this wretched state, then what did?

In spite of his protests I probably should've gone to call an ambulance but I was sure he was right: at the rate he was dying, doctors wouldn't do him any good—and Peter didn't want to die alone.

Over the next hour he suffered alternately from chills and fevers. When he was cold his shivering rattled the entire couch until I put my coat over him and through its tweed material rubbed his skeletal shoulder. When he turned feverish I had to go outside for handfuls of snow to cool his neck, which was hot enough to melt the snow upon touch. During the delusions brought on by his fevers Peter thought I was his father, he spoke of something called the Volter, he called out for Richard to stop hurting him.

At one point when he was rational, relatively rational, Peter asked me how I knew I wouldn't like being a vampire if I never tried being a vampire.

"That's what Mom used to say about asparagus, how do you know you don't like it if you don't try it."

"She was right."

"She was right about *asparagus*, Peter."

He managed a weak laugh.

After repetitive bouts of chills and fever, of coughing blood and vomiting a bilious substance black as tar, Peter became so weakened that we both knew the end was near, that he tottered on the edge. Yet the prospect of his imminent death brought forth no emotion from me other than a guilty weariness that it was taking so long. Was Peter right, was I really that coldhearted?

"Do you remember the osprey?" he asked in the voice of someone dreaming.

"What osprey?"

"Fishermen showed it to us. The osprey had gone after a fish, embedded its talons in the fish's back. But the fish was too big and when it submerged, the osprey drowned. Its talons never pulled loose, the fish just kept dragging the osprey along underwater until the bird's body rotted and nothing was left but an osprey skeleton attached to a fish's back."

"I don't remember that."

"Sure, those fishermen showed it to us."

"I'm sorry—"

"That's all right, Dondo, don't cry, it wasn't your fault."

Peter slept deeply for ten or fifteen minutes, awakening with a start, with a cry of self-hatred. "I'm so fucking despicable! No wonder you can't stand me! I wish I had been more like Richard, tall and blond and sure of himself. I wanted to be like *you*. Oh Roscoe you always had such bonhomie, whereas I was always so little and dark and nervous—"

"Peter—"

"Your wife said you were my friend *faute de mieux,* for lack of something better, that's not true, is it?"

"Where is she?"

"I always wanted you to see me at my best but now this, this *death* is how you're going to remember me."

"No—"

"When we were kids, I used to change clothes a dozen different times before coming over to visit you, in fact I wanted to call and find out what you were wearing so I could dress in a similar outfit, but I knew you'd consider that dorky. I wanted my hair to be like yours, the way it fell down over your forehead and made you look tough and cool, your hair was always perfect. I wanted to be just like you."

I tucked my coat up around his neck.

He blew out his yellow breath and rested awhile before asking, "How did you find me?"

"Richard."

He was surprised. "How did you find *him?*"

"Johnny Laflin's detective work."

"Did Richard instruct you to come here alone?"

"Yes."

Peter nodded as if I had just confirmed something for him.

"Richard said they locked up the wrong brother, he said he's not insane."

Peter smiled. "He would say that, wouldn't he?"

"What happened after we left Hambriento, why was Richard sent away, does any of that have anything to do with my father's death?"

"Have you ever looked into a mirror?"

"What?"

"I mean really *looked* into a mirror, staring at your reflection for an hour straight, looking as deeply as you can into that face that's looking back out at you with an equal intensity. Something very strange starts happening if you do it long enough, intensely enough. The reflection becomes another being and you feel detached from it, you sense its separate presence. When I was little, six or seven, Richard would stand

the two of us in front of a full-length mirror and we would remain
there for the longest time staring at the two who were staring back at
us. He wouldn't allow me to say anything or fidget, I had to stand
there and just look. And then this one time, after an especially long
session in front of the mirror, Richard asked me something, perhaps
the strangest and most life-altering question I've ever been asked."
Silent for a moment, Peter continued with a sense of awe. " *'Which one
are you?'* That's what he asked. And do you know what, Roscoe? I
wasn't sure. Do you understand what I'm telling you, I wasn't sure
which of the four beings was me, the real me, the me that held a soul,
because that *me* had slipped away and could've been anywhere,
could've gone into my reflection or Richard's or into Richard himself.
After that Richard could take me out of my body whenever he pleased.
Sometimes things were done to me, to my body, things I found horri-
fying—until Richard showed me how to escape my body, exist apart
from it. He tried that with Donald too, only Donald was too young.
Richard got him out of his body but couldn't get him back."

I didn't know what Peter was talking about, didn't know who Donald was, but rather than questioning Peter any further I told him he
should try to rest, save his strength, he could survive this night after
all.

"No, there's some information you need."

"About Marianne?"

"About vampires."

"Peter—"

"The beast is wily, not to be trusted. You try manipulating him and
you'll end up being seduced yourself. The only way to withstand him
is to harden your heart, you're good at that—harden your heart and
believe in your God, in the sanctity of your immortal soul."

"Try to rest."

"To kill the beast is difficult but not impossible, I lie here as dying
proof of that. Keep in mind that driving a stake through the vampire's
heart is simply a way of ensuring death, ensuring that no mistakes or
misses are made. There's nothing magical about the stake, about it
being wooden, a stake through the heart is a guarantee that the job

has been done properly, thoroughly. Driving an iron bar through the brain would accomplish the same end. Cutting off his head, burning him. But you can't just take a quick shot with a pistol as you did to me and hope that will do the trick."

"I'm sorry—"

"You don't understand what I'm telling you. *Make sure.* Six bullets in the brain, crushing the skull—whatever method you use, perform it thoroughly."

"Does this have something to do with Marianne?"

"It might."

"How?"

He shook his head as if I was distracting him. "There are several ways to become a vampire. The passing of blood between master and neophyte is the traditional route of course, which is what I offered you tonight, a chance to both give and receive *life.* But the transfer can also be accomplished, albeit more slowly, by passing other bodily fluids. Mucus under certain conditions, semen, and the secretions from the vagina of a female vampire can be a rich medium for transfer."

"Why are you telling me this?"

He shook his head again, impatient with my denseness. Then whatever was worrying him, whatever he was trying to convey, he gave it up. "I'm useless. I've never held a job, never married, never had children, never contributed anything, never harbored a decent emotion in my life except loving you. How pathetic it is, to die useless."

I sat there patting his shoulder, trying to think of something reassuring to say. "Do you know why tarpon run today in nearly the numbers they did a hundred years ago? Because the tarpon's flesh is inedible, gray and gristly, not 'good' for anything except sport. If the tarpon hadn't been useless to everyone except sportsmen, it would've been fished out a long time ago."

"This is supposed to be making me feel better?"

"You weren't useless to me, Peter. I never had so much fun, never laughed so hard, was never so scared as I was with you, when we were kids on Hambriento."

"Truly?" He was looking away from me but smiling. "I was good for something, as sport for you, I was fun?"

"You were a blast."

"Roscoe?"

"Yes?"

"I suppose . . . I suppose I can legitimately hold no hope for heaven."

"It's not too late." But would I remember the words?

Before I could recite them, however, Peter said, "It's too late."

And with that he arched up from the couch as both eyes rolled back in his head until only the bloody whites showed.

"Peter?"

He moaned pitifully.

"Don't die!" As soon as I said those words, a memory fingered my heart: when Johnny Laflin came to take me out of high school history class he said that my father had been shot, not that Dad had killed himself but "your father's been shot," those were Johnny's exact words. I thought Laflin was taking me to the hospital where Dad was in intensive care or being operated on at that very moment so as I rode in the patrol car I kept saying to myself over and over, Don't die, Dad, don't die, don't die, please don't die. As if by saying it enough times with enough conviction I could somehow will it to be so. But of course Johnny wasn't driving me to the hospital, he was taking me home and my father was already several hours dead and my saying *don't die*, even saying it endless times with infinite conviction, was useless, was too late.

"Don't die, Peter!" I had him by the shoulders.

His white-coated tongue came out to make a vain dry pass over his cracked lips.

"Don't die."

He opened his fingers to show me that tattoo, then made a fist, and, holding me in the palm of his hand, Peter died.

THIRTY-EIGHT

Standing at a pay phone waiting to be put through to a homicide lieutenant I knew only as Jim, I felt something in my mouth, caught it on my tongue, and touched a finger to the tip of my tongue. Still holding the phone I looked down and saw on that damp finger a lone rat hair. I bent over to vomit but there was nothing left.

Forty minutes later I was back outside the trailer and in a world of police. Six squad cars, more arriving. The coroner's wagon. Uniformed officers everywhere. Truncheonlike flashlights with blinding beams, radios that squawked. Serious dogs snuffling in the snow.

Lieutenant Jim-something, the older detective with white hair and acne scars, touched my shoulder. His voice explained what his eyes were already telling me: "We've found the bodies of two women under the trailer."

On top of everything else I had borne that night I felt then the additional weight of inevitability.

"You said you thought that Tummelier had arranged your wife's kidnapping." He waited a moment. "It's up to you."

I knew exactly what he meant. "Where?"

"Around here," the lieutenant said, holding out his arm like a maître d' showing me to my table.

I followed him to the back of the trailer, where, next to Peter's Mercedes, two zipped-up black body bags lay in the snow.

As the zipper came down on each of the two faces, I felt all eyes on me, courtiers watching for the king's decision: yes or no?

No. (The first woman was middle-aged, her face pudgy.)

No. (The second woman, although Marianne's age, had curly stringy hair; her face was battered, mouth hanging open to show a gap where certain teeth were missing.)

"Neither of these women is my wife," I said, sounding stupidly imperious even to myself; I had no idea how I sounded to Jim, who patted my shoulder congratulating me I suppose on the excellent job of identifying the two women as not my wife.

Returning to the front of the trailer I heard a group of uniformed officers laughing and I wondered what could produce laughter at a place such as this, at a time like this. Yet I wasn't offended, perhaps laughter here, now, was a hopeful sign. They were gathered around someone.

It was Johnny Laflin. I overheard him regaling the troops with the story of how he and I managed to put one over on the Evergreen's formidable Ms. Tanya Allfrey. Johnny was illustrating how he faked insanity to give me a chance to slip onto the grounds, the cops laughing again as he flapped his arms and made strange noises.

"Roscoe!"

He excused himself from the circle, shaking a few hands before coming over and hanging a big arm around my neck. "I don't know whether to kiss you or kick you. It was a dirty trick you played there at the Evergreen, but it got the job done, didn't it."

"Yeah."

"What'd Peter tell you before he died?"

"Not much that made sense."

"About your wife?"

"Nothing helpful. He said Marianne is safe, someone's holding her. But I don't know where or who. Peter promised me she'd be released."

"I ain't goin' back to Florida till we find her, you got my word on that."

I thanked him, then waited for Johnny to tell me what we were going to do next. When he didn't speak, I took the lead: "I think we should see Richard again, I was only with him a few minutes, just long enough to find out about this trailer, but if I talked to him again maybe he'd tell me who else Peter was associating with here in Washington, who might be holding Marianne. I bet he knows *something*."

Johnny nodded but said nothing.

"Surely, with all that's happened tonight, surely you can get authorization for us to see Richard."

Although he listened patiently, I could tell by Johnny's expression that he had no intention of taking me to the Evergreen. "The detectives are already on it, Roscoe. They'll be interviewing Richard, tracing Peter's car, who he rented this trailer from, *everything*. Now that they've got something to go on it won't take long to find her."

"But Richard won't open up to strangers the way he will to me, that was the whole reason you took me to the Evergreen in the first place, remember?"

"Yeah but—"

"Yeah but you've already got your killer, already cracked the case, and now the pressure's off, right?"

"No, that ain't it at all, you know it ain't."

We watched two men from the coroner's office carrying a stretcher out the trailer's door.

I asked Johnny if he had seen Peter's body.

"Yeah. Hard to believe somebody in his condition had the strength to kill a cop and then Maring too, not counting his trips back and forth to Florida to commit those murders down there. How long's he been sick like that?"

"Peter hasn't been sick, not until tonight."

"What do you mean? I *saw* his body. Christ, talk about the living dead."

"I'm telling you, Johnny, when I saw him last night, when I shot him there on Connecticut Avenue, he was fine, he looked normal, physically normal."

Laflin turned us so we faced away from the other cops. "What are you saying?"

"I'm saying when Peter first came to my house last Sunday he was completely healthy and he remained completely healthy all the way up until tonight. I'm saying that whatever happened to him, it took less than twenty-four hours to happen."

"But you can't go from healthy to the way he looked tonight in less than twenty-four hours."

"Exactly. It's impossible."

"I don't know what you mean."

I didn't know what I meant either, not exactly.

Johnny was called over to speak with a detective, leaving me alone to wonder about Peter and what he told me in that bar Sunday night, the point he tried to make about having a close encounter with an extraterrestrial or with the supernatural, how you couldn't do anything about it if there was no evidence to back you up, no one would believe you. So you've had this profound, life-altering encounter and then what? Whom do you tell? Peter told his best friend but I laughed in his face.

Laflin returned and said it was all over. "That patrolman who was knifed outside Maring's house, his uniform stolen? They just found the uniform behind Peter's couch. And they're still looking through some papers they found in a box but apparently there are records of Peter chartering flights back and forth to Florida. That's what they were asking me about just now, when the killings on Hambriento took place so they can match the flight times with when the Burtons and Kate Tornsel turned up missing. I guess you saw that he covered one entire wall with pictures of you."

"Yes."

"Well, it's all settled now, that poor sick fuck was the killer, just the way you—"

"I wish you'd stop saying it's all over, it's all settled. Nothing's over or settled until we find Marianne."

"You're right. I didn't mean . . . Hey, no one considers this settled until she's found, believe me."

"So where do we go from here?"

"You go home, I'll give you a ride."

"*Home?* Right this minute some lowlife Peter hired is holding Marianne, we can't just all go home and call it a night."

"We both need some sleep."

"You think Marianne's sleeping?"

"I don't know what possibly could be done to find her that ain't already being done, do you?"

"Yes! Getting Richard's ass out of bed to answer a few questions."

"They're going to do that."

"Now? Tonight?"

"I don't know, it's their case—"

"It was their case when you took me to the Evergreen too, you didn't mind interfering then."

"Roscoe—"

"But now of course you're a big hero, the pressure's off, time for war stories about how you did it. Have you already called the boys down in Florida, told them to rest easy 'cause Big Johnny Laflin got his man?"

He took my elbow. "I'll drive you home."

I shrugged him off.

"What're you going to do, Roscoe, you going to start knocking on people's doors, you going to go house-to-house asking if anybody's seen your wife?"

"If I have to."

"Maybe she's already been released, found her way home, and now she's sitting there worried about where *you* are."

"I called the house the same time I called the cops, nobody answered."

"Maybe she got home since then, let's go see."

I was still shaking my head no but this time when Johnny took my elbow I followed along.

"If she ain't at your house when we get there, then we'll decide what to do next."

"I want someone to go out and talk to Richard, search his cottage."

"They will."

"I want you to make sure they do, and if he clams up on them, then I want you to arrange for me to talk to him."

"Okay."

"Promise me."

"I promise." He held open the front passenger door on the rental car and asked me for the keys. I handed them over and Johnny walked around and got in behind the wheel. But before he started the engine he turned to me and said, "I got your dad's pistol, it's on the backseat there."

"Okay," I answered, dazed.

"Considering everything, there's not going to be any charges brought against you for what happened on Connecticut Avenue and since you didn't use the pistol for anything that went on in that trailer tonight, they let me take it, professional courtesy and all that."

"Yeah."

"But they also said my ass is on the line to make sure you put the pistol in storage."

"Okay."

"Or maybe you can send it to your mom in Saint Louis or let one of your sisters keep it for you, you ain't allowed to have a pistol in the District."

"I know."

"Anyway it's there on the seat for you."

"That gun keeps being given back to me, why is that?"

The question surprised him. "I thought you wanted it. You know, 'cause it was your dad's."

"Why would I want the gun that killed him?" I asked it more of myself than of Johnny.

"Roscoe, you're the one that kept it all these years, not me."

"I know. Take it back to Florida with you when you go."

"Okay. I'll keep it for you. Then someday when you have a son and he gets old enough you can pass it along to him."

The idea struck me as both appealing and singularly bizarre.

THIRTY-NINE

We got to my house at four that Friday morning but found no sign that Marianne had been there, my note to her exactly where I'd left it and no messages on the answering machine other than mine.

Johnny said he'd go pick up his luggage, then find a motel room, but I insisted he stay the night with me. Johnny looked at my face for a few seconds, then said, "Sure."

When I asked him if he wanted a drink Johnny said he was tired enough to pass out on his feet but, yes, he would have a drink, after what we'd been through we both deserved one.

We drank Scotch standing in the kitchen.

I said I was trying to think of who else saw Peter, who else could confirm that he had been in perfect health before tonight. "There's Marianne of course. And Richard, but I don't know the last time he saw Peter."

"Why is this worrying you?"

"Because something strange is going on here, something that can't be explained. For Peter to lose that much weight, to become covered in sores, to be ravaged the way he was—and all in less than a day's time? *You* explain it."

"I think what happened was, he was sick all along but kept it hidden from you, kept up a good front. I remember I had this uncle once who died of cancer but nobody in the family knew he had it, he didn't complain anything was bothering him, but after he died they opened him up and the doctors said that the kind of cancer he had, it must've been causing him incredible pain for a long time, he just didn't let anybody know."

"No, it's not the same. You didn't see Peter last night the way I did. He was *perfectly fine*. He was running through the snow, pulling people out of their cars, he wasn't sick or weak, hell even getting shot didn't slow him down much."

"You missed."

"Bullshit, I saw where it hit."

"I don't think so. I was there in the trailer while the coroner looked over his body and we didn't see no gunshot wounds. That's why the detectives were willing to cut you some slack on what happened there on Connecticut Avenue. You might've fired the pistol but you didn't hit Peter."

"I'm telling you I did."

"Okay, all right, maybe the coroner missed the wound, considering the condition of Peter's body, all those sores and bruises, I suppose you could overlook a gunshot wound, though a three-fifty-seven Magnum tends to make a hole that's pretty fucking undeniable—but what does it matter anyway?"

"It matters because if I shot Peter and the wound mysteriously healed at the same time he was being transformed overnight into a living cadaver, then . . ."

"Then what?"

Then maybe vampires do exist and Peter was one. Not that I said this to Laflin. I wasn't ready to admit to vampires, not yet.

"It'll all come out in the autopsy," Johnny said. "If there's a bullet wound, what he died of, everything."

"When will it be done, the autopsy?"

"I don't know, maybe tomorrow, maybe not until Monday."

"Monday?"

"We got jurisdictional problems, homicides both in Florida and here in the District. Right before we left they found a purse that apparently belonged to one of the women whose body was under the trailer and her I.D. gave a Virginia address, so if Peter killed her there, that's a third jurisdiction that'll be staking a claim. The FBI will probably be called in, so by the time all this is settled it might be a day or two before the autopsy is performed."

"Where's his body now?"

"Why?"

Because I remembered what Peter said about making sure a vampire is dead, that while you don't necessarily have to drive a wooden stake through his heart, you have to do something just as definite, just as final. Cutting him open and removing his organs during an autopsy would do it of course, but if that wasn't to take place for another few days, then maybe Peter would . . . Jesus I couldn't believe I was thinking this: that Peter might come alive and escape from the morgue.

Seeing the distress in my face, Johnny asked what was wrong.

"Can you get me into the morgue?"

He quickly downed the remainder of his drink. "Show me where I'm sleeping."

"Did you hear what I said, can you get me in to see Peter's body?"

He shook his shaggy head. "You're distraught—"

"Distraught?" I wondered if he picked up that word at a police sensitivity training program.

"I realize you been through a lot, you're spooked by what happened tonight and worried about your wife, okay, but you can't be going around talking about vampires."

"I didn't say anything about vampires."

"I know what you're thinking. Peter talked a good game, he convinced you he was into something supernatural—"

"No, he never convinced me, I laughed at him when he said he was a vampire. What convinced me was seeing him tonight."

"Well, they ain't going to let you put a stake through his heart or whatever it is you have in mind. You're stressed out, it's four-thirty in the morning, you won't be thinking this way after a night's sleep."

"I need to know he's dead."

"He is."

"Really, irretrievably dead."

"I saw the body. The coroner examined it. He's dead."

"Nobody believed me when I said Peter was killing people here and in Florida both, but I was right. So maybe I'm right again and maybe we should go to the morgue—"

Johnny walked over and took the glass from my hand. "You're talking nonsense."

He was right, I was talking nonsense.

"We're going to bed. And in the morning I don't want to hear no bullshit about vampires or morgues. If you're not careful you could end up at the Evergreen with Richard."

"Call one of your detective friends."

"And ask 'em what, ask 'em is the suspect still dead?"

"No. Ask if they've found out anything about Marianne."

"I gave them the number here, they'll phone us if—"

"Will you just do it for me?"

He put our glasses on the counter. "We go right to sleep after I make the call?"

"Deal."

FORTY

I awoke at noon Saturday hearing someone down in the kitchen, thinking, hoping Marianne had come home, but it was only Johnny Laflin rattling around in the cupboards looking for coffee. When I joined him in the kitchen he gave the answers before I could even ask the questions: Yes, he had already checked in with the detectives but, no, there wasn't any information on Marianne's whereabouts. Which is the same thing Johnny was told when he called right before we went to bed last night: No one knows anything.

While I made coffee Johnny said he planned to spend the day with the D.C. police. He'd come back to the house for dinner and give me a complete status report.

The rest of the day I waited by the phone for a call that never came. It was March 19th, the sun hot at work melting snow along with hope. And when I saw Johnny shuffling up our walk at dusk looking as tired as he had the previous night, I knew without asking that he carried no new information about Marianne.

I felt so numb during dinner that I don't remember what I prepared or how it tasted; Johnny had to keep repeating himself because I didn't always register the meaning of what he said, as if he spoke a language I was only just learning to understand.

We waited up until past midnight, Johnny making one last call at my request—still nothing about Marianne.

I arose Sunday morning facing the same hopeless routine.

Laflin was gone until late afternoon and when he came in the door he started in on a speech he had obviously rehearsed, saying he had received a call from Florida and had been ordered to return home Monday morning to file his report.

"I thought you were going to stay here until Marianne was found, that's what you said, that's what you promised."

"Either I go home or I get fired, that's the way they put it to me."

"When are you coming back?"

He raised his shoulders.

"Oh I see, you're *not* coming back."

"I ain't allowed to work on the case here, all I'm doing is shuttling information back and forth between you and the detectives, and now they say I'm making a nuisance of myself. As soon as they hear anything, they'll tell you."

"Sure."

He kept avoiding my eyes so I knew there was more bad news coming.

"What else?"

"Well, tonight. My wife's uncle lives over in Baltimore and I thought I'd, you know, spend the night there with him and his family, I ain't seen 'em in years, then I could leave right from their house for the airport first thing tomorrow morning."

With that I became convinced that the search for Marianne, like a political campaign a day before the election but already lost in the polls, had been abandoned in spirit, and I could too easily imagine never hearing from her again, never knowing what happened to her until, maybe, years from now, construction workers uncovered some human bones from a shallow grave or a jogger came across human remains, and tests are done that prove the remains are all that is left of my wife.

"Yeah, you go ahead, Johnny, don't let me keep you from visiting your wife's uncle."

"Everything that can be done *is* being done, nothin' I can add to it. You got friends, why don't you call 'em and have somebody come over to stay with you."

"Sure, we'll have a party."

Ignoring my sarcasm Johnny said there was something he had to warn me about.

"I know, I know. There's a chance she'll never be found, that's what you're going to say, that's going to be your cheerful little parting message, right?"

"That's a possibility, yeah, but what I was going to say was, there's talk, and it's just a theory right now, no one's taking it seriously, but there's talk that maybe you and Peter were in this together after all, that maybe since he was sick and was about to die anyway, you two had an arrangement that he'd do all those killings for you, including your wife."

I thought I had lost my capacity to be astonished but obviously I hadn't. "You're not serious."

"Someone turns up dead or missing, the spouse is always a suspect."

"This is incredible, this is un-fucking-believable. Now along with worrying about Marianne, I have to consider the possibility I might be arrested again?"

"Get yourself a lawyer."

"Yeah, I'll do that, thanks." Then under my breath I called him a sonofabitch.

Before he left, Laflin gave me the names of the detectives who were in charge of various aspects of the search for Marianne, telling me not to hesitate calling them for updates.

"Or if I feel an urge to confess," I said before thanking him as insincerely as I could. I stood at the door watching him leave, wanting to call him back.

For the next hour I sat alone in the living room feeling guilty for my ingratitude toward Johnny and wishing I had his wife's uncle's number in Baltimore so I could call and apologize. I didn't bother fixing anything to eat and television made no sense at all. Nothing left to do except wait in an empty house for something else to happen.

It finally did at ten P.M. with a light tapping knock on the front door.

FORTY-ONE

Dressed all in black—turtleneck sweater, woolen trousers, double-breasted jacket—he carried under his arm a large box wrapped in shiny red foil.

"I'm not insane," he said before I had a chance to invite him in or even speak his name.

"It's still a good line, Richard. I'm glad you're here." I was convinced Richard knew more about his brother's activities and associates than he ever told the police, but I hadn't been allowed to talk to him after Peter's death. Now I could.

He still hadn't stepped over the threshold so I said, "Come in, come in."

"Thank you, Roscoe."

I led him into the living room, then asked what was in the box.

"Something for you."

I waited for a further explanation but Richard said nothing as he placed the box on our couch and turned to look at me with those bulging gray eyes.

I said I was sorry about Peter.

Richard smiled. "He was troubled."

No disagreement there.

"Have they found your wife yet?" he asked cheerfully.

"No, but I was hoping you could help."

"Of course—how?"

"Do you remember anything Peter might have said about people he had hired or houses he had rented, somewhere he might have taken Marianne after he kidnapped her, someone who might have helped him?"

"The police have questioned me about that relentlessly."

"I know they have."

"They even act as if *I'm* the guilty party."

"Hell, Richard, they're thinking I'm guilty of something too."

"Are you?"

"Am I what?"

"Guilty of something."

"You mean Peter's death?"

He smiled. "I'm afraid I can't help you find your wife."

"There must be something—"

"*No,* there's nothing. But don't worry, I'm sure she'll be found—and not dead either."

"I hope so. Are you . . ." I wasn't sure how to phrase it. ". . . on leave from the Evergreen?"

"Actually I have been graduated from the Evergreen."

"Released?"

"Ooo, that sound's so animalish—'the creature was released into the forest to fend for itself.' Released, yes."

"Congratulations. Will Ralph miss you?"

"Ralph?"

"Your suite mate."

"Ah."

I waited for some more illuminating response but none came and

I figured I might as well be talking to that box he'd put on the couch.

"Where are you going from here?" I asked. "Back to Europe?"

"Peter bought a boat, did you know that?"

"Well, he said—"

"I plan to cruise the Caribbean, are you interested in coming with me?"

"I—"

"Just joking. Actually I've already hired a crew, an entire little family, Captain Daddy, Cook Mommy, and Little Mate Sis. They should last me a while, don't you think?"

"I—"

"All these years the wrong brother has been locked up as insane. The Tummelier family crisis that precipitated this mistake occurred simultaneously with your own family crisis, were you aware of that?"

This time I didn't even try to reply, I just let him talk.

"Our parents had brought a little adopted brother back from Europe, Donald showing up the selfsame week your father committed suicide, but you never knew about little Donald because we kept him a secret. In any case there was an accident, a tragic but wrongful death, and I was blamed for little Donald's passing, though in fact Peter was responsible. But rather than allowing Peter to be tucked away in Switzerland, I went in his stead. How wonderfully generous I am."

Was any of this true? I tried to question Richard but he kept giving spectacularly obscure answers and in the end I was too battered to process any new revelations about wrongful deaths and who might be responsible for them. I settled for telling Richard that Peter never mentioned anything to me about an adopted brother.

"No, he wouldn't, would he? Well, I simply must be off. This box contains something of Peter's, I'm sure he would want you to have it."

When I reached for the box, Richard roughly grabbed my wrist. "I couldn't *bear* to see it again, do open your present *after* I've left, won't you?" Then he hurried for the door, saying just one word before he left: "Dondo."

Where had I heard that name before?

FORTY-TWO

I opened the package to see a face staring out at me. It was ugly: menacingly, turgidly, bone-mud-mean ugly. Pulling the little beast partially out of the box for a better look, I saw it was dressed in a black velvet Little Lord Fauntleroy suit. Two feet tall with an oversized head and protruding ears, the doll almost made me laugh it was so wonderfully bizarre and I could easily believe it had been Peter's. But why did he want me to have it—or had Richard told the truth about that? The Tummeliers were so unreliably strange you never knew what was sincere, what was a joke.

When I looked at the the doll again, at that hard painted face, I got the spookiest feeling that something wasn't right, that the doll was a message of sorts, a warning.

With my heart feeling suddenly large in my chest, I went around to make sure all the doors and windows were locked, wishing I had called someone to come over and stay with me now that Johnny had gone.

What time was it? Eleven-thirty. I could still call some of our friends and tell them what had happened to Marianne, what I've been through these past several days, friends who would be happy to come over at this hour, I wouldn't even have to ask. I decided to telephone three couples. I wanted people with me, lots of people.

I picked up the phone to make the first call and heard Laflin's voice in the earpiece. "Roscoe, that you?"

"Jesus!" I exclaimed with an anxious laugh that came out like a cough. "I just put the phone to my ear, getting ready to punch in a number, and I hear *you.*"

Unimpressed by this telephonic phenomenon, Johnny spoke in breathy hesitation. "I'm calling from Baltimore . . . a few minutes ago I checked in with the detectives and they told me . . . well, there's this . . . there's a *situation.*"

"They've found Marianne, they've found her body."

"No, nothing new about her."

"Then *what?*"

"You haven't talked to anyone about Peter thinking he was a vampire, have you?"

"No. Why?"

"Now, don't go getting all weird on me when I tell you, 'cause there's a perfectly logical explanation, the detectives think that Peter was involved in some kind of cult, vampire believers or Satan worshipers or whatever, and to build up the mystique about Peter being a vampire, to give some status to the cult, you know, to bring in more members—"

"Will you please tell me what's happened!"

"Peter's body is missing from the morgue."

And at that very moment I felt eyes on me. Turning quickly I saw no one in the room, no one except that hideous doll still half in its box, propped up on the couch and facing in my direction, exactly as I had left it but appearing now as if it were climbing out of the box.

"Roscoe?"

"You have no idea how I feel at this exact moment."

"Yeah I do. Peter almost had you convinced he's a vampire, you even wanted to go put a stake in his heart, and now the body has turned up missing—I can imagine how you feel."

"No you can't." My oversized heart grew larger with each terrified pump.

"Just keep in mind that somebody *stole* the body, it didn't get up off the slab and walk out on its own."

"How do you know, were you there?"

"Of course not, I'm in Baltimore."

"Then you can't be sure."

"I know what's possible and what's not—"

"And you also can't be sure Peter's not stalking his way over to my house right at this moment."

"I could call in and have a squad car—"

"Park outside my house? A lot of good it did us last time, didn't help Maring either. I'm going to have about two dozen friends come over, that's what I'm going to do."

"Good idea. But don't mention to them about Peter's body being stolen, the homicide squad is keeping this quiet, you can imagine the publicity if it gets out that the body of a multiple killer who claimed he was a vampire is missing, I ain't even supposed to be telling you."

"I don't give a rat's ass about bad publicity, I'm worried about looking out a window and seeing Peter standing there!"

"Hey come on, Roscoe."

"Come on yourself!" Did I have to say it, did I have to fucking say it? Peter's a vampire.

"Roscoe—"

"He's coming back for me. That's why Richard checked out of the Evergreen, so he and his vampire brother can leave together on that boat *but first they're going to come here and shanghai me!*"

"What do you mean, Richard checked out of the Evergreen?"

"I just wonder what they've done to Marianne."

"Roscoe, what do you mean about Richard checking out of the Evergreen?"

"He was here."

"He can't check himself out, he's under a criminal commitment order."

"Well, he was here. Do you know anything about Richard and Peter having an adopted brother?"

"No, what's that got to do—"

"I don't know. Jesus, Johnny, *Jesus.*"

"I'll come there."

"You're in Baltimore for chrissakes."

"You got the names of those detectives I gave you, call whichever one is on duty tonight and tell them about Richard being out, that he was at your house and you want a uniformed officer to be *in* the house with you. Then call your friends like you said, your neighbors, anyone you can convince to come over at this hour. Ain't nothing going to happen to you in a house full of people. You do that, I'll leave right now."

"Okay."

But the first thing I did after hanging up was get rid of that doll, no way was I going to have it staring at me. Picking up the box as if it contained nuclear waste, I hurried it out the kitchen door and to the garbage cans at the alley. After dumping the doll in, I pressed down on the garbage can's galvanized lid with both hands.

Watching shadows and half expecting Peter to intercept me before I made it back to the house, I ran through the grass, made wet and muddy by snowmelt, and slipped once to my knees. Panting through the kitchen door, I quickly turned around and locked it. Had Peter gotten into the house while I was out? Was he waiting for me, sitting on the couch where the doll had been or about to step around a doorway, still cadaverous, still holding that stained sheet around his wasted body, reaching out for me with a bony hand?

I grabbed for the phone as if it were a life ring, fearing the line would be dead, yes, of course, they've cut the line, isolated me from help—but when I placed the receiver to my ear I heard a strong steady dial tone.

I spent nearly twenty minutes on the phone, going into far more detail than I'd intended with various friends who hadn't known about

Marianne's disappearance and were appalled, asking for details. After I got a commitment from three couples to come to my house just as soon as they could, I called a homicide detective who promised to drive over right away, to question me about Richard Tummelier being out and about, *that's impossible,* the detective kept saying.

I still wasn't at ease when I finally put the phone down, but at least I had reason for hope: six of our friends and a police officer would all be here in less than half an hour, maybe fifteen minutes. I felt almost safe.

Until I heard something outside: the clattering of a metal garbage can lid, followed some seconds later by the sound of shattering glass in the kitchen.

FORTY-THREE

Tap, tap.

I want to scream. It swells inside me like something I need to get rid of, a piercing, head-back, two-handed scream, but instead of giving it release I choke it down, keeping that scream swallowed as I hurry to the hall closet and take out a softball bat.

Tap, tap.

Coming from the kitchen, someone—something—tapping on the tile floor.

I stand in the hallway and listen.

Tap, tap.

Hefting the bat in my right hand I take the eighteen most agonizing steps of my life, reaching the swinging door that leads into the kitchen. Is Peter waiting for me on the other side? It's impossible. Slowly pushing the door open, I see something on the floor.

The doll lies facedown in front of the outside door, which has had a pane of glass broken. But the greater horror isn't seeing the doll lying there, the greater horror is noticing that its little velvet slippers are covered in mud.

It has climbed out of the garbage can to run across the backyard and break through a windowpane of my door, to hurl itself inside my house. Then it tapped porcelain knuckles on the tile floor to get me in here with it.

I believe this. Impossible, but with heart and soul I believe it to be true. I need something more deadly than a softball bat, I need my dad's pistol. One last time. It's back up in the bedroom, I had forgotten to give the pistol to Laflin to take back to Florida with him and had in fact been sleeping with it under Marianne's pillow. But first, I think, before I go upstairs to arm myself, first I should walk over and stomp the doll's head into shards, making sure it can't follow on little muddy feet.

"Roscoe."

Marianne.

"Roscoe."

Softly calling my name from upstairs.

"Roscoe."

Still carrying the bat, I run through the hall and take the steps two at a time, turning a corner and pushing open our bedroom door to see arranged there on a chair in the corner of the room a vulgar tableau of Michelangelo's Pietà.

Richard as the Virgin Mother, a torn remnant of that bloody stained sheet from the trailer about his head and shoulders, his face turned down, eyes closed, left arm held low in presentation, the index finger of that left hand pointing, and sprawled across his lap is Peter, Richard's right arm holding the naked corpse of his brother as the slain Christ with head thrown back so that his face is on a plane parallel with the floor, left leg slightly elevated, right foot down, right arm hanging loose in front of Richard's right knee.

This profanity is further mocked by a black homburg jammed tightly on Peter's skull.

The two of them are statues remaining utterly still until Richard

slowly . . . slowly . . . turns his face in my direction and from beneath
that dirty shroud he looks with bulging eyes directly at me, opening
his mouth to speak plaintively in Marianne's voice: "Roscoe."

A great seizing pain blooms in my chest, the pain too large for my
chest cavity to contain, preventing me from moving or calling out or
even breathing. Maybe it's that scream I've been keeping down or
maybe I'm having a heart attack but I know I have never experienced
pain like this, no injury I've ever sustained, no broken bone, none of
the fishhooks I've embedded in my flesh as a child, nothing ever hurt
like this.

"Roscoe," he says again exactly as Marianne would speak my name.

I wait until my heart unseizes, until I can fill my lungs with a ghostly
rattle, then I walk stiffly to the bed and withdraw my father's gun from
beneath Marianne's pillow.

And I stand there, armed with pistol and bat but feeling as naked
as Peter's corpse.

Richard throws off the torn sheet from his head and slowly gets up,
allowing Peter's body to slide-flop onto the floor like so much
butcher's meat. And as he stands I see that Richard is garishly magnif-
icent. Like a colorized movie, everything about him is more intense
than reality would permit, his eyes too gray and his beard too blond
and his skin much too smooth and white, like marble, like alabaster.
He is dressed in costume, his trousers rich black velvet as from the pelt
of some butter-fed mammal, his white shirt all shiny bright silk with
an excess of ruffles and pleats, the cuffs closed by large onyx links that
shine as black as his brother's eyes once did. And Richard's eyes have
changed too, instead of bulging as they normally do, they protrude so
far from their sockets that it seems they will surely roll out onto the
smooth white cheeks.

To avoid those terrible eyes I look down at Peter's body on the floor:
bones sticking up like small, blunt tentpoles under a pocked bluish-
ashen skin that still bears signs of an appalling infection, though most
of the sores have dried. Peter is dead and two days of cold storage have
only advanced his body's physical beggary. I notice, under the brim of
that stupid homburg, that the chewed remnants of his earlobes have
curled and discolored like meat left too long in the refrigerator.

Then I look back at Richard and, keeping the pistol leveled at him, I demand to know what he's done with Marianne.

He half closes his eyes—perhaps that's as far as his eyelids will reach across those massively protruding orbs—and raises his nose to sniff the air. "I smell your fear." He smiles in a kind of exaggerated ecstasy. "Oh but it excites me." And rubs himself across the groin.

"You sick fuck."

"Mmm, I grow erect."

"I'm going to kill you."

"I am *engorged.*"

Do it, I tell myself. He's deranged, he has stolen his brother's body from the morgue and dragged it here. What else is he capable of? *Shoot him.* And the only thing that stops me from firing is the vague hope that he can tell me, that he *will* tell me where Marianne is, what he's done to her.

"Where is she, where's my wife?"

"She resides in a far better place than you could ever provide for her, old chum."

I cock the pistol.

And still, even now when I'm about to kill him, Richard mocks me: "His hands full of weapons, Roscoe Bird promises to assault me with his mighty bat, to pump his hot bullets into me. Oh yes, *do it.*"

I pull the trigger just as Richard opens his left hand letting six cartridges clatter to the floor. "Oh his chambers are empty," he says, "how very limp of him."

I'm lost. It's not just that the pistol is empty, I feel *spiritually* disarmed. What sin do I carry that has caused all this to happen to me, of what am I guilty to be so punished? Sensing my capitulation, Richard holds a hand in my direction and orders, "Come here."

I can't even say no, all I'm able to manage is a childish shaking of my head.

"Don't be petulant."

I'm still shaking my head.

"I mean only to worship you," he says softly in a voice I find strangely appealing. "Your very flesh is life-giving to me. You are my god and I, your terrible worshiper, your supplicant, venerator, deifier.

And faithful too, your exclusive predator, devoted to hunting only you, firing your imagination. You look out into the darkness, night's night, and call, 'Who's there, what do you want?' How unloved you would feel if I didn't answer, you'd have to *invent* creatures lurking in darkness, wanting you, only you, witches and warlocks, werewolves and Frankensteins, horror movies and ghost stories told around a camp-fire. But now, here, tonight, in this room, now when you look into the darkness and ask who's out there, what do you want, it is I who answer, *I* am here, *I* want you, you are still loved, let me humble myself at your life-giving flesh. Oh Roscoe, my eucharist, come, bring me communion."

Mesmerized into obedience, I tuck the empty pistol into my waist-band and step toward him. Although a portion of me is still calculating how, when I'm close enough, I can swing the bat at his head, another portion has already surrendered. I'm a kid again and Richard is the older boy who knows everything; I'm poor and he's rich; I'm small, he's big; I have nothing, he has everything.

"For what is god without psalmsinger, prey without predator? From whom will you run if not me? That's it, closer, let us complete this prayer. It is bone dust and blood lust, it is inevitable."

"Are you going to kill me?" I ask cringingly, advancing another step, starting to raise my hand for Richard to take.

"Like father, like son."

I stop.

"Brother Peter blabbed to Father Curtis what I had done to Baby Donald."

What is he talking about?

"Peter kills exactly as I taught him to, we are indistinguishable in our methods, Peter is my mirror image. But Peter has a soft spot, a low-grade infection of guilt that he could never seem to shake entirely, and I blame your influence for that."

"You killed my father?"

"Oh now who's being the brilliant boy," Richard says, a sarcastic teacher addressing his most doltish student. "Yes, I killed him, using the selfsame gun you have there in your pants."

"Why?"

"Haven't you been listening? I buried little Donald, that noisy child our parents adopted in Europe, it was only a game, burying him, he was supposed to tap against the undersides of the boards I laid on top of him, *tap, tap,* so that Peter would hear it and dig him up, but I suppose little Donald was too young for such games, he suffocated. When Peter and I finally dug him up, I told Peter that Donald wasn't really dead, he was only caught out of his body, the way I'd transported Peter out of *his* body. Peter wanted so to believe me, to believe that I had placed Donald—his spirit, his essence, his soul—in that adorable doll that Father brought back from Europe.

"But guilt tormented Peter. He knew what I'd do to him if he snitched, but he went to your father for protection, begging to be adopted, oh I heard all about it. Then Peter made the mistake of telling Curtis about little Donald's demise, and when Curtis confronted me on the dock, that big pistol in his hand, I broke down crying, confessing, waiting until your father got close enough that I could take the gun from him and blow his brains out."

For the first time since entering this bedroom I experience an emotion more powerful than fear: I hate Richard enough to dismember him with my bare hands.

"Oh I never thought you would captain our boat," he continues, enjoying himself, *"never.* I let Peter play out his fanciful plot simply to keep him amused but I knew his dream of sailing the ocean blue with his friend so true would never pan out. No, I never had any intention of trusting *you* with my immortal life."

He steps to close the gap between us.

"What have you done with Marianne?"

Richard rubs his belly. "Mm-*mm* good."

I raise the bat.

He laughs at me. "At this moment you have some five or six quarts of blood circulating through your body, I need half. Shall I tell you about it? Once I've downed a salty quart of you, you'll go into shock, your pulse will race, you'll experience a cold sweat, your pupils will dilate, you'll suffer a horrible hunger for air, mental confusion, the whole nine yards. Your capillary flow will have shut down but arterial blood pressure is maintained, thank goodness. By the time I drink the second quart and start in on the third, you'll be all but dead. So. Shall we?"

"You killed my father . . ."

"By George I believe you got it!"

"My wife . . ."

"Oh I left her dripping. Any other loose ends need tying?"

I stand there in dumb rage.

"Your turn," Richard says, raising his arms like great wings. Holding them out, he seems to grow taller, somehow to increase his bulk, puffing up with breath and tensed muscle to make himself larger, to grow several inches, to become bigger and bigger until it seems that his head will touch the ceiling, that he will fill the entire corner of that room.

I can't believe it.

He rushes me.

As I brace myself, I see Peter coming swiftly off the floor just behind Richard. And the fact that Peter still wears that homburg makes him not ridiculous but somehow all the more sinister.

Tell me now that spirits walk and I will believe. That ghosts haunt houses where crimes of passion took place, that witches cackle, fairies cavort with fireflies, that if you capture a leprechaun he must tell where his pot of gold is hidden, that some men change into wolves at the full moon: I will believe what is unbelievable because I have seen it to be so.

Peter's naked corpse arises not with the effort of muscle pulling bone but as if that corpse is quickly levitating, arms elevating first, pulled by unseen strings, the body coming erect and grabbing Richard from behind just before he reaches me.

They both scream. Peter's emaciated arms encircle Richard, and the brothers fall to the floor hissing and screeching, feral animals at one another's neck, snarling.

It takes me precious seconds to shake off my paralysis and hurry over to them where, holding the bat with both hands, I take a golf swing that lands with a satisfyingly meaty *thwap* across Richard's back. It doesn't faze him. In fact he turns to grab me and if it weren't for Peter's arms around him, Richard would've had me.

Tossing the bat away and drawing the pistol out of my pants, I gather up the cartridges Richard had dropped, fumbling to get them into the chambers. When the pistol is finally loaded I shout at Peter, "Get out of the way!"

But as I step back to avoid their intertwined bodies—how they shriek, barking and snorting, squealing like pigs, like butchered beef—I see no hope of separating them. Richard is biting at Peter's face, actually pulling off mouthfuls of mortified flesh.

I aim.

The first shot splatters scalp tissue and hair from off the top of Richard's head, yet he continues battling Peter, the two of them still embraced, making charnel-house racket.

I fire again, the sound blasting throughout the room, the bullet blowing a hole halfway down Richard's spine. The pistol is shaking so severely in my hand that I can hear the floating firing pin clatter, but this trembling is more from excitement than fear. Aroused by the explosions, by the thrill of killing the beast, I wish for the noise to be even louder, the buck of the pistol in my hand harder, the muzzle flash brighter. And when Richard finally slips his brother's dead grasp and quickly comes for me, I joyously fire into his face, feeling an urge to whoop as the bullets strike, one of them exploding his bulging right eye, the second ripping open a newly bloodied mouth lower in his beard, the third hitting him in the forehead and blowing apart his skull like a dropped melon.

He falls over on his side, one leg straight out and twitching in death throes. I go to him and kick the monster repeatedly in his temple, kick him until my leg muscles ache and the bones of his skull separate and his brain is out on the bedroom floor.

I feel saturated with death and yet look around for more.

Peter.

I kneel at his side. Necrosis has dried his eyes until they have separated and shrunk back from the surrounding tissue. Looking into those dry, dead eyes I wonder what they see.

Yet not dead because his hand, the one tattooed with a bird in its palm, motions for me to lean close.

I dread to, but I do.

"I've hungered for your touch," he whispers with breath of mold and rot, quoting my favorite song, *"a long lonely time."*

"Peter."

"Kill me again."

I don't argue.

Positioning the muzzle just above the bridge of his nose, between those eyes that were once black and wet, I hold it there long enough for a prayer, then squeeze the trigger onto one final explosion.

In spite of the revulsion I feel, in spite of the old sores that mark him, I take that naked body in my arms and hold it tightly.

I am aware only then of a commotion outside the house. Still holding Peter, I step to the window and see various friends, though there seem to be many more than I called. Unable to get in through my locked doors and having heard gunshots, they stand now in the front yard and out on the street that runs by my house. Some of them have flashlights. And when they see me looking out the window, those lights are shined on my face and on the body I hold in my arms. In the distance a siren sounds, coming closer.

Looking down on that gathering, I imagine a medieval village having been roused in the middle of the night by reports of the beast out and about—such reports would be believed back then of course, back when the beast was real—and now here the villagers gather, torches held high, their blood up, needing to confront what they know in their hearts and souls lurks somewhere out there in the darkness, a beast that worships them by stalking among their number, that needs them to survive, this most faithful and exclusive predator.

Standing at the window, burdened by the body of a friend, the beast who bowed out gracefully, I feel a pair of arms encircle me from behind.

FORTY-FOUR

Marianne was in shock. She kept her arms around me as we went downstairs to let in our friends, their number having grown to a dozen or more because the people I originally called went on to contact others. When they gathered around us and began asking questions—what happened, who was shooting, is anyone hurt?—Marianne buried her head into my shoulder like a weary and overly shy child refusing to look at or respond to anyone.

One of our friends was a physician, an obstetrician, and she finally was able to separate Marianne from me to take her into another room for a cursory examination. Meanwhile an ambulance was called.

The detective I had called—that was his siren sounding—was a tall black man who seemed too young for the task at hand; I hadn't met him before but he assured me he was familiar with the case. On the way upstairs I told him my version of what had happened: that Richard Tummelier had stolen his brother's body from the morgue and had carried the body here. He'd also brought my wife, though I didn't know that until later. When Richard attacked me I defended myself by emptying a revolver into him. One of the bullets apparently went wide and hit Peter's corpse in the forehead. I didn't say anything about vampires.

The death scene in my bedroom clearly shocked the young detective, though he did his professional best to appear blasé.

Leaning over to look at what was left of Richard's skull, the detective asked, "The gunshots do all this?"

"I kicked his head in," I admitted. "He said he had killed my wife. I hadn't seen her yet so I believed him and after I shot him I kicked his head in."

The detective nodded as if he didn't blame me.

After the ambulance arrived, our obstetrician friend called out from the bottom of the steps to say that she would ride to the hospital with Marianne. "Roscoe, Marianne needs you, are you coming?"

I looked at the detective, who apologized but said I'd have to stay around until his lieutenant and captain showed up. So I went to the top of the stairway and told our friend that I'd join her and Marianne at the hospital as soon as I could. Marianne was standing down there looking small and forlorn, all the more waiflike for being barefoot.

"Honey, they won't let me leave just yet," I told her.

She glanced up at me like an orphan who'd just been rejected for adoption.

"I'll come as soon as I can," I said, wondering what Richard had done to her and wishing I had kicked him in the head a few more times, even harder. "Make sure she gets something on her feet," I told our friend.

When the police brass arrived they cleared all of our remaining friends from the house and asked me to sit on the living-room couch and explain everything I knew about the Tummeliers, then go through the events that had just taken place. One of the uniformed officers—there were four or five of them along with a similar number of plainsclothes detectives—held a video camera on me. Everyone was courteous. Never had I faced such an attentive audience and as I looked at all those expectant faces I wondered how their expressions would change if I said that Peter's corpse attacked its brother, that a living corpse saved my life and spoke to me, that vampires were real, would those faces show anger to hear such obvious lies or would they turn away in pity?

"There's a rational explanation for everything that's happened," I opened, explaining how I first met Richard and Peter Tummelier back on Hambriento Island off the southwest coast of Florida. Even as children they were obsessed by the supernatural and apparently experimented with what they believed to be out-of-body experiences that led to the death of a little boy who had been adopted by their parents. Richard was responsible for the child's death but tried to convince Peter that the boy's soul had been transferred to a doll, that the boy therefore wasn't really dead.

"That's the doll you found on my kitchen floor," I told the police. When Peter went to my father with news of what Richard had done to their adopted brother, my father confronted Richard and Richard killed him.

"I want that on the record. My father didn't commit suicide, he was murdered by Richard Tummelier." And although Richard's parents might not have been aware that he killed my father, I speculated, they obviously knew he was responsible for the adopted child's death because they covered up that crime and sent Richard to a mental institution in Switzerland. Peter kept in touch with me sporadically over the years, then showed up here a week ago to ask me to captain a boat for him on an extended cruise. To force me to accept, Peter killed people I had grudges against, hoping to implicate me and thereby force me to run away with him to avoid arrest. The Tummeliers kidnapped my wife, but I didn't know where she was held or by whom.

"At one point Richard had her at the Evergreen," Lieutenant Jim-something explained. "We found one of her shoes there. Rope, tape. And those two bodies under the trailer? There's evidence that Richard killed at least one of them at his cottage at the Evergreen. But we still don't know what Peter died of, how he managed to overpower and murder people in his condition. How long had he been sick like that?"

"A long time," I lied without hesitation. "I don't know how he found the strength to kill, force of will I suppose." After Richard escaped from the Evergreen, I continued, he brought me that doll, which Peter believed contained the child's spirit, and I put it in a garbage can out back. When Richard returned later he dragged the doll's feet across the muddy yard and pushed the doll through a pane of glass and into the kitchen. Richard carried his brother's body here and he had also brought Marianne, though I didn't know this until after I killed him. How he accomplished everything without being caught or seen, I have no idea. The Tummeliers were both crazy but obviously they were also enormously resourceful.

"As I told the detective who first got here, Richard attacked me and I emptied a revolver into him and in the course of doing that I apparently put a round in Peter's corpse. It's bizarre, I realize, but nothing supernatural has happened, there are rational explanations for everything."

The lieutenant asked why I kept insisting nothing supernatural had occurred. "No one has said otherwise, have they?"

"No."

When I saw Johnny Laflin standing at the back of the living room, I requested to speak with him privately. He came over and asked, "How's your wife?"

"She's been taken to a hospital. Do you think you can arrange for me to be released, I'd like to go see her."

"You got it. Mainly these detectives are just tying up loose ends, you ain't being held on any charges. I'll have you out of here in five minutes."

"Thanks, Johnny."

"They didn't get what you were trying to say by insisting nothing supernatural happened but I read you loud and clear."

"You did?"

"Sure. Gettin' your head straight after Peter twisted you around with all his vampire talk."

"Yes." But actually the truth lay elsewhere: As those who witnessed the miracles of Christ went on to deny Him, Faith bound me to deny Satan's magic—it never happened.

"Let me go talk to the lieutenant, then I'll drive you to the hospital."

On the way there, Johnny asked me if I'd been told what had been found among Richard's personal papers stored in a safe at the Evergreen.

"I'm not sure I want to know."

"You do. Believe me, you do. When the parents died, Mr. and Mrs. Tummelier, they left everything to Peter because Richard had been judged mentally incompetent. And Peter's will, which was found in that safe, left everything to you."

"What do you mean, everything?"

"Everything as in millions of dollars stashed in banks all over the world, in coastal towns that can be reached by boat. Property too, beach houses. A big boat. Everything Peter and Richard had set up for that permanent cruise they were planning."

I successfully fought an impulse to say I didn't want any of it.

Johnny hummed tunelessly as he drove. "The only thing that surprised me about the statement you gave was you saying that Peter had been sick all along. 'Cause you swore to me he got in that condition overnight."

"I must've been wrong."

Marianne waited for me not in a hospital room but down in the lobby, sitting with several of our friends who explained that she had been examined thoroughly and appeared to have only superficial wounds: scratches, cuts, and bruises. They said that Marianne obviously was still shaken—confused, frightened—and should stay in the hospital overnight, though she refused to be admitted, insisting she wanted to be alone with me.

I knelt at her chair and told her I loved her.

Marianne's big brown eyes were bloodshot and she looked weary enough to collapse, but when she smiled, her face turned radiant and I knew she'd be okay. Pulling me close for a kiss, she whispered a queer message, "I'm warning you, get me out of here."

Neither one of us wanted to stay in our house that night so I had one of our friends call ahead to reserve a hotel suite downtown. Once we were in the room I ran a tub of hot water and helped Marianne undress. Missing her these past days, worrying that she had been killed, and now seeing her without clothes, so close to me, I was aroused, as if we were lovers on a tryst instead of two victims who came to this hotel suite to recover from crimes that had been committed against us. I wanted to feel between her legs, to touch her small high breasts, to place my mouth on her nipples until they hardened against my tongue. But of course she needed rest and comfort, so as I bathed her, shampooed her hair, and then dried her with a large thick towel, I carefully guarded against touching her selfishly.

I had her sit on the toilet seat so I could dry between her toes, which I resisted kissing. When she asked what was wrong with my eye, I told her it happened when I was being arrested.

"Poor Roscoe."

I took a quick shower. We hadn't brought any nightclothes and settled for putting on the hotel's robes, after which we lay on the king-sized bed, on top of the covers. We didn't talk further about what had happened, we didn't need words, we needed each other. We fell asleep embraced.

Then just before dawn she woke me with her mouth.

FORTY-FIVE

My robe had been opened and Marianne was down between my legs. When she noticed I was awake she came up smiling, wiping her mouth in a manner that was purposely vulgar. "I want you to make love to me." Before I could reply, she corrected herself, "No, that's not exactly right. When you were being so careful with me, giving me a bath and drying me off, you were making love to me then. What I want now is different, what I want now is for you to fuck me."

I pulled her up to the pillows but when I tried to open her robe, she held it closed. "Go out and get some rubbers."

Which confused me. We'd never used rubbers, we wanted a baby.

"You can find an all-night drugstore. Get dressed and go buy some rubbers, a big box of them." She laughed. "A case."

"Are you okay?"

"I'm hot." She reached in her robe, down between her legs, and when she brought her hand out she drew slippery fingers across my mouth. "Now go find those rubbers and get back here quick or I'll start without you."

Although concerned about how she was acting—God knows she had reason enough for not being herself—I got out of bed and dressed, asking once again if she was okay, was she serious about the rubbers, was she sure she wanted to do this.

She insisted she was sure, laughing at her own sexual urgency and prodding me once more to hurry. But then right before I left, Marianne spoke sadly, "If I were me I'd leave me."

Assuming she meant to say, "If I were *you* I'd leave me," I told her I would never leave her, *never.*

When I returned twenty minutes later Marianne was lying naked on the bed, stroking herself and watching with an animal hunger as I entered the room. Seeing her masturbate like that, openly, wantonly, both aroused and worried me. If she was still suffering from psychological trauma, she needed to see a doctor, be given tranquilizers, hospitalized.

"Marianne—"

"Hurry! You be the gladiator, I'll be the slave girl." She grinned. "You can hurt me if you want."

"Maybe we should call—"

"Someone for a threesome? That could be interesting, who'd you have in mind, someone we know or a stranger? I could go out and pick up some guy at a bar, no, you want a whore, don't you, I'll be your whore, come here."

"Honey, are you sure?"

She barked out a rude, loud laugh. "About which part?"

"About wanting to do this?"

"With you or without you, doll," she said, that hand working faster between her legs.

Marianne watched intently as I undressed, making me feel strangely shy. As soon as I knelt on the bed she rolled me over on my back and put the rubber on, knocking away my hands as I tried to help.

When I reached for her she said she changed her mind. Then she laughed at me, saying of course she wanted to fuck—but I wasn't to touch her breasts. Then she insisted I suck them as hard as I could.

And in the end she was right about what she wanted: not to make love but to fuck.

When we finally finished—more accurately, when she finished with me—I got up and headed for the bathroom.

"I'm in love with you," Marianne said from the bed.

"I love you too."

I was just to the bathroom door when she spoke again, "And, Roscoe?"

"Yeah, hon," I answered without turning around.

Came the voice: *"When I say I'm in love you best believe I'm in love, L-U-V."*

ABOARD THE TRAWLER YACHT *R&R VAMP*
SOMEWHERE IN THE CARIBBEAN ISLANDS

With an array of electronics that would put a spy ship to shame, since dawn I have tracked the sailboat from a discreet distance. I spotted the couple onshore two days ago. He is intense and gawky, she is pretty and unhappy. As they walked along the beach, he tried to hold her hand, she wouldn't let him. They're ripe.

Now at dusk their sailboat, a twenty-eight-footer, approaches windward of a small green island, drops sails, and motors through a deep-water inlet leading to an isolated cove.

I follow. The sailboat's captain, this thin young man in his late twenties, sees me just as he's setting anchor. Outraged that I've invaded his privacy with my fifty-five-foot trawler, he wastes no time hailing me on the radio.

"Captain," he says after we've made contact, "would you *please* find anchorage elsewhere? You're being incredibly discourteous. This cove is too small for both of us. If you try to anchor here and if the wind picks up, we'll swing into each other. Over."

I tell him that I'm having trouble with my hydraulic steering mechanism and must remain in protected anchorage until I've corrected the problem.

"This is exactly why you smudgepots have the reputation you do. Out!"

O petulance.

After setting my hook I watch through a nightscope ($2,859, worth every penny of it) as the young man goes about his duties, coiling lines and securing sails, while his unhappy friend stands in the cockpit with her arms crossed over her breasts. She's staring in my direction. He occasionally turns toward her and says something, perhaps suggesting that she pitch in and help, Come on it'll be fun, I'll tell you what all these lines are called, but she doesn't bother answering, she ignores the geek.

Some hours later I hail him on the radio and quietly listen as he berates me again for interrupting their privacy, then I apologize and say I'd like to make it up to him. "My wife suggests having you aboard for dinner. Over."

He immediately declines and signs off but a few minutes later calls back and, obviously at his mate's insistence, reluctantly accepts the dinner invitation. "Can we bring anything?" he asks without enthusiasm. "Some wine? Over."

Oh no, I tell him, just bring yourselves.

Then during dinner—freshly caught lobster and a lighthearted Moselle—Marianne flirts with the young man outrageously, smiling when he speaks, laughing openmouthed at his wooden witticisms, nodding seriously as he explains the computer programs he's designing for an environmental group. She takes every opportunity to touch him, a hand on his wrist, a breast pressing his upper arm when she leans in close as if to avoid missing a word of what he says.

The young sailor—Andy, I think, but there've been so many of them—is clearly flummoxed by all this attention from my wife, her large dark brown eyes riveted on him, her perfume in his nostrils, her hands on and about his person. When Marianne invites him topside to look at the stars and listen to some Wagner, Andy glances over at his sailing partner as if to ask, *Should I?* She waves him off, she couldn't care less.

I watch as they leave, an improbable couple: Andy wearing cutoff jeans, a Greenpeace T-shirt, dirty sneakers; my barefoot wife in a beautiful white cotton Mexican peasant dress that rests low on her smooth brown shoulders. He wears glasses that keep sliding down his hooked nose, which, combined with his overbite, makes his face unfortunately ratlike; Marianne has never been more beautiful, wearing a bold red lipstick, her eye shadow a light blue, looking dramatic.

Once they're topside I turn my attention to Andy's sailing mate, Linda, I believe it was. Seeing that the Moselle is gone, I check the wine cabinet. "I bet you'd like some liebfraumilch, I keep some just for young women like you."

Linda looks at me dumbly until I show her the picture on the label, then she nods yes-please. She's wearing a wraparound blue skirt and a bikini top that displays what she apparently considers among her leading assets. She has light red hair, a lot of it, and actually Linda is quite pretty in a bouncy, healthy, California-American sort of way.

She doesn't hesitate telling me how terribly disappointed she's been in this sailing vacation. Back in Chicago, where she and Andy both live, she never even dated him, not her type, too nerdy, but she agreed to go on this sailing vacation because he made it sound like so much fun, *sailing through the Caribbean,* and of course he was paying for everything except her airfare. But it's turned out to be a disaster. Andy spent all his money on the boat charter and has been trying to get through the vacation on the cheap, avoiding tying up at docks because of the fees, refusing to take her to nightclubs or restaurants.

"He sails and I do the cooking," Linda tells me. "If I wanted to cook I could've stayed home, at least my kitchen is bigger than a closet and doesn't stink. I mean we haven't even had a tropical drink yet, he says why pay five bucks for a drink when he's got a whole box of cheap wine on the boat."

I commiserate with her, agreeing that there's nothing quite as unattractive in a man as parsimony.

She asks if I own this boat or am I chartering it.

I laugh a little, charmed by her naïveté. "Not to put too fine of a point on it," I tell her, "but the truth of that matter is, I'm rich. Filthy rich." I manage to elongate that final word into two syllables and laugh again.

Linda laughs too, leaning toward me in a way that causes her breasts to spill forth and nestle together, creating an absolutely intriguing line of cleavage, over which her pale blue eyes appraise me as she asks, "Why is your wife coming on to Andy?"

"Oh you noticed."

"You guys aren't into kinky stuff like switching partners, are you?"

"Of course not."

"Because if you are, your wife is getting the short end of the stick."

"Is that a comment on your friend's endowment?"

She giggles and pushes my arm as if to say, *Oh you rogue.*

I pour her some more liebfraumilch.

Linda assures me she's pretty old-fashioned when it comes to matters sexual, can't be too careful these days, but if the truth be known, the idea of trading places, my wife going off with Andy in his dinky little sailboat so that she, Linda, could spend the rest of her vacation with me on *this* boat, why, gosh, she finds that mighty appealing—not that she's suggesting it of course.

"Of course not," I agree. "Actually my wife is more adventuresome in this area than I would ever dream of being. I'm kind of old-fashioned, just like you."

We nod together, co-conspirators in our elevated morality.

Overhead we hear the opening strains of "Ride of the Valkyries," followed quickly by the slap of sneakers and of barefeet making a short run on the deck, then a scream and a shriek, fear and delight, music up.

"What are they *doing?*" Linda asks, rolling her eyes.

"God knows."

When she gets up from the table I ask if she's going topside.

"Not on your life. I don't care what they're doing, he means nothing to me. If it wasn't for having one of those airplane tickets you can't change without paying a penalty I would've flown home days ago. Who's doll is this?"

"It belonged to a friend of mine."

"Ugly, isn't it?"

"Yes, rather."

"What kind of boat is this?"

"Goes by different names. The configuration is along the classic trawler lines but I suppose the power plant and the appointments qualify it as a true motor yacht." Anticipating her next question, I tell Linda the boat cost a million dollars. A *mill*-yun dollars.

She can't help grinning. "How come you call it *R&R Vamp?*"

"Ah, there hangs a tale."

"Pardon?"

"Tell me, Linda, do you believe in vampires?"

She scrunches up her pretty little face. "You mean like Dracula?"

"Yes."

"It's like a folk tale, isn't it? Like goblins and trolls?"

"You don't think vampires actually exist, you don't think they really walk among us?"

"Gosh, do you?"

"Here's what I think, I think that if someone *believes* she is a vampire, believes she needs the blood of a living human victim to survive, believes she will die without it, and then if she acts upon that belief to the extent of killing people for their blood, and if, for whatever reason, she thrives on this regimen, then for all practical purposes she *is* a vampire. Or at least, given the premises I've just outlined, it makes little difference either to the victims she feeds upon or to the husband who, to protect her, finds himself serving as her daytime guardian, it makes little difference whether she is truly a vampire or 'merely' believes herself to be one."

As I speak, Linda holds a half smile on her lightly freckled face. She thinks I'm putting her on.

"Are you a natural redhead?" I ask.

Linda squeals a little, delight and shock performed exclusively for my benefit. She lowers her face and looks up seductively. "That's for me to know and you to find out." Her eyes are *invitational*. I say nothing. Realizing I haven't taken the bait, she wiggles it a little. "But I guess there's *one* way to find out."

"I'd love to but Marianne has warned me never to cuckold a vampire."

"Huh?"

"She once said, 'If I were me I'd leave me.' I thought she had misspoken and meant to say, 'If I were *you* I'd leave me.' But in fact she meant exactly what she said."

"I still don't—"

Just then Marianne comes down with her eyes glazed and her lipstick smeared, looking like a woman on a drunken sexual spree. Blood is all about the bodice of her dress.

"My God what happened to you?" Linda asks.

Still hungry, Marianne holds out a hand.

Aghast, the young woman looks to me but I'm already standing and turning from her, heading toward a passageway that leads to a cabin with a specially fitted door. It is in here, that heavily barred door closed against the sounds of my wife feeding, that I take down world charts and plot a course.

ACKNOWLEDGMENTS

I wish to thank as much as I possibly can (without actually handing over any money): The Honorable Damian Russell; Barbara Parker; Headline House; and most especially, David Rosenthal.